the christmas trap

shannon myers

contents

Cover design by Kris Duplantier of Limeade Designs

First Printing: 2025

Paperback ISBN- 978-1-7332748-9-0

❀ Formatted with Vellum

also by shannon myers

From This Day Forward Duet

(David & Elizabeth's Story)

From This Day Forward

Forsaking All Others

Operation Duet

(Dakota & Zane's Story)

Operation Fit-ish

(Kate and Nate's Story)

Operation Annulment

Silent Phoenix MC Series

(Main Storyline)

The Deserter (Book One)

The Protector (Book Two)

The Renegade (Book Three)

The Traitor (Book Four)

The Savior (Book Five)

Standalones within the SPMC universe

The Keeper

The Christmas Trap

Fairest Series (Can be read as standalones)

(Charm & Neve's Story)

Through The Woods

(Killian and Ari's Story)

Wait For It

Fictioned Series

(Hayden & Jake's Story)

Protagonized

To those who still believe anything is possible at Christmas…

author's note

This story contains themes of grief, loss, divorce, and trauma, including the death of a child (off-page).

For a detailed list, click the QR code below.

Reader discretion is advised.

terminology

1%er (One-Percenter)- *If 99% of motorcycle riders are law-abiding members of society, the rest is the 1%. Advertised through a patch or tattoo, usually on a diamond shaped back field.*

13 - *Patch worn by a biker, usually a 1%er. May stand for the letter "M" (13th letter of alphabet), and indicate the wearer smokes pot, or uses "crank" (methamphetamine). Can also mean "The Mother Club", or original chapter of a motorcycle club.*

1916- *The nineteenth letter of the alphabet (S) and the sixteenth (P). Stands for Silent Phoenix.*

3-Piece Patch- *Configuration of back patches, consisting of: a top rocker (club's name), a center patch (club's emblem), and a bottom rocker (geographical territory).*

69 - *Patch indicating someone who has performed cunnilingus with witnesses present.*

Air Condition- *Riddle with bullets*

ATF- *Bureau of Alcohol, Tobacco, Firearms and Explosives.*

Broad- *A female whose sole purpose is being used as a sexual object; similar to a one-night stand.*

Cage- *Non-biker's car/truck.*

Church- *Club meeting.*

Club Whore- *Also known as a Mama. Sexual equivalent of a public well. Anyone can dip into her, at any time, as often as he wants. These are woman who belong to the club at large. They belong to every member and are expected to consent to the sexual desires of anyone at anytime. They perform menial tasks around the clubhouse, however do not attend club meetings.*

Colors- *Patches, logo, or uniform associated with a motorcycle club.*

Fly Colors - *To ride on a motorcycle wearing club's kutte.*

Gathering: *A scheduled social event or meeting. This is not Church.*

Grocery-getter- *A biker's car/truck.*

Hang Around- *a person that hangs around a motorcycle club and may be interested in joining.*

Jacket- *Arrest record*

Kill-Light- *A flashlight used as a weapon.*

Kutte- *A jacket which has had the sleeves cut off. All club patches are sown onto kuttes, which are worn as the outer-most layer of clothing. Most, if not all, outlaw clubs have kuttes as their basic uniform.*

Mother- *Founding/original chapter of the club.*

Nomad- *1) "Nomad" on a bottom rocker patch means that motorcycle club member travels between geographical chapters. Kind of like working in a secretarial pool, a Nomad goes where he's needed. 2)"Nomad" on a top rocker patch or car plaque means "Nomad" is the name of that club.*

Ol' Lady- *Wife or long-time girlfriend of club member. She is considered property of the member and is off-limits to other club members.*

Property Of- *displayed on a shirt, patch or tattoo to show who the woman "belongs to." Example: Monica wore a "Property of Torch" vest in Renegade. That meant that she associated herself with Torch and would do anything he needed/wanted.*

STRUCTURE WITHIN CLUB

National President- *Many times the founder of the club. He will usually be located at or near the national headquarters. He will be surrounded by bodyguards and organizational enforcers.*

Territorial or Regional Representatives- *In some cases called the National Vice President in charge of a specific region or state.*

National Secretary / Treasurer- *He is responsible for the club's money and collecting dues from local chapters. He also records any by-law changes and records any minutes.*

National Enforcer- *This person answers directly to the National President. He acts as a body guard and gives out punishment for club violations. He has also been known to locate former members and retrieve colors or remove the club's tattoo from them.*

Chapter President- *This person has either claimed the position or has been voted in. He has final authority over all chapter business and members.*

Chapter Vice President- *This person is second in command. He presides over club affairs in the absence of the president. Normally, he is hand picked by the Chapter President.*

Chapter Secretary / Treasurer- *This is usually the member with the best writing skills and probably the most education. He will maintain the chapter roster and maintain a crude accounting system. He is also responsible for collecting dues, keeping minutes and paying for any bills the chapter accumulates.*

Chapter Sergeant (SGT) at Arms- *This person is in charge of maintaining order at club meetings. Because of the violent nature of outlaw gangs this person is normally the strongest member physically and is loyal to the Chapter President. He may administer beatings to fellow members for violations of club rules. He is the club enforcer.*

Road Captain- *This person fulfills the role of a logistician and security chief for club sponsored runs or outings. The Road Captain maps out routes to be taken during runs, arranges the refueling, food and maintenance stops. He will carry the club's money and use it for bail if necessary.*

Members- *The rank and file, fully accepted and dues paying members of the gang. They are the individuals who carry out the President's orders and have sworn to live by the club's by-laws.*

Prospect- *These are the club's hopefuls who spend from one month to one year in a probationary status. They must prove during that time if they are worthy of becoming members. Some clubs have the prospect commit a felony with fellow members observing in an effort to weed out the weak and stop infiltration by law enforcement. Must be nominated by a regular member and receive a unanimous vote for acceptance. They are known to carry weapons for other club members and stand guard at club functions. The prospect wears no colors and has no voting rights.*

Associates or Honorary Members- *An individual who has proven his* *value or usefulness to the gang. These individuals may be professional people who have in some manner helped the club. Some of the more noted are attorneys, bail bondsmen, and auto wrecking yard owners. These people are allowed to party with the gang, either in town or on their runs; however, they do not have a voting status or wear colors.*

1

Six Days Until Christmas

kelsey

THE RENTAL CAR'S wipers scraped uselessly over the thin layer of ice building up on the windshield, and I wondered—not for the first time—why I'd ever agreed to spend Christmas in Colorado.

The answer—and reason I did most things—lay with the daughters who'd tag-teamed me with a 'tiny, little request.'

Addie's practical arguments and Sky's emotional pleas had worn me down until saying no would have been tantamount to canceling Christmas and disowning them both.

Now, gripping the steering wheel as the GPS cheerfully announced my arrival at what appeared to be the lost set of a Hallmark movie, I couldn't shake the feeling that I'd been played.

I killed the engine and sat for a moment, watching the sleet dance across the glass. The cabin loomed before me like something out of a Thomas Kinkade painting with its warm wood and glowing windows. The only thing missing, as far as I could tell, was a statuesque plume of smoke rising from the chimney, but that could be remedied after a hot bath. After multiple flight delays, a never-ending rental car line, and a white knuckle drive up icy mountain roads, my body felt as though it had been put through a woodchipper.

The cold hit me the second I opened the car door, sharp enough to steal my breath and sting my eyes. Texas winters hadn't prepared me for this. I hauled my suitcases from the back, the wheels immediately useless in the ankle-deep snow. Because why would anything about this trip be easy?

By the time I managed to wrestle the luggage to the front porch, my designer boots—purchased in a fit of post-divorce retail therapy—were soaked through. I also invented several new curse words when the key code Addie texted me didn't work before realizing I'd transposed the last two digits in my half-frozen state.

Inside, warmth curled around me like a hug I hadn't asked for but desperately needed after the day's events. I dropped the bags by the door and paused to take it all in.

String lights wrapped around the exposed wooden beams overhead, casting a soft glow over the living room. A pine wreath hung on the far wall—not the fake, perfectly symmetrical ones found in every craft store, but a lopsided one braided together with real greenery.

Throw blankets in deep reds and forest greens were neatly folded on a leather sectional that had seen better decades but looked comfortable enough to swallow you whole.

Someone had clearly put a lot of effort into transforming the rental into a cozy Christmas cottage. I peeled off my wet boots and ventured further inside, eagerly soaking up every little detail, from the hand-carved wooden reindeer lining the mantel to the collection of holiday mugs lining the open shelving in the kitchen. None of them matched, like they'd been collected over years of Christmases.

Pine-scented candles dotted various surfaces, unlit but still managing to perfume the air with that sharp, clean scent that never failed to remind me of him.

I pulled out my phone and started snapping pictures before my mind could detour too far down memory lane. The mismatched mugs. The reindeer with a malformed antler. A ceramic Santa that looked like it had been around since the seventies, complete with a chip in his beard that had been painted over.

Once everything was documented, I opened the group chat Addison had named 'Riggs Girls ' and uploaded the photos.

Me
How cute is this? The owner of this place really went all out.

The response was immediate.

Sky
you made it
isn't it PERFECT??!! 😎

Addie
We knew you'd love it. It's so you.

So me?

What did that even mean? My Christmas mugs matched, every piece of decor on display back home perfectly arranged and in pristine condition.

My mind immediately went to the reindeer with the wonky antler. Before, I would have made up a funny story about how he injured it to entertain the kids and asked Teddy to help me fix it. He would have laughed it off and told me it wasn't worth the glue to fix.

Somewhere along the way, I became the chipped antler. Easier to leave broken. Not worth fixing.

Me
It's lovely. Have you landed? The rental car line is a beast, so you might be there a while. I was thinking of picking something up for dinner and doing all the grocery shopping in the morning. What sounds good?

There was a lengthy pause. The kind that made my stomach tighten with the same maternal intuition I got anytime they were up to something.

Sky

okay before you get mad, we have the MOST BRILLIANT PLAN.

Addie

It's practical.

Sky

SO BRILLIANT

Addie

If someone would stop chiming in, I could explain it properly.

Sky

fine

but I came up with it

Addie

We BOTH came up with it.

Mom, we found a solution to the whole Christmas situation.

I sank onto the couch, still in my damp coat. The leather creaked under me, my fingers shaking as I typed.

Me

What solution? I thought we agreed that if I came to Colorado, you'd spend Christmas Eve and Christmas morning with me, then you'd drive to spend the rest of Christmas and the 26th with your dad.

Sky

but that is so SAD

driving away on Xmas!

like we're abandoning you

Addie

What Sky means is that we found a way to spend Christmas with both of you without anyone feeling left out.

My thumbs hovered over the keyboard. The tightness in my stomach had graduated to a full knot.

Sky
the rental is literally only twelve minutes away from dad
we mapped it

Addie
Eleven minutes and forty-three seconds, actually.

Sky
NOW WE DON'T HAVE TO CHOOSE!
we can do Xmas eve dinner with you, breakfast with dad, lunch with you, dinner with him, etc.

Addie
Or whatever arrangement works best for you.
The point is, we can see both of you without the long drive.

I stared at the screen until the words began to blur.

Twelve minutes.

There was a time when it was twelve seconds—the time it'd take me to walk down the hall to the living room recliner he dozed off in while watching the evening news. Gradually, the seconds between us became minutes. Then miles. Until the distance could have spanned the Pacific Ocean.

My ex-husband, whom I hadn't seen in two years, was twelve minutes away—eleven minutes and forty-three seconds, if we were being precise. Close enough that I could probably see the smoke rising from his chimney if I looked hard enough.

You said he lived on the other side of the state.

Sky
we know it's unconventional

Addie
But this way, everyone gets time together. We
don't lose a whole day traveling, and neither of
you has to be alone on Christmas.

Everyone gets time together. As if we were a functional, divorced
family who could handle proximity without imploding. Like two years
of silence could be bridged by good intentions and a meticulously
scheduled meal itinerary.

You said he lived down by Durango—

I deleted the text and tried again.

You're out of your goddamned minds if you
think I'm going to—
Eleven minutes and forty-three seconds is not
FIVE HOURS LIKE YOU TOLD ME WHEN YOU
GOT ME TO AGREE TO THIS STUPID TRIP—
Christmas is canceled—
No more DashPass, and you can forget about
the Netflix login—

I deleted each one before sending, smashing the little x in the
corner of my screen like I wanted to do with their heads. Teddy and I
hadn't had a reason to speak to each other since the divorce was
finalized. Our daughters were in their twenties and more than capable
of communicating with their father without a middleman.

After several long, deep breaths, I managed to type:

Me
Wow. That's very thoughtful of you both. I'm
sure we can make it work.

Sky
YAY!!!!!!!
mom you're the BEST
this is going to be perfect

Perfect wasn't the word I would have used to describe any part of
their plan.

Addie
Thank you for being flexible. We know this isn't
easy.

Flexible. Right. I was a yoga-practicing, gym-going, flexible woman now. I could handle this. I could handle anything.

Me
Have you landed yet?

Addie
About that...

I knew—with the kind of certainty that came from twenty-five years of parenting her—that I wasn't going to like whatever she was about to say.

Addie
Our flight out of Austin got cancelled due to
storms in Dallas. We're trying to get on standby
for a later flight, but it's not looking good.

Sky
stupid winter weather 😭😭😭
if we don't make it tonight, we'll be there
tomorrow morning!
first thing! promise!

I stared at the phone, feeling something between a laugh and a sob building in my chest. Of course. Of fucking course. I'd stood in line with grumpy travelers and driven through crappy weather all to sit alone in a Christmas cabin, twelve minutes from my ex-husband.

Me
These things happen. Travel safe. Love you
both.

Sky
love you too
try to relax tonight & enjoy the cabin

Addie

There's a fully stocked wine cabinet just off the laundry room. Help yourself.

Me

How do you know that?

Addie

I asked the owner. I'm nothing if not thorough.

In line to talk to the gate agent about getting on a different flight now.

Sky

WE LOVE YOU

don't be sad

tomorrow will be AMAZING!

Me

Love you more. Let me know if you get on an earlier flight.

The cabin settled around me with little creaks and sighs, like it was trying to fill the silence.

A bottle of wine on top of the altitude-induced headache I already had sounded like a great way to spend the remainder of the trip with my head in a toilet.

Tea it was.

In the kitchen, I went through the motions as if it were just another day. Locate kettle. Fill with water. Set on burner. Turn knob. Each movement deliberate, controlled, betraying no hint of the absolute chaos churning beneath my ribs.

I thumbed through a selection of teas in a wooden box near the coffee maker before selecting chamomile—the obvious choice for people who wanted to appear calm—and waited for the water to boil, idly drumming my fingers against the counter to a Christmas tune.

Mug in hand, I grabbed the romance novel I picked up in the airport bookstore and settled into the armchair by the window.

The heroine stood in an empty parking lot, chest caving as she realized the man she trusted wasn't showing up. My heart ached in sympathy—the storyline too familiar, too sharp.

She wanted to run, to put miles between herself and that hollow, humiliating moment. I remembered that same restlessness settling into my bones once Teddy started spending more time at the clubhouse than at home, when the glowing red taillight of his bike disappearing into the darkness became a more familiar sight than his face. Holidays and birthdays turned into performances. Carefully choreographed for the girls' sake. Hollow. Both of us playing our parts to perfection. Until we could no longer remember our lines.

I snapped the book shut and pressed my fingertips to my eyes, brushing away the moisture. Some wounds didn't need prodding, especially not when I was already raw from the day's revelations.

The girls thought splitting Christmas would make things easier. It wouldn't, not really, not since—

I shook my head hard enough to make my vision blur, but the memories were already seeping in through the cracks I hadn't managed to mortar shut.

The way we'd all frozen when Sky found Levi's stocking in a box in the attic and hung it beside the others the first Christmas after. The pained sound Teddy had made when he saw it—not quite a word, not quite a sob. How Addie had jumped in with frantic cheer, changing the subject to favorite cookies and which Christmas movie we should watch next—anything that wasn't a reminder of the gaping void we all carried in our chests.

I'd done everything right after it happened. Hadn't I? Given Teddy space when he needed it, kept the house running while he disappeared into himself. But grief wasn't something you could fix with comfort food or clean clothes. It was a living, breathing thing that moved into your home, unscrewing light bulbs and rearranging all the furniture every time you turned your back. We'd both stumbled around lost in the dark, crashing into each other until we were too bruised to try anymore.

I abandoned the book and the chair, needing to move. The cabin wasn't large—a circuit from the living room to the kitchen to the small hallway took maybe thirty seconds—but I walked it anyway.

Straightened the already-straight blankets. Aligned the mismatched mugs so all the handles faced the same direction. Wiped down the spotless counter.

The girls should have been here with me, arguing over which toppings to put on the pizza. Instead, I had a whole night of waiting ahead, trapped with the same silence that had driven me to ask for the divorce in the first place.

The Christmas music I'd turned on while cleaning suddenly felt oppressive. Bing Crosby dreaming of white Christmases he'd never have to spend alone. I shut it off and stood in the quiet, watching as sleet continued to fall past the window in lazy, drifting patterns.

Darkness came early in the mountains. By five-thirty, the world outside had been reduced to what the porch light could reach—a small circle of illuminated snow, everything beyond it lost to black. I brewed another cup of tea I wouldn't drink. Picked up my book again. Put it down. Checked my phone for messages that weren't there.

When headlights swept across the front window, I bolted upright so fast I caught the small side table with my knee, nearly tipping my mostly full mug.

They'd made it. Somehow, my brilliant, stubborn girls had found another flight or driven through the storm or—God, I didn't care how they'd done it. They were here.

I didn't bother with my coat. Didn't even slip on shoes. I yanked open the door and launched myself down the porch steps, only to stumble to a stop as soon as the Ford Bronco came into view.

A baby blue 1972 Ford Bronco, to be exact. One I'd ridden in a thousand times, my hand on the driver's thigh as we flew down dirt country roads with the music cranked up. I'd lost my virginity on the long tan bench seat after the homecoming dance.

The engine cut. The door opened. And Teddy stepped out. Sleet immediately started collecting on his broad shoulders as he stopped to retrieve something from the passenger seat.

Our eyes met across the snowy driveway, and the expectant smile slid off his lips. I couldn't remember the last time he'd smiled at me. A real, genuine smile—not the cruel smirk he'd pasted on anytime we disagreed. Which had been often.

The silence stretched between us, filled with years of unspoken everything, while flakes of ice fell around us like the world's most picturesque disaster.

"Kels?" His voice was rougher, maybe, like he'd taken up smoking again, but underneath it was exactly as I remembered it. The sound of it hit me somewhere between my chest and my stomach, a punch I should have seen coming, but like everything else, had missed entirely.

Unable to find the words, I opened and closed my mouth like an idiot, while our daughters' brilliant plan crystallized into perfect, terrible clarity.

2

kelsey

"WHAT ARE YOU DOING HERE?" The words scraped out of my throat, rough and accusatory. Years of therapy and finally feeling as though I was healing, and all it took was the sight of Teddy's face for all the rage and hurt to come bubbling back to the surface.

My wet feet were going numb the longer I stood, but I couldn't move. Couldn't process anything beyond the fact that my ex-husband stood in my driveway—no, not mine, someone else's driveway—looking like he'd rather be anywhere else.

He raised his arm, the light hitting a large brown paper bag. "Addie texted and asked if I'd mind picking up chicken parm while they settled in."

The Romano's bag might as well have been a grenade for all the damage it threatened to do to my carefully reconstructed life. No surprise they'd convinced him to bring chicken parmesan—my favorite, once upon a time when favorites mattered, and we ate dinner at the same table instead of in separate states.

His hazel eyes narrowed, taking in my wet feet and lack of coat. "Didn't mention you'd be here, though."

"Me?" A laugh bubbled up, sharp and bitter. "The only reason I agreed to come at all was that I was told you lived down near Durango. You were supposed to be five hours away, not—" I gestured wildly at the space between us, which felt simultaneously too vast and not nearly vast enough.

His jaw muscle flexed, a telltale sign that he was grinding his teeth. "Been living here since right after—"

He didn't finish. Didn't need to. Right after the divorce. Right after he'd packed up his life and disappeared into the mountains without so much as a forwarding address. Not that I'd asked for one.

"Well, this has been fun." The cold had moved past my skin and taken up residence in my bones.

Teddy shifted the bag to his other hand, and I caught the way his leather kutte pulled across his shoulders. Still wearing it, even when no one was around to see it. Some things never changed.

"Speaking of..." He glanced past me into the warm glow of the cabin, then back to my face. "You gonna make me wait out here to see my kids? In a blizzard?"

"Please." I rolled my eyes. "It's hardly a blizzard. More like aggressive sleet." But even as I said it, ice pellets stung my cheeks, and wind whipped hair across my face. Teddy's presence made everything feel more intense—the cold, the awkwardness, the stupid flutter in my stomach that had no business existing after two years of silence.

"Kelsey." He pinched the bridge of his nose, sounding put out, like I was the unreasonable one. Which was rich, considering he was the one who'd given up on us first.

"The girls aren't here," I said, crossing my arms over my chest. Partly for warmth, mostly for armor. "Their flight to Dallas got canceled due to weather, so they're still in Austin. Supposedly, they found another one early tomorrow morning."

"Supposedly? Addie texted me not an hour ago, saying they were here." Understanding dawned on his face, followed quickly by something that looked suspiciously close to amusement. "Jesus Christ. They set us up."

"Give the man a prize," I muttered with a slow clap.

We'd been played. Expertly. By our own children.

He lifted the bag again, and the smell of garlic and marinara chose that moment to waft toward me. "Least they made sure we didn't starve while they parent trapped us."

My traitorous stomach growled. "This is ridiculous." I was talking to myself more than him, but he nodded anyway. "They can't just— we're adults. Divorced adults who have successfully avoided each other for two years."

"One year, ten months," Teddy corrected. "And successful is a bit of a stretch. You sent my lawyer a Christmas card photo of you and the girls last year."

"That was a mistake." It hadn't been. I'd been feeling petty and wine drunk when I'd addressed the cards. But he didn't need to know that.

We stood there, the space between us filled with everything we weren't saying. The sleet picked up, driving sideways now, and Teddy hunched his shoulders against it. He looked older in the porch light— more lines around his eyes, more gray threading through the long dark hair that escaped the low knot he'd always favored. Still beautiful in that rough-hewn way that made me as bubbleheaded at fifty-one as I had been at fifteen.

My mother's voice echoed in my head, all Southern propriety and social graces. *You don't leave a dog outside in weather like this, Kelsey Dawn, much less a dinner guest.*

Even if that dinner guest was my ex-husband. Even if having him in my space—temporary as it was—felt like inviting a tornado into a house of cards.

"Come in, Theodore." The formality was childish, but I was feeling prickly. "The girls would be disappointed if I left you to freeze to death."

He stopped mid-step toward the door, a barely-there smirk I knew too well playing at the corner of his mouth. "Theodore? What are you, my mom now?"

"God knows I cleaned up enough of your messes to earn the title." I turned on my heel, not waiting to see if he'd follow. "And take off your boots. I'm not mopping up after you."

His low chuckle followed me inside, a sound I'd forgotten. Or maybe I'd just buried it with everything else I couldn't afford to remember.

The kitchen shrank the moment Teddy entered it. Not literally—it remained the same modest galley with its granite counters and narrow butcher block island. Then again, maybe I'd just forgotten how much space he took up—not just physically, though his broad build and six-foot-two frame certainly commanded attention. I became hyperaware of every movement, every breath, the way my body automatically adjusted to accommodate his as we fell into patterns worn smooth by decades of practice.

He set the Romano's bag on the counter and started unpacking the food containers one by one while I grabbed a couple of serving spoons from an enamel canister next to the stove. We moved like dancers who'd memorized the steps so thoroughly that muscle memory overrode the fact we hadn't performed together in two years—or *one year and ten months*, as he'd been so quick to point out.

"Forks are in the drawer to your left," I said without thinking, then caught myself. This wasn't our kitchen. This wasn't our home. And I had no idea where anything was.

But he pulled open the drawer all the same. Different kitchen, same layout. Same silverware drawer. Countless hours of dinner preparations, thousands of shared meals, and now here we were, strangers playing house with takeout containers.

The space between the counter and the small island meant we had to slide past each other. Once, twice, three times, we managed it without contact, just the whisper of air between us. But the kitchen was too small for two people who were trying so hard not to touch each other.

I found the plates on the open shelving to the right of the sink and rose onto my toes to grab them. Without a word, Teddy moved behind me, the heat of his body seeping through my sweater.

"I've got it." His fingers skimmed the small of my back as he reached around me, the kind of casual touch that used to occur on an almost daily basis. But now the contact shot through me like an electric current.

I was close enough to smell the leather of his kutte along with the unmistakable scent of pine and spice—the cologne he'd worn since we were kids. One that never failed to remind me of Christmas.

The smart thing would have been to step aside. The safe thing. Instead, I leaned back into him with a soft sigh, the tension instantly leaching from my body.

The plates trembled in his grip above us. His chest expanded against my back, and I felt more than heard the soft curse he growled into my hair. For one terrible, wonderful second, his fingers tightened on my hip, and he tugged me closer.

Then reality crashed back in. We jerked apart the same way we had when we were teens, and my parents flashed the porch light at us. My hip connected with the handle of the silverware drawer hard enough to make me wince while Teddy collided with the island at his back, nearly losing his grip on the plates in his haste to escape.

"Sorry," I said, though I wasn't sure what I was apologizing for. The touch? Leaning in? The last year and ten months? All of it?

"Don't." His voice came out deeper than usual. He cleared his throat and nodded to the table. "Let's just eat."

He set the plates down with more force than necessary, the sound of ceramic clattering against the counter as loud as gunfire in the sudden silence.

I transferred the chicken parmesan onto our plates, willing my hands to stop shaking.

One dinner.

I just had to get through one dinner.

Then, I'd pawn him off on the girls, and things would go back to normal.

Teddy dumped the breadsticks into a glass mixing bowl and deposited them on the table before grabbing a couple of glasses. We moved around each other with exaggerated care now, maintaining a buffer zone that felt both necessary and ridiculous.

Once everything was laid out, he stripped off his kutte and draped it over the back of his chair, leaving him in a fitted black Henley. It should have been illegal for a man in his fifties to look that good. My mind drifted to the wine cabinet in the laundry room before I thought better of it.

We sat across from each other at the small dining table, and I immediately regretted not insisting on the breakfast bar where we would have been seated side by side, able to avoid eye contact. Instead, we were face-to-face with nowhere to look but at each other.

The only sounds were the scrape of knives against ceramic and the occasional clink of a fork finding its way back to the plate. We ate like prisoners, heads down, focused on the task of consumption rather than companionship.

Five minutes in, Teddy gestured at the breadsticks with his fork, a grunt that apparently passed for communication in his world.

"I'm sorry, did you say something?" I kept my tone light, sweet even.

Another grunt, more emphatic this time, fork now actively pointing.

"Oh, you want the breadsticks?" I leaned back in my chair, making no move toward the mixing bowl that sat directly between us. "Interesting way of asking."

His jaw tightened. "Pass the damn breadsticks, Kels."

"Thirty-two years, and you'd think you'd learn the magic word by now."

"Magic word?" The fork hit his plate. "Right. Because that's what was missing from our marriage. Please and fucking thank you. Not the fact that you—" He stopped himself, nostrils flaring, but the damage was done. The temperature in the room dropped ten degrees.

"Please, finish that sentence," I said, my voice deadly quiet. "Tell me what I did to ruin our marriage. I'm dying to hear this version."

"Forget it." He reached across the table himself, grabbing two breadsticks and sending the bowl wobbling.

"No, really. Was it the part where I held our family together while you were off playing outlaw with the club? Or maybe when I handled every teacher conference, every therapy appointment, every—"

"Jesus Christ, Kelsey. Can we just—" He dragged a hand over his face, looking older, exhausted in a way I felt every single day. "Can we just eat?"

I wanted to push his buttons. God, I wanted to list every grievance, every night I'd waited up, every excuse I'd made for his absence. But what was the point? We'd had this fight a hundred times with a hundred different props. Breadsticks, remote controls, intimacy, the kids, you name it. The subject changed, but the script remained the same.

3

kelsey

WE RETREATED INTO SILENCE, but it wasn't peaceful. It was the kind of quiet that pressed against your eardrums, made you hyperaware of every sound. The way he breathed through his nose when he ate. How I set my glass down too carefully, trying not to make noise. The storm outside providing a percussion backdrop to our mutual discomfort.

I took small, methodical bites, chewed thoroughly, tried not to remember all the times we'd shared this exact meal under more pleasant circumstances.

Teddy cleared his plate first—he'd always been a fast eater, something that used to drive me up a wall when the kids were small and I was trying to teach them table manners. I watched him drag the last piece of bread through the remaining sauce, sopping up every last bit like he might never eat again.

On autopilot, I pushed my chair back and moved toward the kitchen.

"Coffee?" The word came out before I could stop them, habit overriding common sense.

Teddy grunted again—his default response to most questions—and I bit back the urge to throw the coffee pot at his head. Some things, it seemed, were eternal. Death, taxes, and Theodore Riggs communicating primarily through caveman sounds.

I went through the motions anyway, finding filters in the cabinet above the coffee maker, measuring grounds with the same care I'd once used to measure formula for midnight feedings. The familiar ritual calmed something in me, even as my skin prickled under the weight of his stare.

I scanned the mugs, the corner of my mouth twitching as I selected one for him that said, *"Sleigh Queen."*

"Haven't been to the store yet," I called over my shoulder as it began brewing. "So, you'll have to drink it black."

"Since when have you known me to drink it any other way?"

Never. He'd never taken cream or sugar, not once in the entire time I'd known him. I'd gotten so used to experimenting with my own coffee since living on my own that it must have slipped my mind.

"Right." I kept my tone neutral, focusing on the slow drip of coffee into the carafe. "Black it is."

"Unlike some people, I haven't changed." There was an edge to his voice that made my molars grind together. "Still the same boring, predictable bastard you divorced. Must have confused me for your new man."

I spun around to face him. "Excuse me?"

Teddy leaned back in his chair, arms crossed, studying me through narrowed eyes. "Just wondering if that's why you forgot."

"You're fishing." I turned back to the coffee, my shoulders instinctively tensing when his chair scraped against the floor.

"Come on, Kels," he said, leaning against the fridge like he was trying for nonchalant and missing by miles. "You can't expect me to believe you haven't been with anyone since the divorce."

The coffee maker sputtered, matching my inability to form words. Did he really think—after everything—that I'd moved on? Found some nice accountant or teacher to shack up with?

"That's none of your business."

He pushed off from the fridge, closing the distance between us. "So that's a yes."

"No, Teddy. It's a mind your own business." The coffee maker gave one final gurgle, and I grabbed the carafe with shaking hands, sloshing hot liquid onto the counter as I tried to pour.

"Careful," he muttered, reaching out to steady my wrist.

I jerked away from his touch. "I've got it."

"Right. My mistake. You've always got it." His laugh was bitter, hollow. "Perfect Kelsey, handling everything on her own."

"Someone had to. Here." I shoved the mug at him. He frowned at the inscription before taking it but didn't move from the doorway.

"Maybe if you'd spent more time at home than at the clubhouse, I would have remembered how you take your coffee." The words were out before I could stop them, years of resentment distilled into a single sentence. I hated how any attempts to be the bigger person went out the window as soon as he was within six feet of me.

Teddy froze, mug halfway to his lips. "Seriously? We're fucking doing this now?"

"I'm simply pointing out that your absence was so notable, I've forgotten basic details about you." I gripped my own mug tighter, needing something solid to anchor me.

"My absence." He set his coffee down with deliberate control, the kind that meant he was seconds from losing it. "Right. 'Cause I was the one who checked out. Not you, with your gym obsession and your sudden need to 'find yourself' after—"

"After our son died?" My voice cracked on the last word. Levi's name remained locked up in my throat, because if I let it loose—if I said it out loud—everything I'd worked so hard to rebuild would come crumbling down.

"Yes, Teddy, I joined a gym. Shocking behavior, really. I should have been more like you and just run off to the clubhouse every night."

"At least there, no one jumped my ass over every little thing." His voice rose, filling the space between us with decades of accumulated frustration. "Nobody gave me shit about what needed fixing in the house, or how loudly I was breathing, or chewing, or existing. They were just happy to be in my company. Didn't need me to be someone I

23

wasn't. Didn't look at me like I was failing some test I didn't know I was taking."

My stomach pitched, every insecurity I'd buried deep clawing to the surface.

There was no mistaking, *they* were the club girls. Young. Uncomplicated. Draped over every surface of the clubhouse in tiny shorts and tank tops that left nothing to the imagination. Women who were down for anything and everything. Women who didn't have stretch marks from three pregnancies or crow's feet from decades of squinting into the sun at soccer games.

The mug nearly slipped from my hands. I set it down carefully, taking a second to arrange my face into something that didn't scream *You may as well have just gutted me with a butter knife.*

"Makes sense." I forced a laugh. "Why deal with your grieving wife when you could have twenty-somethings serving you beer and hanging on your every word? Good for you."

Teddy rubbed at the back of his neck, and when he looked at me again, there was something raw in his expression. "That's not—Christ, Kels. That's not what I meant. I didn't—"

"Didn't what? Didn't mean to let it slip that you found comfort with women half your age while I was home trying to hold what was left of our family together? Didn't mean to admit to—" I couldn't say it. Couldn't put words to the fear that had haunted me for years, the one that whispered I wasn't enough, wasn't young enough, wasn't fun enough to hold his attention anymore.

My cheeks burned with humiliation, remembering all those nights I'd waited up, wondering if he'd come home at all. Wondering if the distance between us was grief or something else. Someone else.

I pressed my palms flat against the counter, needing something solid to keep me from either throwing my coffee at him or dissolving into the kind of tears that would prove I still gave a damn.

"Never cheated on you, Kels." His voice was low, intense. "Not once. Not ever."

I wanted to believe him. God, I wanted to believe that whatever broke us, it wasn't that. But the way he'd said it—*they* were happy in his company—kept echoing in my head. The casual cruelty of it. The implication that I hadn't been happy with him, hadn't wanted his company, when the truth was, I'd wanted it so badly I'd made myself sick with it.

"It hardly matters now. We're divorced. You're free to screw whoever you want to," I said, proud of how steady my voice sounded when everything inside me was collapsing. "Just like I am."

The lie came easily. There hadn't been anyone else. Hadn't even been the desire for anyone else. I'd been too busy trying to remember how to exist with the weight of his and Levi's absences pressing down on me. But he didn't need to know that. Didn't need to know I'd taken to sleeping in the middle of the bed just to make it feel less empty.

Teddy shook his head. "Jesus, can't even share a meal without it turning into World War Three."

"You're right." I studied the pattern in the granite. If I looked at him, he'd see everything written on my face—the hurt, the humiliation, the pathetic fact that I still cared what he'd done or hadn't done with other women. The pathetic fact that I didn't want to be alone. "We can't. Which is why you should go."

"C'mon, Kels—"

"Please." The word cracked down the middle. "Just go."

I heard him shift behind me, the floor creaking under his weight. Heard him pick up his mug, set it back down. The hesitation in every movement, like he was fighting himself.

"Ain't how I wanted this to go," he said quietly.

I would have laughed if I didn't think it'd come out as a sob. "How did you want it to go, Teddy? What exactly did you think would happen when you showed up here?"

"In my defense, I didn't know you'd be here."

"But if you had?"

Silence. Then, so soft I almost missed it, "I don't know."

The honesty of it somehow hurt worse than anger would have. At least anger was familiar. This—whatever this was—felt too much like grief. Like mourning something that was already dead but kept trying to claw its way back to life.

"We'll figure out how to split time with the girls when they get here." I finally turned around, needing the conversation to move toward logistics, something safe and manageable. "They mentioned some elaborate schedule. Christmas Eve dinner with me, Christmas morning with you, but Christmas dinner with me, I think. I'd have to go back and look at the text again to be sure."

"Surprised there's not a color-coded spreadsheet." He chuckled before adding, "Bet you anything, Addie's the mastermind behind this."

"Oh, it's definitely Addison," I agreed. "Sky's the hopeless romantic. Addie's the planner."

For a moment, we almost smiled at each other. Almost connected over our daughters' night-and-day personalities.

Teddy shrugged on his kutte and boots before moving toward the window, studying the storm that had graduated from sleet to something meaner. "This is worse than they predicted."

"It'll pass." I didn't know if I meant the storm or the unbearable tension between us.

"Maybe." He turned from the window, and his expression made my stomach drop. "But if it doesn't—if it keeps up—there ain't gonna be a morning flight."

The possibility of getting snowed in alone on Christmas made my skin crawl. Not just without the girls, but truly alone, with nothing but a rental cabin and whatever ghosts had stowed away in my suitcases. The kind of alone that echoed in your chest and made you do desperate things like drink the contents of the wine cabinet and booty call your ex-husband just to remember what it felt like to be touched.

"They'll make it," I said, more to myself than him. "They have to."

"When's the last time you spent Christmas alone?"

Never. The answer came immediately. There'd always been someone—my parents, then Teddy, then our kids. Even that first horrible Christmas after Levi, we'd all been together in our misery, stumbling through traditions that felt like swallowing glass.

"I'll be fine," I lied.

He clicked his tongue against his teeth. "Sure you will."

I walked him to the door, careful to keep some distance between us. Outside, ice coated every surface, turning tree branches into crystal sculptures that would have been gorgeous if they weren't so dangerous. The porch light caught the falling sleet, like static on an old TV.

"Drive careful," I said, because someone had to say something to end this nightmare of an evening.

"Always do." He lingered, neither in nor out, letting cold air flood the entrance. "Kelsey..."

"What?"

He shifted his weight, jaw working like he was chewing on words he couldn't quite spit out. Then, finally, "You look good. Really good."

The compliment hit me sideways, unexpected and unwanted. The corner of his mouth tipped up in that barely-there smile I'd fallen in love with as a teen.

"Guess all that money I had to pay you in the settlement went to good use," he added.

The warmth that had started to bloom in my chest withered and died. Of course. Of fucking course he couldn't just leave it at something nice. Had to twist the knife, remind me that our divorce had cost him—as if I hadn't paid in ways money couldn't measure.

"Goodnight," I gritted out as I reached for the door.

His hand caught the frame, stopping me. "That came out wrong."

"Bullshit. It came out exactly how you meant it."

"Kels—"

I slammed the door in his face. Not my finest moment, but better than the alternative, which was doing something monumentally stupid like crying or admitting that everything I'd changed about myself had been an attempt to become someone who didn't miss him.

I leaned against the door, forehead pressed to the wood, listening to his footsteps on the porch. Waiting for the sound of his truck starting. It took longer than it should have, and I wondered if he was sitting in the driver's seat, staring at the cabin like I was staring at the door. Two idiots separated by walls we'd built ourselves.

The engine finally turned over, the familiar rumble of his ancient Bronco that had survived longer than our marriage. I stayed pressed against the door until the sound faded, until I was sure he was gone, until the burning in my eyes faded and my legs started to ache from standing still.

The cabin immediately felt larger without him in it. Emptier. Like his presence had briefly filled all the hollow spaces before leaving them to echo.

My phone buzzed from the pocket of my cardigan.

Addison
Looks like the weather's getting worse up there.
Do you have everything you need?"

I looked around the cabin—at the remains of our dinner, at the two coffee mugs on the counter, at the dining room chair Teddy hadn't bothered to push back in when he got up. Evidence of an evening that shouldn't have happened.

How could I explain that their father had just left? That their elaborate plan had already started its spectacular collapse.

Me
I'll handle it tomorrow. I just checked, and the bands of heavy snow aren't supposed to move in until after mid-afternoon. Hopefully, you'll be here long before then.

Love you both. Stay warm.

The sleet continued its assault on the windows, promising a long night ahead. I could clean up, wash the dishes, pretend this was just another evening in my new life. Or I could pour myself a glass of wine and admit what I'd known the moment I saw Teddy standing in the driveway.

Some doors, once opened, were impossible to close again. Even if you slammed them in someone's face. Even if you leaned against them with all your weight, trying to keep the past from flooding back in.

Especially then.

4

Five Days Until Christmas

teddy

WEAK SUNLIGHT FILTERED through the dense clouds, painting everything the color of dirty dishwater. I stared at the spot where Kelsey's rental SUV should have been, the coffee turning to acid in my gut.

I'd barely slept after leaving last night. Kept replaying our conversation—if you could call that disaster a conversation—wondering how we'd gone from touching in the kitchen to her slamming the door on me like I was some door-to-door salesman. The look on her face when she thought I was confessing to spending my time with the club whores. Christ. Like I'd confirmed every fear she'd ever had about us.

And then I had to go and make a shitty comment about the money, had to get another dig in, as if I was hurting for cash.

The thing was, I'd come here to make amends. Or explain. Or something. I'd rehearsed it on the drive over, had a whole speech about how I hadn't meant what she thought I meant, how there'd never been anyone else—ever—how the guys at the club were just easier to be around because they didn't look at me like I'd killed our son.

But her car was gone, and with it, any chance of fixing what I'd broken.

I killed the engine and climbed out, boots crunching through the fresh powder. Maybe she'd just moved it. Maybe the girls had told her about the large shed I'd built around back. The cold bit through my jacket as the wind picked up again, sleet peppering my face like tiny shards of glass.

No tire tracks leading around the cabin. The shed revealed nothing but a stack of firewood and some rusty garden tools. I circled back to the front porch, noting the single set of footprints already being erased by the storm.

She was gone.

I pulled out my phone, thumb hovering over her contact. We hadn't spoken on the phone in almost two years. Every communication had been filtered through lawyers or the girls. But this was different. This was about safety, not our failed marriage.

The call went straight to voicemail. Her professional message, the one she'd recorded for work contacts. "You've reached Kelsey Riggs with Home Again Transitions. Please leave a message, and I'll return your call as soon as possible."

I hung up without leaving anything. Tried again. Same result.

"Come on, Kels," I muttered, hitting redial. "Don't do this."

Four more attempts. Four more trips to voicemail. By the sixth call, I was pacing the porch, my free hand clenched into a fist. The sleet had graduated to something meaner, ice pellets that bounced off the wooden railing like bullets.

I switched to texting, typing with numb fingers.

Me
Where are you?

No read receipt. No delivered notification.

Storm's getting worse. Just let me know you're okay.

Same thing. The messages hung in digital limbo, which meant one of two things: either she had no service, or she'd blocked my number.

Given how we'd left things last night, I had a pretty good idea which one it was.

My jaw tightened until my teeth ached. Figured she'd blocked me. God forbid we act like adults about this. God forbid she let me explain or apologize or do any of the things I'd driven here at dawn to do, like offer to grab what she needed from the store, so she didn't have to get out in this mess. No, better to just cut me off entirely, like the past three decades meant nothing.

My phone buzzed. For a second, hope flared. But it was only a weather alert. The winter storm had been upgraded to a blizzard.

…BLIZZARD WARNING IN EFFECT FROM 9 AM MST SATURDAY TO 6 AM MST SUNDAY FOR THE CENTRAL ROCKY MOUNTAIN REGION.

Snowfall: 2–4 inches per hour, with total accumulation expected between 24–36 inches.

Winds: Sustained at 30–40 mph, gusts exceeding 55 mph.

Visibility: Near zero at times due to blowing and drifting snow.

Travel: Extremely dangerous to impossible. Road closures are in effect.

Warning: If you become stranded, remain with your vehicle. Emergency response may be delayed due to hazardous conditions.

I stared out at the swirling white. It was just after eight, but knowing Kelsey, she'd probably left for the store at first light to avoid getting caught in the storm.

Two to four inches of snow an hour, whiteout conditions, roads already closing—she didn't stand a chance. I tried calling one more time, knowing it was pointless, but unable to stop myself. This time I left a message.

"Kels, it's me. I know you're pissed about last night, and you have every right to be. But the storm's getting bad. Really bad. If you're heading to town—" I paused, swallowing past the sudden knot in my throat. "Just call me back. Please."

There. I'd even used the magic word on the off chance the etiquette gods were watching.

I ran a hand through my damp hair, sick at the thought of her navigating mountain roads in a rental car she wasn't familiar with, in conditions that were deteriorating by the minute. She'd learned to drive in West Texas, where snow was rare and measured in scant inches, not feet. To her, it was a thing of beauty, not something that could kill her if she didn't respect it.

A part of me hoped she'd know to turn around when conditions got bad, but this was also the same woman who'd once driven through a tornado warning to get Sky from dance class. Stubborn didn't begin to cover it.

Summit Ridge was only twenty minutes down the mountain in good conditions. Maybe thirty in this weather. I could check the grocery store parking lot, make sure her rental was there, then leave before she even knew I'd been worried.

Not worried. Just... concerned.

The way you'd be concerned about anyone driving in this mess. It had nothing to do with the way my chest had gone tight when I'd seen her standing on the front porch last night, or how good she'd looked in that tight sweater, or how, when she'd leaned back against me in the kitchen, everything in my life made sense again.

No, this was just basic human decency. Making sure the mother of my children didn't end up in a ditch somewhere.

I headed back to the Bronco, already second-guessing myself. She'd blocked my number. The message was clear: *Leave me alone.*

But as I started the engine and pulled out of the driveway, I couldn't shake the feeling that something was wrong. Call it intuition, call it knowing someone well enough to sense when they were in trouble, but something in my gut was screaming at me to find her.

The twenty-minute drive took almost forty, with visibility dropping to ten feet in places. The Bronco's four-wheel drive was the only thing keeping me from joining the collection of vehicles I passed—some abandoned at odd angles, others creeping along like they were trying to sneak under the blizzard's radar. Black ice lurked under the fresh snow, revealing itself only when my back end started to slide, that sickening weightless feeling before the tires found purchase again. The kind of conditions that would terrify someone who'd learned to drive where ice meant the stuff you put in your sweet tea.

She'd be fine. She had to be fine.

By the time I reached the grocery store parking lot, my shoulders ached from tension, and my jaw hurt from grinding my teeth. The place looked like the last helicopter out of Saigon. Cars were parked at angles that suggested their drivers had abandoned any pretense of following the painted lines.

I cruised the rows slowly, looking for a white SUV with New York plates. Kelsey always parked in the same general area—not too close to avoid door dings, not too far because she hated walking in bad weather—creature of habit, even in unfamiliar places. But there was nothing.

No white SUV. No New York plates. No Kelsey.

Inside, tinny Christmas Muzak played over the speakers, some synthesized version of "Silver Bells" that sounded like it was being performed by dying robots. The contrast between the cheerful music and the barely controlled panic of the shoppers would have been funny if I weren't one of them—scanning faces, looking for one in particular.

The produce section had been picked clean except for some sad-looking Brussels sprouts and a few bruised apples. An elderly woman clutched the last bag of potatoes like someone might wrestle her for them. Maybe someone would. The storm had everyone spooked, turning neighbors into competitors for the last loaf of bread.

I moved systematically through the store, trying to look casual while my eyes searched for dark brown hair with highlights. Streaks of blonde that caught the light, making her look ten years younger. Not that she'd needed them. Kelsey had always been beautiful to me, even during the brutal months leading up to our divorce when grief had left her with dark circles beneath her eyes and a permanent shell-shocked expression.

The breakfast aisle turned up nothing but a harried mother with three kids arguing over Pop-Tarts. In the dairy section, two men were playing tug-of-war with a gallon of whole milk.

Each aisle I checked without finding her made the knot in my stomach pull tighter. Maybe she'd already come and gone. Maybe she was back at the cabin right now, blissfully unaware I was out looking for her.

But that meant I would have had to have passed her on the way down, and I was damn sure I hadn't.

A stock boy pushed past with a cart full of canned goods, and I grabbed his arm. "Hey, you been here all morning?"

He looked about sixteen, with acne and an expression that suggested he'd rather be anywhere else. "Since five, yeah."

"You see a woman with brown hair, about this tall?" I held my hand just under my collarbone.

The kid shrugged. "Man, I've seen about two hundred people this morning. They're all starting to look the same."

Fair enough. I released his arm and headed for the checkout lines, all six of them packed with people whose carts overflowed with supplies. Like they were planning to be snowed in until spring.

The elderly cashier at register three looked familiar—Helen or Ellen. She'd been working here since I'd moved to town. I waited until she'd finished ringing up a man with enough bottled water to fill a swimming pool.

"Morning," I said, trying for casual. "Place is crazy today."

"Tell me about it." She pushed her glasses up her nose. "Haven't seen anything like this since that storm in '06. You stocking up too?"

"Actually, I'm looking for someone. Woman about my age, long brown hair? She would have been driving a white SUV with New York plates."

Her face scrunched in thought. "New York plates? Can't say I've seen any. But I've only been on register for the last hour. Maybe check with Carl in the parking lot. He's been helping people load their cars."

Carl turned out to be as useless as a screen door on a submarine. Hadn't seen any New York plates, hadn't noticed any woman matching Kelsey's description, hadn't really been paying attention to anything except trying to keep his fingers from freezing off.

The parking lot was even more chaotic now, cars sliding on the ice, horns honking, people abandoning their carts in the middle of traffic lanes. I headed back to the Bronco and pulled out my phone. No messages. No missed calls. Just the two texts I'd sent earlier, still undelivered.

My thumbs moved across the screen, opening the group chat with the girls.

Me

Either of you heard from your mom this morning?

The response was almost immediate.

Addie
Not since last night. She said she was going grocery shopping this morning. But she hasn't responded to any of our texts.

Sky
you're not mad we tricked you last night, are you???

Addie
It seemed like the only way to get you two in the same room.

I scrubbed a hand over my jaw, the wind blowing hard enough to rock the Bronco. Of course, they'd ask about that now. I wasn't about to unload thirty years of marital failure in a goddamn text message, and sure as hell not while their mama was out in this storm.

Me
We can talk about that later.

Sky
so, you ARE mad

Me
Mad, no. Cold, yes. Roads are hell here. Any luck at the airport?

Addie
The flight situation here is a nightmare.
Everything's being canceled due to the blizzard.

Me

Not surprised. They're shutting the highways
down, so even if you managed to make it to
Denver, you'd be stuck in the airport.

Addie

They're saying maybe tomorrow afternoon, but
honestly, I'm not optimistic. This storm system
is massive. At least we're still in Austin, so we
can go home and wait it out. Better than being
stranded in an airport.

Sky

what if we miss Xmas??? 😭

My chest tightened. The girls missing Christmas was bad enough.
But if something had happened to Kelsey, if she was hurt somewhere
and they couldn't get to her...

Me

Don't worry about it. We'll figure something out.
Your mama and I can handle things here. Y'all
focus on staying safe.

Sky

does this mean you're going to see each other
again???

Addie

She didn't mean that.

Sky

what

it's a legitimate question!

Me

We can manage.

Addie

Okay. But it's not like her not to respond to a
text. Are you sure everything's okay? Is
she mad?

I stared at the screen, weighing how much to tell them. They were adults, technically. Addie was twenty-five, Sky twenty-two. Old enough to handle the truth. But they were also two states away, helpless to do anything except worry.

Me
I'm sure she's fine. Probably just taking her time at the store. You know how she gets about comparing brands.

It was a weak lie. Kelsey had never been one to linger over grocery decisions. She shopped like she did everything else—with ruthless efficiency and a mental list organized by aisle.

Sky
tell her we love her when you see her

Addie
And remind her to charge her phone. You know she always forgets.

Me
Will do. Love you both. Keep me posted on the flight situation.

The rational part of my brain offered explanations. Maybe she'd driven to a different town. Maybe she'd decided to abandon the holiday plans and catch the first flight back to Texas.

Maybe she was holed up at a coffee shop somewhere, reading one of those romance novels she thought I didn't know about, oblivious to the approaching blizzard.

But the irrational part—the part that had lived through finding our thirteen-year-old son—that part was starting to scream.

Something was wrong.

I could feel it in my bones, the same way I had that early morning I'd woken up in a sheer panic for no reason I could explain. Just a feeling that I needed to check on Levi. And I'd been right then, even if it had been too late to change anything.

I wouldn't be too late again.

The engine roared to life, and I pulled out of the parking lot faster than was safe, tires spinning on ice before finding grip. If she wasn't in town, and she wasn't at the cabin, then she was somewhere between the two.

Somewhere on winding mountain roads that were getting worse by the minute.

I just had to find her before the storm did.

5

teddy

THE MOUNTAIN ROAD disappeared completely about halfway up.
Not gradually, the way fog rolled in, but all at once. Like the world had
been swallowed up by a wall of white.

One minute, I could see twenty feet ahead of me. The next, I might
as well have been driving through dense fog. I leaned forward,
gripping the wheel hard enough to make my knuckles ache, trying to
spot the reflective markers that lined the road's edge.

If they were still there. If I was still on the road.

The wipers shrieked against the windshield, fighting a losing battle
against the ice that formed faster than they could clear it. Every few
minutes, I had to slow to a crawl, riding the rumble strip when I could
find it, using the vibration to ensure I wasn't drifting into oncoming
traffic. Not that anyone else would be stupid enough to be out in this.

Anyone except Kelsey, with her Texas understanding of winter and
her stubborn refusal to back down from anything.

The defroster was cranked all the way up, blasting heat that made
the cab feel like a sauna while doing fuck-all to keep the windshield

clear. I could see maybe three feet ahead. Maybe. The rest was just white on white on white, hypnotic and disorienting.

The radio crackled with weather updates, each worse than the last. "I-70 closed at Vail Pass... multiple accidents reported. Stay off the roads unless absolutely necessary..."

Easy for them to say. They weren't looking for someone. They hadn't driven away from an argument that might have been the last conversation they'd ever have.

My phone rang through the Bluetooth—Addie. I hit ignore. Whatever she needed could wait until I wasn't playing chicken with the side of a mountain.

A shape loomed out of the white. Guardrail. I jerked the wheel left, felt the back end slide, corrected into it like I'd learned to do in my first Colorado winter. The Bronco steadied, but my heart was hammering hard enough to hurt.

This was insane. I needed to pull over and wait for a break in the storm. But there was nowhere to stop safely, and the thought of Kelsey out here, maybe hurt, maybe trapped in her car...

The windshield was icing over again. I couldn't see shit.

I eased onto what I hoped was the shoulder, threw the Bronco in park, and grabbed the scraper from behind my seat. The second I opened the door, the storm tried to rip it off its hinges. Wind-driven snow hit my face like buckshot, stealing my breath and making my eyes water.

I worked fast, scraping enough of a viewing hole to continue, but by the time I got back in the cab, my fingers were numb and my jacket was soaked through. Worse, the cleared spot was already starting to ice over again.

"Come on, Kels," I said out loud, needing to hear something besides the wind and the laboring defroster. "Where are you?"

Up ahead, the mountain road curved—or I thought it did. Hard to tell when everything looked exactly the same. I dropped into first gear, creeping forward at a snail's pace. Any faster and I'd be driving blind.

I came up on the familiar switchback near Miller's Point faster than expected, the one with the stone memorial for some kid who'd taken it too fast in the 90s. I knew this road. Had driven it hundreds of times. But in this white hell, it felt alien, dangerous in a way it hadn't before.

Last time, the world hadn't been white but pitch black. Levi's bedroom door had been closed. That should have been my first clue—he never closed it completely; always left it cracked so the cat could come and go. But as I crept down the hall, eyes still bleary with sleep, Luna was meowing at his door, her back bristling.

When I'd knocked and gotten no answer, I told myself he was asleep. But the knob wouldn't turn beneath my hand. I threw my body into the door, my shoulder breaking through solid wood as if it were particleboard.

He'd been wearing his new sneakers. That was what I remembered most about that night. A pair of Air Jordans he'd begged for when we were shopping for something to wear to his end-of-year banquet and dance at school. Like the right shoes could make him fit in, could armor him against whatever demons had taken up residence in his head.

They'd been too expensive. Kelsey had given me that look when I came home with them, the one that said we'd be discussing financial responsibility later. But Levi's face had lit up for the first time in weeks, and that was worth any lecture.

He'd worn them once. To the banquet, where he'd made the A honor roll and been voted most kind by his classmates.

The Bronco's tires hit a patch of ice, snapping me back to the present as the back end started to drift toward the guardrail again. I managed to keep it on the road. Barely.

My hands were shaking. Not from the cold. I was still back there. Back in that bedroom, bargaining with God. Take me instead. Take the house, my bike, everything I own. Just let him be okay. Let those shoes walk down the stairs one more time.

But God hadn't been interested in bargaining.

Now I was searching again, through different blindness, for someone else I couldn't afford to lose. The parallel was too sharp, too close to the bone. But this time would be different. Had to be. I couldn't find Kelsey like I'd found Levi. Couldn't live through that again.

Hell, I'd barely survived it the first time.

The windshield was freezing up again. I pressed my palm to the glass, accomplishing nothing. Everything was closing in—the storm, the memories, the crushing certainty that I was already too late. Just like before. Always too late to stop the people I loved from slipping away.

During the final months of our marriage, I'd watched helplessly as Kelsey faded like an old photograph. The girls were home for the summer. She'd thrown herself into routines—gym at dawn, meal prep on Sundays, planning their schedules like organization could fill the void Levi left. But I'd seen the truth in the moments between tasks. The way she'd pause at the top of the stairs, staring at his bedroom door. How she'd stop mid-sentence when his name almost slipped out. The way she flinched and pulled away when I tried to touch her.

I couldn't fix it. Couldn't fix her. Every time I tried, she'd pull further away. Built her walls even higher. Until I was watching her drown behind glass I couldn't break.

We'd become each other's walking triggers, living reminders of the worst day of our lives.

So, when she asked for a divorce, I gave it to her. Signed the papers, wrote the check, packed my shit, and moved over five hundred miles away. Better to be the bad guy than to watch her disappear one gym session, one pound, one perfectly organized day at a time.

Not because I'd stopped loving her. Christ, I'd never stop loving her. But because I thought maybe, without me, she could find a way to live again. Maybe without the weight of my grief added to hers, she could surface long enough to take a breath. Maybe we both could.

The joke was on me, though. Two years later, and I still couldn't breathe. Still woke up at two every single morning, my heart racing. Still thought of those fucking Air Jordans every time I passed a shoe store.

The Bronco lurched again, tires spinning on ice. I'd drifted too close to the edge, could feel the road falling away to my left. I corrected hard, maybe too hard, fishtailing across to the other side. The guardrail appeared like a ghost, clipping the front tire.

"Fuck." I stopped in the middle of the road, hands shaking violently against the wheel. My breath came in rapid, panicked puffs.

Get it together. Can't help her if you're dead.

I got out and scraped the windshield again, fingers numb despite my gloves. The storm showed no signs of letting up. If anything, it was getting worse. But somewhere out here, Kelsey was driving through the same hell. Alone. Probably scared, though she'd never admit it. Too proud to call for help, even if her phone worked.

Just like she'd always been too stubborn to admit she wasn't okay. Too proud to let me see her break.

Back in the truck, I inched forward. Five miles an hour, maybe less. At this rate, it would take hours to cover the route. But what else was I going to do? Go home, pour a whiskey, relive every word I'd said to her last night, wondering if they were the last words I'd ever say to her?

No. I'd failed her too many times already. Failed Levi. Failed our family. But not today. Today, I'd find her, and she could hate me all she wanted as long as she was breathing to do it.

The radio static cleared for a moment: "—record-breaking accumulation expected. This is a life-threatening situation—repeat: Stay off the roads. Emergency services are suspended until—"

I turned it off. Emergency services might be suspended, but I wasn't. Not until I found her. Not until I knew she was safe.

"Please," I said to whoever might be listening—God, the universe, the Ghost of fucking Christmas Present. "Please let me find her. Please let me get there in time."

The words disappeared into the white void outside, swallowed by a storm that didn't care about second chances or broken hearts or fathers who'd already buried one person they loved.

But I kept driving anyway, searching for a white SUV in a sea of blinding white snow, for the woman I'd let go because I thought it would save her.

Some part of me would always be looking for her, ready to drive into the storm of the century if she needed me. We'd filed papers, divided assets, moved to different states, but we'd never really figured out how to stop loving each other.

At least I hadn't.

The wipers groaned against the ice, and I leaned forward, peering through the small, clear patch I'd scraped, looking for any sign of her.

Then, through the white, a flash of twisted metal where the guardrail should have been.

My heart stopped.

My brain, numbed by an hour of staring into nothing, almost dismissed it as another phantom—like the dozen false alarms before. I hit the brakes harder than I meant to, sliding sideways before the tires found purchase against the ice-covered asphalt.

And there, less than ten feet from where I stopped, sat a white SUV with New York plates.

It had gone through the guardrail at an angle, taking out twenty feet of metal barrier before being stopped by a massive pine tree. The front end was accordioned, steam still rising from the exposed engine block.

How long had she been here? Minutes? Hours?

"No, no, no—" The words ripped from my throat as I threw myself from the vehicle, not even bothering to shut off the engine. My boots slid on the ice, nearly sending me down, but I caught myself against the guardrail—what was left of it. The wind drove icy snow into my face, and I had to shield my eyes just to see where I was going.

The driver's side door of the SUV was jammed from the impact, the frame bent inward. The window was still intact, but a layer of ice made it impossible to see if she was still inside. My gut told me she was.

"Kelsey!" I yanked on the door handle. Nothing. Not even a budge. "Kels, can you hear me?"

I braced my foot against the back door and pulled harder, using all my weight. The metal groaned but held. My hands were beyond numb, gloved fingers slipping on the ice-covered handle.

"Come on, you piece of shit." I repositioned, got both hands on the handle, and pulled with everything I had. Something in my shoulder popped—an old rodeo injury roaring back to life, but adrenaline had taken over, and I wouldn't stop until I got it open.

The door shrieked as it gave way, opening maybe eighteen inches before catching on the bent frame. It was enough.

Inside, the deployed airbags hung limp like deflated ghosts. I shoved them aside, my stomach turning at the sight of Kelsey's body slumped sideways, her seatbelt the only thing keeping her upright.

Blood. So much blood, I couldn't tell where it was coming from. It covered her face, matted her hair, soaked through her pale pink sweater.

"Kels?" My voice broke on her name. I squeezed through the gap, contorting myself to fit, and reached for her with shaking hands. "Baby —open your eyes."

She groaned, the most beautiful sound I'd ever heard. Her lashes fluttered, the deep green eyes I'd fallen in love with at seventeen finding mine through the haze of pain and confusion.

"Teddy?" she whispered, her ice-cold fingers brushing against my wrist as I checked her pulse. "I—I crashed."

"Yeah, baby. I can see that." My hands moved over her, trying to find the source of the blood.

"Pretty sure I totaled it," she mumbled, her voice thick and slurred. "Never gonna let me rent a car again. Blacklisted. Is that a thing?"

A laugh that was half-sob escaped my throat. She was trying to joke. Even now, bleeding and hypothermic, she was trying to deflect with humor.

"That's what insurance is for." My hands shook as I brushed her hair back, blood smearing across my palm. A gash near her hairline was still bleeding freely, but head wounds always bled like a bitch. What worried me more was how cold she was, her lips tinged blue, body shaking.

The windshield had a spider web of cracks I hadn't noticed before, and a gap at the top where it had separated from the frame. Snow was drifting in, already accumulating on the dashboard. The engine was dead, so there was no heat.

How long had she been sitting in the cold?

"Baby, look at me." My voice cracked, and I had to swallow hard before continuing, "I need you to stay awake, okay? Stay with me."

Her eyes had started to drift closed again, but they snapped open at something in my tone. "You're scared."

"I'm not—"

"You are. You're using your scared voice." Her bloody hand came up to touch my face. "I'm okay, Teddy. I promise."

"You're as blue as a goddamned Smurf and bleeding." The words came out harsher than I meant them to, driven by the fear that was crawling up my throat. "That's pretty fucking far from okay."

"But I'm here." She said it so quietly I almost missed it. "I'm still here."

"We need to get you out of here."

"Wait—the eggs," she said suddenly, her eyes going wide with panic. "Fought a woman for them. Free-range. They're in the back."

"Forget the fucking eggs, Kels."

"But Christmas breakfast—" Her teeth were chattering so hard I could barely understand her.

The seatbelt wouldn't release. I pressed the button harder, jamming my thumb against it repeatedly. Nothing.

"It's stuck. I tried… but I couldn't—" When I pulled back, she pawed clumsily at the air, her teary eyes going wide with panic. "No. Please don't leave me here!"

"Not going anywhere." I pulled the hunting knife from the sheath on my belt. "Hold still."

I sawed through the seatbelt, the fabric parting with a wet ripping sound. She sagged forward the second it released, and I caught her against my chest, her blood immediately soaking through my shirt.

"I've got you, baby," I murmured as I maneuvered her through the gap in the door, trying to be gentle while urgency screamed at me to move faster. Every second in this freezing tomb was stealing more of her body heat. "Can you stand?"

"Of course I can." She tried to prove it by shifting her weight, then immediately swayed. "Maybe. The world's a little spinny."

"Spinny ain't a medical term, Kels."

"Sure it is. Right between 'owie' and 'fuck, that hurts.'"

The loopy, unfiltered version of Kelsey typically only came out when she was drunk or heavily medicated, which told me she was definitely hypothermic.

The storm hit us full force once we cleared the vehicle, the wind threatening to knock us both down. I tucked her against my side, using my body to shield her from the worst of it.

"The groceries," she mumbled against my shoulder as I guided her arms around my neck and bent to scoop her up. One arm under her knees, the other around her back. "We can't forget the groceries."

"Kelsey Dawn Riggs, swear to God, if you don't forget about the fucking groceries..." I growled.

"Don't yell at me." She was crying again. "I'm trying to make it nice for them even though everything's broken and wrong and—"

"Shh." I pulled her closer, tucking her head under my chin. "I'm sorry, darlin'. I'm not yelling. And I promise I'll come back for the groceries. But first, we need to get you out of the cold."

"I can walk," she protested, but her arms tightened around my neck.

"Humor me."

"Since when do I do that?"

Since never, I thought, but didn't say it. The trip back to the Bronco was treacherous. Ice under snow, wind trying to knock us sideways, Kelsey's weight throwing off my balance. Twice I nearly went down, and both times she gasped and clung tighter, her face buried in my neck.

"Almost there," I said, though I wasn't sure if I was reassuring her or myself.

The truck was still running with the driver's door hanging open. I kicked it shut before moving around to the passenger side. When I reached for the handle, she caught my hand.

"I can't—I'll get blood on the seats." She stared down at the worn leather as if it were sacred. "I know how you are about the Bronco."

"Are you seriously worried about that right now?"

"This is your baby. You've had this truck longer than you had me."

The words stung, even though I didn't think she meant them to. "Kels, I don't give a flying fuck about the seats. It's just a vehicle. You're—" I stopped, jaw clenching.

You're everything. You're the mother of my children and the love of my life and the only person who's ever really known me.

Not the time, asshole.

"Just get in the damn truck."

She laughed or maybe cried—hard to tell with all the blood and ice on her face. But she let me help her up, let me guide her legs in, let me reach across to buckle the seatbelt. My hands shook so badly that it took three tries to get it latched.

I pulled a bandana off the dash and pressed it against the cut on her head. Still bleeding, but slower. Maybe.

"Hold this." I guided her hand up to maintain pressure. "Tight as you can."

Kelsey finally leaned back, exhausted, the bandana already darkening with blood. I cranked the heat to maximum, angling all the vents toward her.

"Still so bossy," she grumbled through chattering teeth, head tipping back against the headrest. "Don't forget the groceries."

Ten minutes, fifteen curse words, and one busted ass later, the groceries, purse, and cell phone were safely loaded into the Bronco. I eased back onto what I hoped was the road. Visibility was worse than before, if that was possible. We started the slow crawl up to my place, the engine rumbling in displeasure at the pace.

Kelsey had moved to the middle of the bench seat while I was getting everything out of the SUV, and her head now rested against my shoulder.

"Hey." I reached over when she went quiet, gently squeezing her thigh. "Talk to me. How many fingers am I holding up?"

"You're driving," she said without opening her eyes. "Both hands on the wheel, Theodore."

"Don't fall asleep," I said when her breathing started to even out.

"I'm not." But her voice was drowsy, soft. "Just resting my eyes."

"Kelsey."

"I'm okay," she murmured. "We're okay."

We weren't. We were about as far from okay as two people could be. But with her head on my shoulder and her breath on my neck, I could almost believe her.

Almost.

6

kelsey

THE COLD PORCELAIN of Teddy's bathroom counter bit through my wet clothes, but at least I'd stopped shaking. Mostly. My feet dangled like a child's as he rummaged through the medicine cabinet, muttering about hydrogen peroxide and where the fuck he'd put the good bandages.

The overhead lights were softer than I expected—a warm golden—nothing like the harsh bulbs that had lit up every one of Sky's skinned knees and Addie's split lips from soccer headers gone wrong.

"Found them." He emerged with a rectangular white box that looked untouched, probably bought during some optimistic grocery run where he'd convinced himself he'd take up mountain biking or whatever men did when they moved to Colorado to forget their ex-wives.

The bathroom was exactly what I'd expected from bachelor Teddy —utilitarian but clean, a single toothbrush in the holder, one towel on the rack. No decorative soaps or coordinating bathmats. Just the essentials, arranged exactly how he'd kept them when we lived together. Even his razor sat at a perfect right angle to the sink edge.

"This is gonna sting," he warned, dabbing a cotton ball with antiseptic.

"I'm not five, Teddy. I can handle—"

I hissed through my teeth as soon as it touched my skin, the burn drowning out my ability to think rationally—

I was back inside the SUV, metal crumpling as the pine tree caught the hood. The airbag exploded, powder burning my throat, my eyes, coating everything in a chalky white film. Blood slid into my lashes, warm at first, then freezing as snow drifted in through the broken windshield.

The seatbelt locked, cutting into my ribs like a vise. I jabbed at the release repeatedly, but it wouldn't budge. And help wasn't coming.

My thoughts turned sluggish, drifting to Addie and Sky— imagining them arriving only to find me gone. To Teddy, wishing I could take back every word from the night before. And finally, to Levi. Had he been this scared? Had regret clawed at him in his final moments, the same way it clawed at me now?

Then Teddy's face appeared, snow tangled in his hair, eyes wild. And for one horrible second, I thought he'd turn back and leave me to the elements. That he realized saving me wasn't worth it. That I wasn't worth it.

The terror of abandonment had been worse than the crash itself.

"Hey." Teddy's thumb brushed my cheek, pulling me back to the present. "You disappeared on me. You okay?"

I blinked, finding myself not in the SUV but in his bathroom, fingers locked around his wrist, tears streaming down my face. Great. Just what I needed—to fall apart in front of the man who'd already seen me at my absolute worst.

"I'm fine." I let go and wiped at my eyes with the back of my hand. "Just the antiseptic. Zero out of ten, do not recommend."

He didn't call me on the lie but worked more gently. This close, I could see the concern etched deep in his hazel eyes.

I watched his hands. Broad, calloused, the same hands that had cradled our children, braided hair, built dollhouses. The same hands that had struck his youngest brother in the funeral home parking lot after Dane took the blame for Levi's death.

I'd hated Teddy for that—for losing control when I needed him to hold me together. But as he worked now with the same care he'd once used on splinters and scraped knees, I wondered if maybe I'd rewritten our history to make my pain easier to carry.

Memory was selective like that. I'd told myself Teddy had checked out, had chosen the club—and the club girls—over family. But other memories surfaced, too. His thumb tracing lazy circles on my hip at club gatherings, claiming me even in a room full of leather and testosterone, as if the *Property of Crow* patch embroidered on the back of my tank top hadn't been enough. The kisses he'd press to my neck while I cooked, arms wrapped around my waist, swaying to whatever was on the radio. The way his arms quieted the chaos and anxiety in my head, wrapping around me like a promise that we'd get through it together.

Only we hadn't.

"Bleeding's slowing some," he said, frowning at the cut. "You anemic again?"

Three viable pregnancies, three battles with iron pills and medium-rare steaks grilled every single night because Teddy had read somewhere that red meat helped. He'd hover while I ate, making sure I finished every bite, even when morning sickness—which had lasted all day with Sky—made everything taste like copper pennies.

"Blood thinners."

His hands stilled against my temple. "Blood thinners? Why?"

"Oh, you know. The usual middle-aged woman stuff." I waved a hand, trying to deflect with humor the way I always did when things got a little invasive for my liking. "Next thing you know, I'll have a house full of cats and be watching murder documentaries in my bathrobe. I mean, I'm already halfway there. Just need a couple more cats and—"

"Kels," he said with a pinched expression, silently demanding the truth.

"AFib," I said, like it was nothing. Like I hadn't spent three months terrified my heart would stop working. "Couple dizzy spells, one spin class face-plant. Very graceful. I took a header into the mirror in front of a bunch of twenty-somethings in Lululemon."

He scanned me head to toe, like he could fix it by sheer will. "When?"

"I don't know—a year ago?" Which was also coincidentally the last time I'd been in a gym.

His jaw ticked. "And you didn't think to tell me?"

"You know, I meant to include it in the Christmas card I sent to your lawyer. Must've slipped my mind."

"I thought I lost you!" The words burst out of him, raw and jagged.

"Teddy..."

"When I saw that guardrail torn apart, when I found you covered in blood and half-frozen—" His voice cracked. He turned away, rinsing the bloody washcloth under the faucet.

I wanted to joke. Deflect. But nothing came.

"You're not getting rid of me that easily," I said finally, forcing lightness into my voice.

He didn't smile. Didn't even offer the signature half-smirk that used to drive me crazy.

"Hey, I'm okay," I added, even though we both knew it was a lie. I was a lot of things—frozen, confused, slightly concussed, having feelings I'd specifically forbidden myself from having—but okay wasn't one of them.

His hand cupped my cheek as he placed the bandage over the cut. "You're always okay."

I fought the urge to lean into his touch; to pretend we were still the people who knew how to love each other without destroying everything in the process.

Teddy went quiet then, turning back to the sink. Blood—my blood —had dried in the creases of his knuckles, under his nails, streaking up his forearms like abstract art. Our eyes met in the mirror—once, twice, a third time—each glance loaded with all the things we'd never say. This was his way. He never spoke when he was angry, never raised his voice when grief threatened to swallow him whole. He'd just... disappear. Pull away until I was left grasping at shadows, trying to hold onto something that was already gone.

My therapist once said the people closest to us were mirrors, reflecting the wounds we refused to face. At the time, I'd rolled my eyes at the fortune cookie wisdom, but maybe she was right.

Maybe we'd both been drowning, but instead of reaching for each other, we'd clung to our own lifeboats—his made of motorcycle exhaust and clubhouses, mine constructed from treadmill miles and perfect meal prep—neither particularly seaworthy.

Perfect Kelsey—that was what he'd called me. But Perfect Kelsey was just scared Kelsey in designer jeans, terrified that if she showed even the slightest cracks, he'd confirm what I'd long suspected—that I wasn't worth saving.

The water ran pink, then clear, but Teddy kept scrubbing, cleaning under each fingernail as if he were prepping for surgery. "The meds in your purse?"

I shook my head, feeling stupid for having ventured out in a blizzard without an emergency bag. How many times had I harped on the kids about having a plan... about using their brains and thinking things through?

"I'll take the snowmobile as soon as the storm eases up and get whatever you need."

"Or you could just drop me off—"

"Need to get you warm," he interjected as if I hadn't spoken. "You're shivering again."

I hadn't noticed. The bathroom wasn't cold—if anything, the steam from the sink had made it humid—but my body couldn't seem to regulate temperature anymore. The same way it had forgotten how to do basic things, like stay warm or maintain a steady heartbeat or not fall apart the second my ex-husband touched me.

He helped me down from the counter, pausing to grab some clothes from the dresser in his bedroom before guiding me toward the living room, his palm steady and warm against the small of my back.

The living and kitchen areas opened before us, all exposed beams and a massive stone fireplace I'd admired on the way in. But where the rental cabin had been cozy and cluttered with holiday charm, Teddy's place felt hollow. No twinkling lights here. No festive wreaths or mismatched holiday mugs. The cabin was spotless but utterly impersonal, like he'd been living in a very expensive, very clean purgatory.

His boots stood in a perfect line by the door—work boots, motorcycle boots, the ancient cowboy boots I'd bought him for his thirtieth birthday. Everything exactly parallel, toes aligned like soldiers awaiting inspection. A single coffee mug sat upside down in the dish rack in the open concept kitchen.

A tree stood in the corner, half-wrapped in a single strand of lights that hadn't even been plugged in, boxes of ornaments stacked beside it. Waiting. Unfinished. Abandoned. Even Charlie Brown would have shaken his head and told Teddy to get his shit together.

It was the loneliest thing I'd ever seen.

This was what Christmas looked like when you were alone. When there was no one to perform for, no reason to pretend the holidays meant anything more than the end of another long year.

Through the floor-to-ceiling windows, the Rockies stretched endlessly, a million-dollar view that only emphasized how empty the space was. How alone he'd been, staring at all that beauty with no one to share it with.

"Sit." He eased me onto the couch in front of the roaring fire, then dropped to his knees.

"Teddy, you don't have to—"

"Hands."

I extended them reluctantly. His palms dwarfed mine, rubbing small circles until the blood began flowing again.

"Better?" he asked, like it was just another task on his to-do list.

Defrost the ex-wifesicle. Check.

When I nodded, he moved to my feet, muttering a curse at their mottled bluish-purple color. His hands engulfed my left foot, coaxing life back into my frozen toes.

The sudden sensation was excruciating, and I bit down hard on my bottom lip to keep from crying out. If frostbite didn't kill me, the pins and needles would.

"I know, baby," he murmured. "I know it hurts."

Baby.

The familiarity of it—the pet name on his lips, his hands on my skin, the automatic way he knew exactly where to press—threatened to undo me completely.

This was the man who'd rubbed my feet through all my pregnancies, when they were swollen and achy. Who'd sat on the floor of our bedroom at two in the morning, kneading the cramps out of my calves with a patience most men didn't possess.

Now he was doing it again, and I couldn't bear the tenderness of it. Not when I was already so raw, so close to falling apart completely.

"You really don't have to do this," I whispered, even as my body betrayed me, relaxing into his touch.

"Yes, I do," he insisted before switching to my right foot. "Can't have you losing toes. The girls would never forgive me."

The girls. Always our safe topic, our neutral ground. But even that felt loaded now, sitting in his empty cabin while they pulled the strings for this little reunion from two states away.

"Speaking of," I said, wincing as another agonizing wave of feeling returned. "I need to call them back. Addie texted earlier—"

"Already texted them."

I lifted my head to peer down at him. "What'd you say?"

He shrugged, his face the picture of innocence. "Told them your phone was dead, but that you were riding out the storm here, which is technically true."

My brow rose. "That's it?"

A ghost of a smirk tugged at the side of his mouth. "Might have mentioned I had to rescue some crazy woman who drove her rental into a tree in the middle of a blizzard."

"I'll have you know I didn't drive into the tree, Theodore," I said primly. "I drove into the guardrail. The tree was collateral damage."

He ran his tongue over his teeth, fighting a full-on smile. "My mistake, Kelsey Dawn. The tree was just an innocent bystander."

It was strange how easily we'd slipped back into the easy banter that had been a staple of our relationship. Even stranger was how badly I wanted it to last.

He stood abruptly. "Come on, Speed Racer. Let's get you out of these wet clothes."

Panic coiled around my chest like a python. The practical part of my brain knew he was right. The wet fabric was leeching what little body heat I'd managed to generate. But the thought of undressing in front of him, of being that vulnerable when I was already hanging on by a thread—

"I can do it," I rushed to say.

He sighed, a bone-deep weariness that came from fighting the same battles repeatedly. "Let me."

I let him peel the bloodstained sweater off, obediently holding my arms up like the kids used to when we got them undressed for bathtime.

When his calloused fingers grazed the sides of my breasts as he pulled off my bra, everything changed. Not the slow, subtle shift of tectonic plates, but the sudden crack of lightning splitting a tree in half. My body, which had been half-frozen and stuck in survival mode, suddenly remembered it was alive. More than alive—it was hungry in a way I hadn't felt in years.

Goosebumps scattered across my skin, and his pupils expanded, the muscle in his jaw twitching before he moved onto my jeans. His knuckles brushed against my belly as he unzipped me, and a small moan slipped past my lips.

"Sorry," Teddy muttered, mistaking the sound for pain. "Hands are probably still too cold."

Cold?

They felt like brands against my skin, each touch leaving invisible marks I'd be feeling for days.

The denim clung to me like a second skin, forcing him to work it down slowly. When the red lace came into view—purchased post-divorce in a desperate attempt to feel desirable—he rasped, "Jesus, Kels."

Which, for the record, was not the review the salesgirl promised. I'd bought them to prove to myself I was more than a grieving mother, a discarded wife, a woman who'd spent four decades at war with her body. They were meant to be a confidence booster. Standing in front of my ex-husband now, I only felt ridiculous.

Especially like this. One year since the AFib diagnosis, one year since I'd stopped working out. When Teddy left, I'd been a gym rat, all sharp lines and tight muscles. Now, softer curves had replaced the body I once weaponized against him.

He probably thought the lace was a pathetic attempt to be something I wasn't. Or maybe he was cataloging the ways my body had changed, the gym-honed results that had vanished as soon as I stopped chasing them.

Shame stung my eyes when he knelt again, his breath warming my thighs as he peeled them off, instructing me to lift one leg, then the other.

Even when I stood bare, Teddy stayed on his knees, forehead resting against the curve of my belly, shoulders rising with ragged breaths. My fingers slipped into his hair, threading through damp strands at the crown of his head before he jerked back, blinking up at me as though waking from a dream.

He cleared his throat and grabbed a navy flannel shirt off the couch, wrapping it around my shoulders.

The fabric fell to mid-thigh and was saturated in his scent—wood and leather and something I'd never been able to identify but had long associated with him. I had to fight the urge to bury my nose in the collar like some lovesick teenager.

After working my arms through the sleeves, he buttoned me in, one by one, eyes never quite meeting mine. I lost track of my breathing somewhere around the third button. His hands lingered at my collarbone, thumbs resting in the hollow of my throat where my pulse hammered as fast as a hummingbird's wings.

I caught his wrist without thinking, and his eyes flashed to mine, our faces frozen inches apart. His breath ghosted across my lips. All I had to do was lean forward. Close that insignificant distance and feel his lips against mine again.

"You need to rest."

The abrupt withdrawal stung. I dipped my chin in a nod and let him lead me to the couch, my cheeks warm with embarrassment. What had I expected? That he'd pull me into his arms and tell me he'd never stopped loving me? That we'd fall into bed like the last two years hadn't happened.

Teddy tucked me beneath a pile of heavy quilts that smelled like the cedar closet back home before stripping off his shirt. He tossed it next to mine on the floor before undoing his belt, and I tried to look away.

Really, I did.

Once upon a time, we couldn't keep our hands off each other—in the backseat of the Bronco, at the clubhouse, in every motel we ever stayed in. But toward the end, even sex had become a rarity, another item on the endless list of things we couldn't get right.

Looking at him now as he slipped on a pair of sweatpants—his body harder and leaner than I remembered—I ached with memories of the wildness as much as the loss of it.

There were tattoos I'd never seen before—roman numerals lining his rib cage, a black feather on his thigh, and swirling script over his heart. My eyes snagged on the first letter, trying to make it out in the shifting shadows from the fire—an H?

My heart dropped. Hannah? Heather? Some Colorado mountain woman who didn't come with three decades of baggage and a dead son between them?

Something that felt suspiciously like jealousy snared in my chest, which was ridiculous for a man I once told I hoped never to see again.

"Move forward," Teddy said, voice rougher than gravel.

"I'm fine where I am."

He stared down at me, hands on his hips, every inch the frustrated father who could stop the kids' bickering with a single look.

"What? I'm comfortable." I wasn't. The angle was wrong, the heat from the fire only reaching one side of me while the other stayed stubbornly cold. But sharing a couch with him, pressed together under blankets while the storm raged outside? That was a special kind of torture I wasn't sure I could survive.

"I'll be fine. Just need a few more—"

"Your teeth are chattering loud enough to wake the dead," he grumbled, all six-foot-two inches of him squeezing in behind me on a couch that suddenly felt doll-sized.

My breath hitched as his bare chest pressed against my back, solid and warm through the flannel. Every muscle in my body went rigid. "Teddy, no."

"It's not—Christ, Kels. Just trying to get your body temp back up. This is the fastest way." Something in his voice suggested he was trying to convince himself as much as me. "Stop squirming."

"I'm trying not to fall off," I bit out, hugging the edge of the cushion to keep our bodies from touching.

A low sound escaped his throat when I shifted again, too far this time. The couch edge disappeared beneath me, and I started to slide.

In an instant, Teddy's arm shot out, hauling me back before I could introduce my face to the hardwood floor. Thirty-plus years of reflex took over—protective, automatic. He flipped me over and tugged me back until we were breathing the same air, every inch of me touching every inch of him.

The eleven minutes and forty-three seconds our daughters had calculated between our cabins collapsed into the span of a breath.

We were as close as two people could be without actually becoming one. My breasts crushed to his chest; my hips aligned with his in a way that made it painfully clear this was affecting him as much as me.

It was a standoff, a strange game of chicken neither of us wanted to lose. Who would pull away first? Who would admit this was more than survival?

My thighs parted instinctively to accommodate him. Teddy released a rough exhale, dropping his hand to my thigh beneath the blankets and hitching it higher. His hips rolled forward in response, the hard press of him leaving no room for misinterpretation.

His eyes darkened at the sound it drew out of me, and for a wild second, I thought he was about to shove his sweatpants down and erase the last sliver of space between us. *God help me, I wanted him to.*

Then his mouth flattened, and the hand on my thigh retreated, fisting in the quilt instead.

"Better?" he asked, the word rumbling through his chest into mine.

"Not really, no," I squeaked, unable to find the words to explain how every point of contact felt like touching a live wire, electricity arcing between us with nowhere to ground itself.

"Your fingers are digging into my bad shoulder," Teddy grunted, but made no move to shift them.

I immediately loosened my grip, embarrassed by how desperately I'd been clinging to him. "Sorry."

"Don't apologize." His hand came up to cradle the back of my head, fingers threading through my tangled hair. "Just try to relax."

Relax. Right. Like I could do that with the ridges of muscle pressing into me with every expansion of his chest, his thumb tracing absent circles at the nape of my neck, the same way he used to when I couldn't sleep.

"What are you thinking?"

I almost laughed. What was I thinking? That I'd spent two years trying to convince myself I was over him, only to fall apart the second he touched me. That my body remembered his like a language I'd once been fluent in. That the careful walls I'd built were felt about as solid as tissue paper.

I settled on, "I'm thinking this is a really bad idea."

"Probably." But his arms tightened around me anyway, like he couldn't help himself. "But when's that ever stopped us?"

Never.

We'd been terrible at stopping when things were a bad idea. Like when I was sixteen, and I snuck him into my bedroom window, convinced my parents wouldn't hear us. Or when we decided to try for a third baby despite the multitude of complications with my previous pregnancies. Or when we kept pretending everything was fine long after our foundation had cracked beyond repair.

"Earlier, you said you thought you lost me, but you've—" My throat gave a painful squeeze, and I took a deep breath before forcing the words out. "You've always had me. Since the night you showed up at the homecoming dance, even though you hated them. You've had every piece of me since I was fifteen, Teddy. And I haven't moved on— I can't. I gave it all to you."

His chest rose sharply beneath mine, the fire casting enough light for me to see the glossy shine of emotion in his eyes.

"Kels," he murmured.

"I need to tell you something—"

"Whatever it is, it can wait," he said softly.

I'd been carrying this awful truth around since Levi's death, and now that I'd finally worked up the courage to say it—to tell him that the divorce wasn't his fault, that it was my shame eating me alive—he was shutting me down.

"Please. I need you to know—"

"It can wait until morning." His voice was gentle but final. "When you're warm and thinking straight again."

"I am thinking straight."

Lie.

His hazel eyes searched my face, seeing through me the way he always had. "Are you? Because less than a day ago, you slammed a door in my face. Now you're telling me I've always had you. Which version am I supposed to believe?"

He was right—I was all over the place, my emotions swinging like a pendulum between anger and longing, between the urge to run and the desperate need to stay exactly where I was.

"Get some rest."

My chin wobbled, the ache behind my eyes building with the tears I was holding back. His rejection—gentle as it was—still cut deep. Here I was, offering him my heart again, and he was telling me to sleep it off like a bad hangover.

"Right," I managed, already regretting the confession.

Our daughters had orchestrated this entire scheme because they still believed in fairy tales—believed two broken parents could be forced back together with nothing more than good intentions and a little Christmas magic.

But real life was never that simple.

I tried to pull away, but Teddy's arms tightened, refusing to let me go.

"Stay, Kels. Please." His voice was gruff, but there was something underneath it. Something that sounded almost vulnerable.

The please undid me completely. Teddy Riggs never begged for anything.

So, I stayed.

Tomorrow would come with all its complications and regrets. But tonight, with my face tucked into the hollow of his throat and a blizzard raging all around us outside, I let myself pretend that maybe our daughters had it right.

Just for tonight.

7

Four Days Until Christmas

kelsey

THE BLANKETS HAD MULTIPLIED OVERNIGHT. That, or I'd been too frozen to notice that I'd been cocooned in enough layers to survive an arctic expedition.

My body ached in new and creative ways, a symphony of complaints from the wreck, combined with the soreness of sleeping pressed against someone on a couch after two years of having a king-size bed to myself.

I sat up slowly, cataloging the damage. The cut on my head throbbed dully beneath the bandage, my ribs protested where the seatbelt had pinned me, and my neck had developed an interesting crick from using Teddy's chest as a pillow. But underneath all that, something else registered—something so foreign it took me a moment to identify.

I'd slept through the night.

Not the restless, broken sleep I'd grown accustomed to, where I'd wake every hour like clockwork, my body trained by grief to remain vigilant. Not the medicated unconsciousness that came from the sleeping pills I'd finally given up because they left me feeling sluggish and foggy the following day.

Real sleep.

The kind where you closed your eyes in one moment and opened them in another, with nothing but darkness in between.

Two years and seven months of nightmares I wouldn't wish on my worst enemy—dreams of beating my fists bloody on a heavy iron door while Levi screamed for me from the other side, never reaching him before his cries for help stopped. In another, I raced down the hall to his room, only to find Teddy's body instead.

But last night, wrapped in quilts and my ex-husband's reluctant embrace, my body had apparently decided to take a night off from its regularly scheduled programming.

After confessing to the nonexistent state of my love life and being gently rejected, I'd fallen into an exhausted sleep. Teddy woke me some time after dark, his voice low as he coaxed me upright long enough to eat.

Bleary-eyed, I'd managed to choke down a few spoonfuls of sausage potato soup before pushing the bowl away. He'd pushed it right back, his brow lifting in challenge. "All of it. You need the protein."

I'd been too tired to argue and let him spoon-feed me like I was one of the kids. Afterward, he'd handed me a mug of herbal tea that smelled like Mentholatum but had tasted surprisingly good.

Once every drop was gone, he'd tucked me back under the quilts before moving to the armchair near the fireplace. Of course, he'd choose to spend the night cramped and uncomfortable rather than risk the intimacy of lying beside me again.

"Cold," I'd mumbled, the word slipping out before I could stop it. I patted the space beside me for good measure, refusing to dwell on the reasoning behind my need to have him close.

Teddy had hesitated for what felt like an eternity before climbing back under the quilts with me. I'd curled into him the moment the couch dipped under his weight, my cheek finding its familiar place against his chest, his heartbeat steady and strong against my ear. And for the first time in years, the darkness hadn't felt so heavy.

Now, gray morning light filtered through ice-covered windows, but the space beside me was cold. Empty. The fire had been recently stoked. Which meant he was probably showering. Or maybe outside, checking on the damage from the storm.

The flannel shirt had twisted around me in my sleep, riding up to expose damn near everything to the morning chill. I tugged it down and padded from room to room, my voice still rough with sleep as I called out for Teddy with no response.

In the kitchen, a mug had been set out next to the coffee maker, just waiting to be filled. And propped against it like the world's least romantic love note was a piece of paper torn from what appeared to be an envelope.

HAD TO RUN OUT.
-T

That was it. No explanation of where he'd gone or when he'd be back. No acknowledgment of last night—not the confession I'd made, not the way we'd slept tangled together like we used to.

Nothing.

I stared at each word, trying to decode hidden meaning from his familiar handwriting—still the same cramped scrawl that had signed thirty-two years' worth of anniversary cards and grocery lists and excuse notes for school.

Had to run out where?

The hurt that bloomed in my chest was as familiar as it was unwelcome. The worst part? I couldn't even pretend to be surprised. It was what we'd always done—circled each other in an endless dance of almosts and not-quites, getting close enough to remember why we'd fallen in love before pulling back and rebuilding our walls even higher.

Whatever softness had existed between us last night had evaporated with the storm, leaving behind an empty kitchen and a note that might as well have been signed by a stranger.

I mashed the button on the coffee maker, staring blankly out the window above the sink while the machine burbled to life. Outside, the world had been transformed by feet of blinding white snow, reminding me of the snow globes Levi once collected. Everything pristine. Perfect. Beautiful...if you didn't think too hard about being sealed inside it.

Before I could spiral too far into old resentments, my phone buzzed to life on the counter where it had been left to charge last night.

Teddy's mother's name flashed across the screen, and I groaned, wishing I could ignore it. But Lucy had raised four boys and could smell avoidance from two states away. If I didn't answer, she'd reach out to Addie and Sky, and I was nowhere near ready to face their line of questioning.

I scrambled to clear my throat, forcing brightness into my voice as I answered. "Hey, good morning!"

"Good morning, sweetheart." Her voice wrapped around me like one of her famous hugs. "Girls said you made it there in the nick of time. Just wanted to check in, see how you're holding up. We've been watching the weather channel, and it just looks awful. Lord knows Paul and I worry about you kids up there in all that snow."

Kids.

As if Teddy and I were still the teenagers she'd busted going at it on the pool table in their basement.

"I'm... good," I said, which was true if 'good' meant 'I crashed my rental into a tree, spent the night pressed against your son like a barnacle, and woke up to a note that suggested he'd rather brave a blizzard than stay in the same room with me.' "I think the worst of it passed through overnight."

"I've been trying to reach Teddy all morning to check in, but you know how he is."

I did. The man would rather perform his own root canal than have an actual conversation, phone or otherwise.

"Hope he hasn't left you to fend for yourself," she added, as subtle as a freight train.

"Oh, no," I said quickly, willing the coffee maker to brew faster. "I'm, uh, I'm actually riding it out at his place."

"Good, good. Well, put him on." The hopeful lift in her voice sent a pang of guilt through my chest.

"He's actually outside," I said quickly, the lie rolling off my tongue before I could stop it. "The drifts are pretty high, and he wanted to get them cleared."

"In this weather?" Paul's gravel-rough voice cut through the speaker, and I could practically see his and Lucy's eyes narrowing the way they did anytime one of their boys tried to pull something over on them. "That boy never did have the sense God gave a goose. I hope you're keeping him in line."

"Trying to," I managed with a weak laugh. I hadn't been able to keep their son in line when we were married. The chances of doing it now were somewhere between zero and when hell froze over—which, given the view outside, might have happened.

"Well, I'm just glad you two are getting a chance to reconnect," Lucy chimed in, like Teddy and I were star-crossed lovers in a romance novel instead of two people who'd signed divorce papers in separate rooms because we couldn't stand to look at each other.

"We're not," I started, then stopped, aware my former mother-in-law's bullshit detector was top of the line.

The coffee maker sputtered its last drops into the carafe, giving me something to focus on besides the fact that our families continued to treat our split as if it were a phase or a break, convinced we'd come to our senses eventually.

I poured myself a cup with shaking hands, adding a splash of the oat milk creamer I'd managed to snag during the pre-storm frenzy at the store while Paul rumbled something in the background about meddling.

She shushed him before continuing. "I'm just saying, Christmas has a way of working things out. And a blizzard forcing you two together? Sounds like a sign to me."

"Lucy," I warned, but it was too late. She was already off to the races, convinced she could fix whatever had broken between us with a few words of wisdom and a little holiday magic.

"What? You two were always better together than on your own. Whatever happened, whatever drove you two apart—it doesn't have to be permanent. People who love each other the way you two do find their way back. Sometimes they just need a little push."

Or a full-on shove off a cliff, apparently, which was what this felt like.

"It's not that easy," I protested weakly.

We'd been a lot of things together—young, reckless, passionate, broken—but better? That was debatable. Unless better meant perfecting the art of mutual destruction.

"Seems to me," Lucy's voice took on the thoughtful quality that usually preceded something I didn't want to hear, "that you two oughta simplify things then. Life's too short, sweetheart. Trust me, at our age, Paul and I know that better than most."

"Speak for yourself, Luce," he grumbled. "I'm at my peak."

"Honey, Carter was still president when you were at your peak," she teased.

Their gentle sparring continued, but I barely heard it.

Life's too short.

Such a simple phrase, but it landed like a lead balloon. Life was too short—Levi had proven that. Too short for what, though? For second chances? For forgiveness? For admitting that waking up in Teddy's arms was the first time I'd felt whole in two years?

"You can't tell me you haven't thought about it," she continued, like a shark who'd scented blood in the water. "All those years together, three beautiful children who would love nothing more than to see their parents—"

"Two," I corrected quietly, the word catching in my throat. "We have two children."

The line went silent for a heartbeat too long. The kind of quiet that came when people realized they'd stepped on the landmine everyone else was tiptoeing around.

"Oh, honey." Her voice cracked. "I didn't mean—"

"I know," I said softly, gripping the counter edge until my knuckles went white. Because if I let her apologize, if I let her say his name, I'd lose it. And falling apart over the phone with my former mother-in-law while standing in my ex-husband's cabin and wearing his clothes was not on my Christmas bingo card. "It's okay."

But it wasn't. Nothing about it was okay. Not the way grief could still ambush me in the middle of a perfectly normal conversation. Not the way everyone—including me—kept forgetting to subtract one when counting our children.

But that was the script we all followed now—pretending the wound had healed when really, we'd just gotten better at not acknowledging the gaping hole in our family.

"We just want you both to be happy," Paul rumbled, clearly trying to rescue his wife from the conversational quicksand she'd stepped into. "Both of you. That's all we've ever wanted."

Happy.

Such a simple word for such a complicated thing. I'd forgotten what it even looked like, let alone how to achieve it. Was I happy all alone in our old house in Lubbock with its brand-new furniture and rooms I couldn't walk into? Was Teddy happy in his empty cabin with its half-decorated Christmas tree and bare walls?

I pressed my free hand to my sternum, trying to ease the ache that had taken up permanent residence there. "I should probably go check on Teddy," I lied, desperate to end the conversation before it veered into territory I couldn't navigate. "Make sure he hasn't gotten himself buried in a snowdrift."

Paul cleared his throat. "That boy never stopped loving you, Kelsey. Not for a goddamn minute. Don't give up on him."

The tattoo on his chest begged to differ, but I wasn't about to drop that bombshell on them.

"And we love you," Lucy fervently added. "Always have, always will. You're family, baby girl. No matter what."

My throat closed completely. I managed something that might have been "love you too" before ending the call with a shaky exhale.

They still considered me family. After everything—after I'd failed to keep their son happy, failed to save their grandson, failed at the one job that had ever truly mattered to me—they still claimed me as theirs.

Lucy was wrong about one thing, though. I'd gotten very good at being alone. I'd had years of practice. What I wasn't good at was being around my ex-husband without wanting things I couldn't have. Remembering things I needed to forget. Feeling things I had no business feeling.

I stared at the mug on the counter. *World's Okayest Hunter.* Not world's best, not world's worst. Just okayest. If that wasn't a metaphor for where we were now, I didn't know what was.

Snow had begun to fall again, the fat flakes adding to the apocalyptic accumulation from last night. The drive hadn't been shoveled, which meant that Teddy had likely walked to wherever he'd gone.

An image of the tattoo on his chest flashed through my mind, and anger trickled in, replacing the hurt.

I'd practically thrown myself at him last night, and he'd responded by tucking me in like a child and disappearing as soon as the sun was up.

Message received, loud and clear.

I thought of the name tattooed on his chest, wondering if he was with the mysterious H. The thought of him walking through waist-deep drifts to spend a lazy morning in bed with his girlfriend sent anger flooding through my veins.

I needed to keep my brain occupied, or the next stop was either doomscrolling social media for signs of another woman or dissolving into a puddle of tears on his couch for believing, even for a second, that he would be any different now than when we split.

But busy was my superpower. Busy had gotten me through the aftermath, the funerals, the empty rooms. Busy could handle a storm and an empty house and an ex-husband who might have been screwing his way through Summit Ridge or—at the very least—ghosting me while he figured out what to do with the emotional Chernobyl I'd left on his couch last night.

So, I started cleaning.

Not because it needed doing—Teddy's cabin was nearly sterile, a minimalist's wet dream—but because I needed something to control. Our clothes from yesterday sat in a damp heap near the fireplace where he'd left them. I doused my bloody, dry-clean-only sweater with hydrogen peroxide and hoped for the best, while the rest of our things went into the wash. The machine hummed to life, and I escaped back to the kitchen before I started crying over the sight of his jeans tumbling around the washer with mine again.

After washing the three measly dishes in the sink, I decided the situation called for breakfast casserole. Because nothing said "I'm completely fine with you leaving me all alone after the most confusing night of my post-divorce life" like pork sausage and enough cheese to clog some arteries.

I pulled the carton of eggs from the fridge, the overpriced organic ones I'd risked my life for, along with some bell peppers, sausage, and cheese. I moved through the motions without conscious thoughts, having made the casserole so many times that I could probably do it in a coma.

It was Teddy's favorite, the one he requested every Christmas morning until it became tradition. Even that last horrible Christmas, when we could barely look at each other across the table, I'd made it. Addie had eaten two servings while staring blankly at the empty chair. Sky had pushed hers around her plate and rattled on about her classes, pretending everything was normal. And Teddy and I had choked down every bite in complete and utter silence.

Now here I was, making it again in his kitchen, wearing his shirt. And he was, as usual, gone.

The definition of insanity was doing the same thing over and over, expecting different results. By that measure, I should have been committed years ago.

The casserole went into the oven, with the timer set for fifty minutes. Fifty minutes to figure out what the hell I was doing, why I was still in my ex-husband's cabin, why his mother's words kept echoing in my head.

People who love each other the way you two do find their way back.

Except sometimes love wasn't enough. Sometimes love was the heaviest thing you carried, the weight that pulled you beneath the surface when you were already treading water. We'd loved each other through fertility treatments and pregnancies, through sleepless nights and teenage rebellions, through a thousand small disasters and one enormous one. But that last one had broken something fundamental, turned love into something that hurt to look at directly.

I wiped down counters that didn't need it, arranged dish towels that were already perfectly hung. This was what I did now—played at being useful, at being needed, even when no one was asking. It was easier than admitting that I didn't know who I was when I wasn't taking care of someone. Two years of therapy, and I still couldn't quite figure out how to exist without defaulting to caretaker mode.

The washing machine buzzed, and I transferred everything to the dryer before catching sight of my reflection in the tempered glass on his gun cabinet.

I looked like something from some post-apocalyptic TV series—bandaged head, tangled hair, wearing a shirt that was too big. I needed a shower. Needed to wash off the accident, the night, the lingering feeling of his arms around me. Needed to stop playing house in a life that wasn't mine anymore.

8

kelsey

TEDDY'S GUEST bathroom was exactly what I'd come to expect from his new minimalist lifestyle. White subway tile stretched from floor to ceiling, the dark grout lines giving it a clean, industrial edge. An exposed copper pipe fed into a rainfall shower head behind a glass shower door framed in matte black steel.

Black-and-white hexagon tiles formed a precise pattern along the floor, making the space feel more like a city loft apartment than a mountain cabin.

But it was the collection of bath products in the shower that made my eyebrows climb toward my hairline. Verbena shower gel, lavender shampoo with prebiotic, and even the almond shower oil I used to hide in the cabinet beneath the bathroom sink like contraband.

The same expensive products he'd grumbled about during our marriage, claiming they were identical to the stuff they sold in the drugstore, just with fancy labels.

Either he'd developed a sudden appreciation for luxury bath products, or someone else was using his shower. Someone who shared my affinity for overpriced toiletries and burly bikers.

Of course. The mysterious H probably stayed over often enough to warrant her own shower products. The fancy kind, because Teddy would want to spoil his new woman. Give her all the things he'd complained about giving me.

God, I was a fool. Standing here making his favorite breakfast while he was probably at her place, explaining how his ex-wife had shown up like some deranged stalker.

I cranked the water as hot as I could stand it before stepping under the spray, letting it pound the tension from my neck and shoulders. If only it could erase the memory of Teddy's hands on my frozen skin, the feel of his breath against my neck, the way he'd called me baby like the past two years hadn't happened.

Verbena-scented steam filled the small enclosure as I washed the dried blood and sweat from my skin, hating how it immediately transported me back to lazy Sunday mornings when we still showered together, his hands sliding over my soapy skin while the kids watched cartoons downstairs.

My oat milk latte soured in my stomach at the thought of another woman standing exactly where I stood, giggling at the scrape of his beard against her neck.

Shampoo suds made their way down my forehead and into my eyes. At least, that was what I told myself. The alternative—that I was crying in my ex-husband's shower over the thought of him showering with someone who wasn't me—made me sound unhinged.

By the time I stepped out, my skin was pink and tender, but at least I felt clean. Human, even. After brushing my teeth with his toothbrush —because apparently boundaries meant nothing to me anymore—I knotted a towel around my body and opened the bathroom door, running right into Teddy.

The duffel bag he was carrying hit the floor with a heavy thud, its contents spilling out like evidence at a crime scene—my clothes, medications, and the lingerie I'd packed in a moment of temporary insanity.

"Who's it for?" The words shot out of him before I'd even steadied myself.

"What—what are you talking about?" I clutched the towel tighter, hyperaware of how little it covered. How we were standing close enough for me to see the snow clinging to his hair.

Teddy's eyes tracked the movement, pupils dilating in a way that made heat pool low in my belly.

"The lingerie." He bent to scoop up a handful of lace, waving it between us. "Who's. It. For?"

"Are you serious—how'd you get into the cabin?" I managed to snatch a pair of panties from his grip, heat crawling up my neck.

"Through the door."

"That's called breaking and entering, Theodore." I tried for stern, but it came out breathless. "If there's any damage to the property, so help me—"

"There won't be." His gaze dropped to where the towel gaped at my thigh before jerking back to my face. "I own it."

I blinked; certain I'd misheard. "You what?"

"The cabin you were staying in. I own it."

I stared at him, waiting for the punchline. When it didn't come, when he just stood there with his jaw set and his shoulders tense, the full weight of it crashed over me. The mismatched mugs, the wonky reindeer, the way everything had felt somehow familiar—it was his.

The girls had let me think I was escaping to neutral territory, then literally put me in his house.

"Why didn't you tell me?" My voice came out smaller than I intended.

He rubbed the back of his neck, a tell I immediately recognized. That was the problem with marrying your high school sweetheart, with building a life so intertwined that even two years and five hundred miles couldn't fully separate you.

"If I'd told you that first night, you would've packed your shit and left. Driven off into a blizzard rather than stay in something I owned. Tell me I'm wrong."

He was right, which only made me angrier.

"That's what I thought," he continued when I remained silent. "It wouldn't have been fair to the girls. They wanted one Christmas where we could all be together without the drama."

Everything always came back to what was best for the girls, what would cause them the least disappointment, the least disruption.

"Without the drama?" A laugh bubbled up, tinged with hysteria. "You mean without me ruining everything? Without me being the difficult one? The bad mom who can't keep her shit together?"

All the times I'd thought I was helping, thought I was being the strong one, holding everyone together while Teddy retreated to the club. But maybe I'd had it backward. Maybe I'd been the one they all had to work around, the weak link in our family chain.

The last time I'd seen Levi really smile—not the forced one he wore like armor, but a real smile—had been three months before he died. Teddy had taken him to some motorcycle rally for spring break, just the two of them, and they'd come home covered in mud and grinning like idiots. I'd been furious about the mess, about Teddy encouraging reckless behavior when Levi was already so fragile.

But looking back, maybe that was the problem. I'd treated him like delicate glass while Teddy had treated him like a normal kid. Maybe if I'd been less afraid, less controlling, less desperate to fix everything—

"That's not what I meant." Teddy's hand brushed my shoulder, his voice low, dangerous. "Jesus, Kels. You're not—"

I jerked away from his touch. "Then what did you mean? Because from where I'm standing, it sounds like you all decided I needed to be handled. Tricked into proximity because God forbid anyone actually talk to me like an adult."

He moved closer, backing me against the doorframe. "You wanna talk about being adults? Fine. Let's talk about this." The panties he'd held onto dangled from the end of his index finger. "Because last I checked, you weren't wearing anything like this when we were married."

"Last I checked, we aren't married anymore." I tried stepping around him, but he moved with me, blocking my path. "What I wear under my clothes is none of your business."

"It damn well is when you're—" He stopped, the muscle in his jaw pulsing wildly.

But I wasn't in the mood to hear the rest of his sentence. "I'm not having this conversation with you," I bit out before pushing past him, needing to put some distance between us before I did something monumentally stupid. Like sob uncontrollably. Or worse—admit that the lingerie had been for me. A pathetic attempt to feel desirable after two years of sleeping alone in flannel pajamas that might as well have been a chastity belt.

I made it maybe ten feet before his hand caught my elbow, spinning me back around with enough force to make the towel slip. I clutched at it with my free hand, trying to maintain some illusion of dignity.

"We're talking about this now," he growled, and God help me, the rough edge in his voice did things to my insides that had no business happening when I was this angry.

"No. We're not." I yanked my arm free or tried to. His grip didn't budge. "Let go, Teddy."

"Not until you tell me who he is."

"Who who is?" I knew exactly what he meant but making him spell it out felt like the only power I had left.

"The man you bought the underwear for." His free hand gestured down the hall where he'd dropped the offending scraps of lace. "The one you're—"

"The one I'm what?" I lifted my chin, defiant even in a towel that barely covered the essentials. "Sleeping with? Touching? All the things you haven't done in years?"

His nostrils flared, and something dangerous flashed in his hazel eyes. The kind of look that used to precede either spectacular fights or spectacular sex, sometimes both in the same night.

"Tell me his name."

"You're being ridiculous."

"His name, Kels."

"Do you hear yourself? You sound like a caveman." I tried to step back, but he moved with me again, crowding me against the wall. "What's next, tough guy? Gonna beat your chest and mark your territory?"

"Don't tempt me." Teddy's hand dropped from my elbow to the towel, fingers curling over the knot before he tugged me closer. Until our bodies were flush, until I could feel every hard line of him against me.

His mouth dropped to my ear, his beard scraping against my cheek as he asked, "Wanna know what I'll do if another man touches you, baby?"

My heart hammered against my ribs, every nerve ending suddenly, painfully alive. "Teddy—"

"I'll hunt him down," he murmured, his voice low and dangerous. "I'll break every goddamned bone in his body. Leave him breathing just long enough to regret ever looking at what's mine."

The words should have made me angrier. Should have sent me into a feminist rage about autonomy and toxic masculinity and all the things Sky was always speaking out against. Instead, they sent liquid heat pooling between my thighs, my body apparently having missed the memo that we were supposed to be over this man.

"You don't get to do this," I whispered, hating how my voice cracked. "You don't get to act like—"

"Like what? Like I give a damn who you're planning to let see you naked?" His grip on the towel tightened, knuckles going white. I was one solid tug away from being naked. "Because I do, Kels. I give a very big damn."

"Don't." I pressed my palm against his chest, intending to push him away, but my fingers curled into his shirt instead. "I saw the name tattooed on your chest last night. You don't get to play the jealous ex when you've clearly moved on with your mountain girlfriend."

Teddy pulled back just enough to meet my eyes, and the corner of his mouth twitched. "Mountain girlfriend?"

"H-something. Hannah? Heather? Doesn't matter. I saw the stuff in your shower. I know it's hers."

"Yep," he agreed, not looking the least bit remorseful. "It's hers, just like the perfume in the cabinet."

My stomach plummeted to somewhere around my ankles. Of course he'd admit it. Of course he'd moved on. What had I expected— that a man like Teddy would have stayed celibate since we divorced?

"Every damn thing in that shower is what you used when we were married." He pressed closer. "Same brands, same scents. Bought it all because it reminded me of you. Pathetic, right? Grown man washing his hair with forty-dollar shampoo because it reminds him of his ex-wife."

My mind swam in confusion, struggling to process the idea of Teddy—gruff, practical Teddy—buying lavender shampoo because it reminded him of me.

"But the tattoo—"

"Jesus Christ, woman." Keeping one hand locked around my towel, he tugged his shirt up, baring his chest to the morning sunlight. "Can you read it now, baby? Whose fucking name is that?"

Not Hannah. not Heather. Not an H at all.

Kelsey.

My name. Scarred into his skin in elegant black script, right over his heart. Six letters, a claim, a declaration of something that shouldn't exist anymore but apparently did.

"You…" I couldn't form words. My brain had short-circuited somewhere between seeing my name permanently etched on his body and the realization that he'd marked himself as mine after the divorce. Even after I'd broken us beyond repair.

Without stopping to consider what a terribly bad idea it was, I threaded my fingers through his long hair and tugged his mouth down over mine.

The moment our lips touched, it was like striking a match in a room full of gasoline. Two years of distance, of careful boundaries and polite silence, incinerated in the space between one heartbeat and the next.

Teddy's hand abandoned the towel to bury itself in my wet hair, angling my head to deepen the kiss while his other arm banded around my waist, lifting me clean off the floor.

My legs wrapped around his hips on instinct, and the towel gave up its fight with gravity, pooling to the floor between us. I should have cared. Should have felt exposed, vulnerable, all the things a reasonable person would feel when suddenly naked in their ex-husband's hallway.

Instead, I felt alive. Electric. Like I'd been asleep for years and had finally, blessedly, woken up.

His tongue swept into my mouth—the taste of him something I'd tried to forget, one that had haunted me through six hundred and eighty-two nights of sleeping alone. My body immediately softened, every cell recognizing its other half and sighing in relief.

"Mine," I gasped between kisses, not sure if I was answering his earlier question about the lingerie or staking my own claim. My nails scraped against his scalp, drawing a growl from deep in his chest that vibrated through me.

His beard scraped against my sensitive skin, leaving a trail of delicious friction from my jaw to my collarbone. I'd have beard burn tomorrow, visible evidence of this moment of insanity, and I wanted it. Wanted to wear his marks like a badge of ownership.

"Kels," he breathed against my throat, and I felt the vibration of my name all the way to my toes. "Baby, I need—"

"Yes," I said before he could finish, because whatever he needed, the answer was yes. Had always been yes, even when we were destroying each other. "Please, Teddy, please—"

Time collapsed. We could have been in our mid-twenties, sneaking quickies during Addie's naptime. Or thirty-five, reconnecting after a long stretch of long club runs. Or eighteen, fooling around behind one of the storage buildings at the clubhouse, convinced we'd invented this feeling.

His thumb brushed over my nipple, and I made a sound that would have embarrassed me if I'd had any functioning brain cells left. My body was already tightening, ridiculously close to coming from the slightest touch. I fumbled blindly for his zipper, breathless and half-crazy with need.

And then—because the universe had a warped sense of humor—the oven timer went off.

The shrill beeping cut through the haze of lust like a bucket of ice water. We froze, chests heaving and eyes wide with shock.

"Fuck," he muttered, his forehead dropping to my shoulder.

"The casserole," I said stupidly, as if he couldn't hear the timer screaming from the kitchen.

For a moment, neither of us moved. His body still pinned mine to the wall, my legs still wrapped around his waist, both of us caught between what we wanted and what we definitely shouldn't be doing.

Teddy recovered first, gently lowering me back to the ground before bending to retrieve my towel from the floor. I snatched it from his hand, and he turned away, giving me privacy—like he hadn't seen every inch of me a million times before.

I opened my mouth to say as much when I caught the subtle shift of his shoulders, the unmistakable hitch in his stance, and realized he was adjusting. Trying to get himself under control enough to drag his zipper back up.

When he turned back to face me, his expression was strained, the muscle in his jaw ticking.

I tugged the towel tighter around my body, shaking with the clarity of what we'd almost done and how badly I still wanted it to happen. A few seconds more, and we would have complicated everything exponentially. We would have kept going, up against the wall in his hallway, and I would have let him. I would have soaked up every ounce of pleasure and aftercare he could offer, and then what? Crawled away, pretending it was just one more mistake in a lifetime of spectacular mistakes?

For two years, I'd told myself I didn't want him. Couldn't want him. That Teddy Riggs was my past... that I deserved a future unshackled from all the damage and drama and heartbreak. But one kiss—one second of his mouth on mine—had my entire nervous system revolting.

The digital timer trilled again, more insistent this time, and Teddy raked a hand over his face, deliberately avoiding meeting my eyes. "Kels—"

"Don't." I held up a hand. "Just... don't. Not yet."

Because if he told me it was a mistake, I'd break. If he told me it wasn't, I'd climb him like a Christmas tree and burn through what little goodwill we had left. Neither outcome would improve our situation.

We'd never been able to keep our hands off each other, even when we absolutely should have. Even when we knew it would only end in disaster. Maybe that was our problem all along, why it had all blown up in our faces—he was gasoline, and I was always the dumbass who dropped the lit match. The timer had saved us from making a mistake. Or stopped us from fixing one. I honestly couldn't tell which anymore.

He nodded stiffly before turning and stalking into the kitchen, leaving me half naked in the hallway on trembling legs, still tasting him on my lips.

For one reckless heartbeat, I wanted to believe he couldn't look at me because he was fighting the same battle in his chest. But the grim set of his jaw suggested otherwise. Maybe he was already regretting everything, wishing I'd never set foot in Colorado at all.

9

kelsey

THE FOREST green bodysuit clung to my curves, the V-neck plunging low enough that I reflexively tugged it higher every time Teddy's gaze drifted south of my collarbones.

Which was often.

According to my ex-husband, he'd only had enough time to grab the essentials from the other cabin, wanting to get back before the snow got worse. Turned out, he and I had vastly different views on what constituted "essentials."

In addition to my medications, toiletries, makeup, glasses, and several pairs of socks, Teddy had inexplicably packed the romance novel I'd been reading, all my lingerie, three low-cut bodysuits, and a single pair of jeans.

Not the oversized sweaters or comfortable leggings.

Just silk, lace, and the bodysuits I'd only packed at Addie and Sky's urging, intending to layer them beneath something much warmer. At the time, I hadn't given much thought to their sudden interest in my wardrobe. But it didn't take a genius to see that this had likely been the outcome they'd been hoping for all along.

"Looks like there's another storm system developing," Teddy muttered between bites of casserole, phone glued to his palm.

Great.

"Maybe it'll hold off until the girls make it here," I said, more to break up the silence than any sense of misplaced optimism. Teddy had taken the snowmobile to reach the other cabin earlier and said the roads were completely impassable by vehicle. With DIA shut down indefinitely, the odds of our daughters, much less anyone else, making it today were slim to none.

He offered a noncommittal grunt in response.

We'd been playing this game since we sat down. Polite small talk about the weather, the altitude, how the snow seemed to be picking up again, how good the casserole tasted—as though it were a new recipe and not one I'd perfected in the nineties. Measured tones. Careful distance. As if we hadn't been pressed against each other in the hallway a half-hour ago, my towel on the floor and his hands everywhere.

A flush crept up my throat at the memory, and I turned back to the half-eaten slice of casserole on my plate. The silence felt heavier than the snow piling up outside. Every time I glanced up, his gaze was fixed on me—sometimes on my face, sometimes lower, but always with the intensity of a man trying very hard not to say something. Or do something. Maybe both.

He polished off the rest of the casserole on his plate before taking a drink of coffee, cradling the mug in his hand as his fingers were too large to fit through the handle. I couldn't stop staring at them, couldn't stop the heat that coiled in my belly at the memory of those same fingers threading through my wet hair, cupping my jaw, sliding down to my—

I cleared my throat and pushed my chair back. "There's more. If you want it."

Teddy's head jerked back, his brow furrowed as if I'd suggested something scandalous instead of offering him seconds.

"The casserole," I clarified when the double meaning became clear, the flush migrating up to my cheeks. "Do you want more?"

"Yeah. I do."

The way he said it made me think we weren't talking about breakfast anymore.

I stood, grateful for the excuse to put some distance between us. The kitchen wasn't far—just a few steps from the dining area in the open-concept space—but it felt like crossing a minefield. I could feel his eyes on me as I moved, tracking every sway of my hips.

"Thanks," he said as I passed his plate across the table before settling back into my seat.

"Oh my God. Did Theodore Riggs just thank me?" I asked, dramatically peering out the large window behind him. "Didn't realize Hell had frozen over as well as most of Colorado."

He took a bite, his eyes closing briefly like he was savoring it. Or maybe he was trapped in the same memory loop I was. The movement of his throat as he swallowed shouldn't have been sexy, and yet I couldn't look away. He leaned back in his chair, the corner of his mouth twitching in what might have been a smile. "Been known to have manners. On occasion." His gaze dropped to the V of my neckline, lingering long enough to drive home his point before he licked a stray crumb from the corner of his mouth.

My entire body clenched in response.

This was ridiculous. We were grown adults with decades of history between us. We'd slept in the same bed for more than half our lives, raised three children together, seen each other at our absolute worst. And yet here we were, acting like teenagers who'd just discovered what bodies were for.

My phone buzzed on the table beside me, saving me from whatever was happening between us. I snatched it up, unsurprised to see a series of texts from Addie and Sky.

I knew the brief 'everything is fine' message I sent before we sat down to eat wouldn't be enough to satisfy them.

Sky
PROOF OF LIFE REQUIRED IMMEDIATELY
mom if you can read this and aren't being
buried alive in the snow send a sign or an emoji

Addie

But if you are being buried alive in the snow,
can I have your Le Creuset collection?

Sky

ADDISON GRACE RIGGS! THAT'S SO
MORBID!!!

but hypothetically speaking who gets the
louboutins dad bought you that you never
wore??

asking for a friend.

Even in the worst crisis, they could make me smile.

"The girls?" Teddy asked.

I nodded and passed him the phone so he could read the messages. "The vultures are already dividing up my estate."

It buzzed again, and he swiped his thumb across the screen before drawling, "Skylar."

"Father," she said, deepening her voice to match his register. "Why are you answering Mom's phone?"

"He hasn't murdered me, if that's what you're wondering!" I called from across the table.

"Yet," Teddy added, his eyes holding mine in a way that made my skin feel too warm. Too tight. "Day's still young, though."

"Funny." I reached for the phone, but instead of handing it back, he got up and brought his chair around the table to mine, angling the screen so we were both in frame. His shoulder pressed against mine, warm and solid. I tried not to react to the contact.

Sky's green eyes bounced between us as she scooted over to make room for Addie. Our eldest daughter's long dark hair was twisted into a messy bun on top of her head, her glasses perched low on her nose like she'd just rolled out of bed, which, knowing her, she likely had.

"We got worried when we didn't hear back from you," she said before frowning. "What's wrong with your head?"

My fingers moved over the bandage near my hairline. "Just a little cut from the accident. Your dad patched me up."

"Did he patch up your neck, too?" Sky asked, hiding her smile behind the rim of a cheerful red mug.

I tugged my hair forward, but not before Addie clocked the marks on my throat. "Are those... hickeys?"

"What? No!" The denial shot out of me so fast and high-pitched that even I didn't believe it. Of all the things for my daughters to notice through a grainy video call, it had to be the evidence of their father's mouth on my skin.

"They're from—" I scrambled for a plausible explanation while my brain helpfully replayed every second of our hallway makeout session in slow motion.

Your father's mouth. And beard. And teeth.

"Road rash," Teddy interjected smoothly.

"Weird. I didn't realize you could get road rash when you were inside the car." Sky's voice dripped with sarcasm.

"Seatbelt had your mama pinned. Had to cut through it just to get her out." His hand found my thigh beneath the table, stopping its nervous bouncing before continuing, "Lucky she walked away with just a few bumps and bruises. Could have been a lot worse. Right, Kels?"

I nodded, probably too enthusiastically, trying to ignore the way his thumb had started tracing lazy circles against my leg. "Right," I finally managed, my voice only slightly strained. "Just grateful to be in one piece."

Both girls stared at us through the screen, and I could practically see the wheels turning in their heads. Sky's eyes were bright with barely contained excitement, while Addie wore the satisfied expression of a woman whose carefully laid plans were coming to fruition.

"But to get them on your jaw? Must have been some creative seatbelt placement," she said, adjusting her glasses with a smirk.

"Airbag," I blurted out, my voice going up an octave.

Teddy's hand squeezed my thigh, whether in warning or reassurance, I couldn't tell. The heat from his palm seared through the denim, making it impossible to think of anything but how those same hands had lifted me against the wall earlier. My breathing picked up, shallow and quick, and I had to force myself not to squirm in my seat.

"Well," Sky said, dragging out the word with obvious glee,

"sounds like Dad really had to work to get you free. Must have been very... thorough."

"What's y'all's plan?" Teddy asked, casually rerouting the conversation to a safer topic. "DIA probably ain't gonna be up and running again until tomorrow at the earliest... maybe longer if this second storm is as bad as they're saying it is."

"Yeah, we've been getting the updates," Addie said with a sigh. "Everything north of Amarillo is getting hammered right now. Even if the second storm misses y'all, they're saying it's going to take a while to clear the roads. We've talked about just driving to Lubbock and spending Christmas with LuLu and Poppy."

I'd been so focused on surviving my bizarre reunion with Teddy that I hadn't stopped to consider that the girls might not make it at all. That the elaborate scheme they'd concocted to bring us together for Christmas might end with Teddy and me alone in his cabin while they celebrated with his parents five hundred miles away.

A part of me understood. The drive from Austin to Lubbock was about six hours and much less treacherous than the arctic hellscape they were watching play out on TV. But it didn't ease the hollow feeling in my chest.

Teddy and I, trapped together with nothing but sexual tension and unresolved feelings to keep us company. Days of trying not to notice how his jeans fit or the way his arms and chest had somehow gotten bigger.

"Piper even offered to host a baking day at her and Uncle Dane's house when we get there," Sky added, stopping me mid-spiral. "We're gonna make stollen, and struffoli, and some French sponge cake thing that we can't pronounce."

I forced a smile, even as my heart sank. "That sounds like fun."

But it wasn't fun. It was another Christmas where everything felt wrong. Another year of empty seats. Another reminder that we'd failed at keeping our family together.

My throat clenched painfully, my eyes burning with unshed tears. I'd been looking forward to my time with them for months, had spent weeks planning the perfect Christmas, buying gifts, memorizing all

Sky's new dietary restrictions, and making lists of Addie's favorite desserts for our baking day. All for nothing.

"Are you sure?" Sky's expression softened with concern. "You look like you're about to cry."

"I'm fine," I lied, the same way I'd been lying about being fine for the past two years. "Just tired. Think I'm still trying to get used to the altitude."

Teddy's eyes locked with mine on the phone screen, and for a moment, it was like he saw me. The real me. Not the version of me I'd played for the better part of three decades.

It nearly broke me. I could handle his anger, his frustration, even his desire. But this—this softness, this genuine understanding— threatened to dissolve what little composure I had left.

"It might not even happen," Addie cut in, taking back the wheel. "LuLu said Piper was due at the beginning of January or something, so she could be in labor by the time we get there."

Sky sighed in disappointment, only to perk up at something on the screen. "Dad! Tell me that's not your Christmas tree in the background!"

Keeping his hand anchored to my thigh, Teddy twisted in his chair, following Sky's gaze to the pathetic spruce in the corner of the living room.

"What about it?" he asked, his tone defensive.

"It's naked!" she exclaimed, her horror evident even through the slightly pixelated connection. "And sad! I didn't think a tree could look ashamed, but yours does."

"Skylar," Addie hissed through her teeth, but even she looked troubled by the state of the tree.

"It's not that bad," Teddy muttered, but his hand tightened on my thigh, like he expected me to back him up.

But it was that bad.

Because looking at that tree—listing to the left and half-strung with lights that weren't even plugged in felt too much like a visual metaphor for our marriage.

Something that had begun with high hopes and the best of intentions, only to end up abandoned long before it was finished.

No ornaments. No star on top.

Just green branches and two people who'd given up on making it shine.

"That tree is a cry for help," Sky continued, undeterred by her sister's death glares. "You should do something with it."

"Like what, take it out back and put it out of its misery?" he asked, though something in his tone suggested he already knew where the conversation was headed.

Sky threw her hands up in exasperation. "Decorate it! You know, like normal people do at Christmas?"

"We sent you two whole boxes of ornaments," Addie added, her guilt-trip game as strong as ever. "Do you remember how much shipping costs from Texas to Colorado?"

"Sixty-three forty-seven," Sky answered, nodding solemnly. "That's a lot of ramen noodles, Dad."

"I seem to recall I'm the one who paid for shipping," he pointed out, his jaw tightening with frustration. "It'll get done. Just haven't had time—"

"To what? Hang a few ornaments?" Sky's eyebrows disappeared into her messy bangs. "At the rate you're going, you'll be decorating it for Valentine's Day. Mom, please tell me you're going to fix this tragedy."

I looked at the tree again—really looked at it—and something clicked into place. The other cabin had been decorated to perfection. Every surface adorned with garland and twinkling lights, mismatched ornaments that somehow worked together, stockings hung by the fireplace. Teddy had clearly put thought and care into making that space feel like Christmas for the girls.

Making it feel like home.

Yet his own cabin remained stark and empty, like he'd forgotten he was allowed to celebrate too.

Teddy used to drag the tree down from the attic the week before Thanksgiving, insisting it wasn't fair that the fall decorations got to stay up for months, while his favorite holiday was confined to December. He used to wake up before dawn on Christmas morning, more excited than the kids, pouring pancake batter into cookie-cutter molds shaped like snowmen and trees while Christmas music played in the background.

Something in me needed to fix that tree.

"I'm sorry your dad didn't get the tree decorated while he was busy saving me from a blizzard and ensuring I didn't freeze to death, Skylar Jade," I said, the defensiveness in my tone surprising everyone, including me.

"He wanted to get it done first thing this morning, but I told him it could wait until after breakfast, so why don't you both tend to your own cattle?" I placed my hand over his on my thigh, and he tensed but didn't pull away.

On screen, our daughters' mouths fell open in synchronized shock.

"Did you just..." Sky started, then stopped, her wide-eyed gaze bouncing between us like she was watching a tennis match.

"Tell us to mind our own damn business in Texan?" Addie finished, though her tone held more amusement than offense. "I believe she did."

My cheeks burned, but I didn't take it back. Couldn't, really, not when I could feel the slight tremor in Teddy's hand, the way his breathing had changed. Not when I remembered the way he'd risked his life to find me in that storm, how gentle he'd been cleaning my wounds, how he'd held me through the night even after I'd made that mortifying confession about having no one else.

"We're going to decorate it," I said, trying to sound casual even though my pulse was hammering in my throat. "Together. After we finish our breakfast."

"Together," Sky breathed, her eyes lighting up as though she'd just unwrapped the best Christmas present ever. "You're sitting together. You're going to decorate the tree together."

"No, we'll decorate it in separate rooms and communicate ornament placement using smoke signals," Teddy deadpanned.

I bit back a smile. For someone who communicated primarily in grunts and monosyllables, the man could be surprisingly funny when he wanted to be.

"What Sky means," Addie said, shooting her sister a look, "is that we're glad you're getting along. For Christmas. It's nice to see you two in the same room without looking like you want to murder each other."

Murder wasn't exactly what I wanted to do to their father right now, but I kept that thought to myself.

"Don't sound so shocked. We're both adults." Teddy turned his hand over, lacing our fingers together. His thumb skimmed my knuckles, sending electricity shooting up my arm.

"What are y'all's plans while you're snowed in?" Addie asked as she and Sky exchanged a loaded look.

"All alone in a mountain cabin. God, it's like a movie," Sky added with a grin I didn't trust for a second. "Snowed in with My Ex—no, wait—Christmas Cabin Confessions."

"Ew, that sounds more like a porno," Addie said, her nose wrinkling in disgust.

"What else are they gonna do in a blizzard?" Sky fired back, waggling her eyebrows at us suggestively.

If it had been anyone else, I would have been scandalized. But this was the girl who spent most of her senior prom texting her sister live updates about a couple hooking up in the back of the locker room.

"You should make popcorn garlands, and mulled wine, and watch *Elf*—oh, and bake Christmas cookies!" Sky declared, clapping her hands together.

Teddy lowered his mouth to my ear. "Good to see they're being subtle about their little plan."

The shiver that ran down my spine had nothing to do with the temperature. His breath was warm against my ear, the scrape of his beard against my skin sending a fresh wave of goosebumps across my arms.

"Like a brick through a window," I murmured, trying to keep my expression neutral for the sake of our daughters, who were watching us like hawks.

"Cue the montage," Sky continued, practically vibrating. "Building a gingerbread house. Slow dancing in the kitchen to Nat King Cole. Hot chocolate by the fire. Kissing under the mistle—oh wait. Looks like they already covered that one."

Addie lowered her voice, as if she were doing the voice-over for a movie trailer. "Two people, trapped together in a blinding snowstorm."

"Now, they're forced to confront the past that tore them apart as well as their burgeoning lust," Sky managed in an equally deep tone before dissolving into another fit of laughter.

I could feel Teddy's gaze burning into the side of my face, but I refused to look at him. Not when my cheeks were flaming and our daughters were basically writing erotic fan fiction about their parents' reunion.

"We're hanging up now," I announced, reaching toward the screen with my free hand.

"We'll stop, we'll stop," Addie pleaded through her laughter. "It's just really good to see you two together again."

"Jesus, we're capable of being friendly without it having to mean anything," I protested before catching myself.

Friendly.

God, I hated that word. Hated how it reduced whatever this was— this electricity, this pull, this complicated mess of want and hurt and history—to something safe and sanitized.

We weren't friendly. Friendly was what you were with your neighbor. Your coworker. Hell, even the barista who remembered your coffee order. Friendly didn't grip the backs of your thighs and leave marks on your throat.

But admitting that to our daughters—admitting it to myself—felt like stepping off a cliff with no guarantee of a soft landing.

"Right," he said quietly, his voice carefully neutral. "Friendly."

"Well, whatever you want to call it, there's nothing like a blizzard to make you realize you never stopped loving each other. Okay, we love you. Bye!" Sky rushed to say, ending the call before either of us could respond.

The silence that followed felt deafening. Teddy released my hand and pushed back from the table, leaving me alone and painfully aware that I'd done it once again.

Because apparently, my superpower was taking any moment of connection we managed to build and blowing it to smithereens with my big mouth.

10

kelsey

I WATCHED Teddy retreat into himself, shoulders tensing as he stood and carried his empty plate to the sink. The easy banter from moments before evaporated, leaving behind the familiar chill that had defined most of our interactions toward the end of our marriage.

"Teddy—" I started, but he was already moving toward the living room and the little tree that couldn't.

"Might as well get this done," he said without looking back.

I forced myself to follow him, my bare feet silent on the hardwood. He'd already dragged the first box of ornaments closer to the tree and was stabbing his knife through the packing tape with more force than I would have used.

"You don't have to help," he muttered, ripping the box open and scattering packing peanuts across the floor. "I can handle it myself."

Usually, I'd leave him to brood and find something to do on the opposite side of the house. Sometimes, I'd leave altogether under the guise of running errands, which was nothing more than an excuse to drive around, scream-singing angry rock songs until my throat was raw.

But this wasn't my house, and I'd already made one attempt at driving in a blizzard. I wasn't exactly keen on a repeat performance.

The need to impose some order on at least one part of the chaotic situation we'd found ourselves in was strong. When everything else spiraled out of control—our marriage, our son, our lives—I'd always retreated to what I could manage. Cleanliness. Organization. Decoration.

Control the controllable.

"I know you can." I knelt beside him, reaching for the second box. "But I want to help."

Teddy shot me a sidelong look. "You never could leave well enough alone."

"Please." I bumped his shoulder with mine, using a teasing tone to deflect from whatever was happening between us. "There's not a single part of this tree that's well enough, Riggs."

He didn't smile at my weak attempt at humor, but some of the tension left his shoulders. "Why's it so important to you?"

"Because I miss—"

This.

Miss bickering about ornament placement and why the big ones go on the bottom of the tree, never the top.

I miss telling you that the star's still crooked so that I can smack you on the butt when you climb the ladder to fix it.

I caught myself, forcing a smile. "I missed out on tree decorating this year."

I. Miss. You.

Teddy stared at me for a long moment before pulling a snarl of lights from the box. "You wanna help?" he asked, his voice low but edged. "*Friendly* thing to do would be to sort out the rest of these."

I accepted the tangled mess of lights, grateful for something to do that didn't involve touching him. The silence stretched between us, broken only by the rustle of tissue paper.

"Did the girls just stuff everything into a box and hope for the best?" I grumbled as I worked on a particularly stubborn knot.

"Not everything."

I glanced up to find him holding a silver bell engraved with *"Our First Christmas 1995."*

"Haven't seen this since…" He trailed off, running his thumb over the letters.

Since we were a family. Since Christmas meant something.

Our eyes met over the boxes of memories, and for a moment, the weight of everything we'd lost threatened to crush me. Not just our marriage or our life together, but the future we'd planned, the family we'd built, the son we'd buried before ever getting to see him grow up.

"We don't have to put it up," I said, my voice thick as I worked another section of lights free.

He was quiet for a long moment, turning the ornament over in his hands. "It goes on the tree."

I looked at him in surprise. The man I'd known toward the end of our marriage would have taken any excuse to avoid painful reminders. Would have shoved the ornament back in the box and pretended it didn't exist.

"Teddy—"

"It goes on the tree, Kels." His voice was firm, but there was something fragile underneath it. "All of it goes on. That's what you do with ornaments."

I managed to nod while fighting against the sudden urge to cry. He was right. That was what you did with ornaments. You put them on the tree, even when they carried memories that felt too heavy to hold.

"Hey," he said thickly, catching a rogue tear that managed to slip past my lashes with his finger. "It's part of our story. Good or bad, it's ours."

And just like that, the walls I'd built around my heart toppled completely.

I nodded again before returning my attention to the tangled light strands, shoving my emotions back down.

We worked in companionable quiet after that, falling into the familiar ritual of decorating. I settled cross-legged on the floor, the lights spread across my lap like some kind of holiday puzzle. This was something I knew how to do. Something that made sense, unlike everything else happening between us.

I was aware of his gaze on me as I climbed onto the stepladder to wrap lights around the higher branches, his hand automatically moving to steady it.

The transformation was nothing short of miraculous, considering what we'd started with. The tree glowed with properly arranged lights, and the ornaments we'd placed so far brought much-needed splashes of color to the previously depressing display.

The almost-smile on my lips faded as Teddy passed me another ornament—a clay foot mold painted bright red with "*Christmas 2000*" scrawled in my careful handwriting.

Addie's first Christmas.

My chest squeezed tight. I'd made one for each kid. Sure enough, the next one he unwrapped was Skylar's from 2003, slightly larger and painted a forest green.

The third bundle contained Levi's footprint from 2010, painted a cornflower blue to match his nursery. It was the smallest of the three, because he'd been our smallest baby, barely six pounds at birth.

After taking Teddy's advice and placing it just above his sisters' ornaments, I paused to adjust the pipe cleaners on a Styrofoam snowman head before stepping back. He was watching me again—this time with an expression I couldn't quite decipher.

"What?"

Teddy shook his head with a low chuckle before passing me a glass ball painted with tiny snowflakes—something Sky had made in elementary school. "You could make a tumbleweed look like it belongs on the cover of a magazine. Always could."

"Mm… my therapist would probably say it's my pathological need to try to control the things around me," I said with a snort, carefully hanging the ornament where it would best catch the light.

"Funny," he murmured, his palm meeting my spine as he reached around me to hang a popsicle stick reindeer. "Mine would say the same thing about you, too."

Had his hand not been holding me upright, I likely would have toppled over in shock.

Teddy Riggs, in therapy?

The same man who'd once told me that therapy was "just paying someone to listen to you bitch and moan"? Who'd refused to join me for grief counseling after Levi, saying he didn't need to "talk about his feelings with strangers"?

It seemed about as likely as his father, Paul—the founder and former president of Silent Phoenix MC—taking up ballet.

His mouth twitched like he was fighting a smile. "Jesus. Don't look so surprised, Kels."

"What? I'm just glad to hear you're finally addressing all your... issues. And I'd be happy to provide your therapist with a comprehensive list of things you could work on, if they need suggestions," I said sweetly.

He clicked his tongue against his teeth and moved closer. "Bet you've got that list memorized, don't you?"

"Of course I do," I murmured, tilting my head back to meet his eyes. "And organized into categories."

This time, he did smile, a real one that crinkled the corners of his eyes and made the dimples on his cheeks appear. My stomach flipped. God, I'd missed that smile. Missed the way it transformed his entire face, softened all the hard edges grief had carved there.

By the time I registered what the sudden shift in his expression meant, it was too late. I made a futile attempt to dart around him, shrieking when he looped one arm around my waist and took me down to the rug.

"Don't you dare," I warned when he moved above me, his fingers skimming up my sides.

He tickled me until I was thrashing beneath him and begging for mercy between screams of laughter.

"Stop—I can't—" I gasped, trying to catch my breath as his fingers found the place where my neck met my shoulder that had always been my undoing.

"What's the magic word, baby?" he asked, grinning down at me with the same boyish expression that had first made me fall in love with him at fifteen.

"Please," I managed between helpless giggles.

"Please, what?"

"Please stop tickling me before I pee on your rug!" I wheezed, my sides aching from the assault.

He stopped immediately but didn't move away. We lay there panting, his body caging me against the soft rug, our faces inches apart. The laughter died on my lips as I became acutely aware of every point where we touched—his chest pressed against mine, his thighs bracketing my hips, his hands braced on either side of my head.

The playfulness evaporated, replaced by something infinitely more dangerous. His gaze dropped to my mouth, and my lips parted on a shaky exhale.

We were close enough that I could see the small flecks of gold in his hazel eyes, close enough to watch as his dark pupils eclipsed them. I knew that look. I knew what would come next if I didn't put a stop to it. But my will had always been paper-thin where he was concerned.

"Teddy?" I whispered when he abruptly pulled back with a muttered curse.

His hand moved to the back of his neck, and I pushed myself up into a sitting position while my heart parachuted out of my chest.

Here it came—the rejection, the gentle letdown, the explanation for why he'd been so careful to keep his distance since our interrupted moment in the hallway.

"We can't..." He cleared his throat, looking more uncomfortable by the second. "Think it's best if we hold off—"

"No, you're right," I cut in as I rushed to get up, desperate to save whatever scraps of self-respect I had left. "Let's just forget it happened and finish the tree."

The words came out clipped, defensive—my standard operating procedure when I sensed rejection approaching. Better to be the one who pulled away first. Better to pretend I didn't care than to let him see how badly I wanted him to contradict me.

"That's not what I—" His brow furrowed, mouth tightening at the corners.

"It's fine." I turned back to the tree, my fingers trembling as I tugged the neckline of my bodysuit up. "We got caught up in the moment. It happens."

"Kels—"

"I said it's fine." I reached for another ornament, desperate to keep my hands busy and my voice steady. "We're both adults. We can acknowledge that being in close proximity after two years might create some... confusion."

But my fingers wouldn't stop shaking as I unwrapped what looked like a papier-mâché angel one of the kids had made. The edges were yellowed with age, bits of glitter still clinging to the crooked wings despite decades of careful storage.

"Confusion," Teddy said, his face screwing up like the word tasted bitter. "Is that what we're calling it?"

"A mistake. Lapse in judgment. Temporary insanity. Take your pick. I knew—I knew this would happen. It's your M.O.—we get close, you panic, you pull away. Rinse and repeat." I laughed, but it sounded brittle, even to my own ears. "At least you're consistent."

"And you're still a stubborn pain in the ass," he ground out, his jaw muscles jumping beneath the skin.

"Yeah, well, it takes one to know one." I reached for a felt wreath ornament with Addie's kindergarten photo glued to the center. Once upon a time, there had been a tiny red bow affixed to the bottom, though it was long gone now.

Teddy moved to the other side of the tree, maintaining his distance as we continued decorating. The stilted quiet was punctuated by the occasional crackle and pop from the logs burning in the fireplace, as well as the sound of the wind picking up outside. But the easy camaraderie from earlier had evaporated, leaving behind the familiar dance of avoidance we'd perfected in those final months of our marriage.

I hung ornament after ornament, each one a small piece of our history. The wooden Santa that Sky had made in fourth grade, complete with a scraggly yarn beard and googly eyes. The honeycomb paper ornaments Addie had made in art class, flattened in some places but still beautiful to look at. The Galileo thermometer and collection of snow globe ornaments Levi had amassed due to his desire to be a meteorologist.

Once I was satisfied with the placement of the lower ornaments, I climbed onto the stepladder to finish decorating the top branches.

The star for the top of the tree—a silver and crystal piece that had been a wedding gift from one of Teddy's great aunts—sat in its box on the coffee table.

"Can you hand me the—"

Before I could finish, he was there, passing me the star, our fingers brushing in the exchange.

I turned back to the tree, stretching to place the star, and felt the ladder shift beneath me. My foot slipped, and suddenly I was falling backward, a startled yelp escaping my lips. Strong hands caught me immediately, Teddy's reflexes as quick as they'd always been. One hand slid behind my knees while the other went to my back, steadying me as I fell against his chest, the solid wall of him stopping my descent.

"Guess this is why you banned me from getting on ladders after the Porch Lighting Fiasco of 2012," I said weakly, attempting to lighten the moment with humor even as my heart hammered against my ribs.

We stayed frozen like that—me cradled against his chest, his arms tightening as he stared down at me with an expression I couldn't quite name.

"You okay?" he asked, his voice like gravel.

I nodded, though I wasn't sure that was entirely true.

"You can put me down now," I whispered, though I made no move to extract myself from his arms.

"Sure about that?" His thumb brushed against my spine, just above the waistband of my jeans. "Because last time I tried to be the responsible one, you accused me of pulling away."

My breath caught. "Teddy…"

He gently set me back on my feet, his palm lingering at my waist before he jerked it back. "Christ," he muttered, dragging a hand through his hair. "What the fuck are we doing, Kels?"

I shook my head, my ears burning as I admitted, "I don't know."

He searched my face before sighing. "Every time I get close to you —every damn time—I remember what it felt like to lose everything."

The raw honesty in his voice, the pain etched into every line of his face—it stripped away all my defenses, leaving me exposed and aching.

I wrapped my arms around myself as if it could somehow hold me together.

That was what I was to him now—not the woman he'd loved for over thirty years, not the mother of his children, not even the person who knew all his secrets. I was a reminder of loss—a walking, talking symbol of everything that had gone wrong in his life.

11

Three Days Until Christmas

teddy

THE WIND HOWLED AS it tore through the surrounding pines, stripping the warmth from my face even through a fleece gaiter and a beanie tugged damn near over my eyes. Shoveling feet of new snow from the cabin's drive while more drifted down from the sky should have felt futile.

But freezing my ass off was a hell of a lot easier than talking.

The steel shovel bit into the icy drift with a sound like splitting bone. I found a rhythm. Heave, twist, throw, repeat. Every scoop was another round of the same fight, different winter.

My gloves—the heavy-duty ones I kept on my snowmobile—might as well have been made of mesh. They were soaking wet at the seams, each shift of my fingers sending cold needles into my palms.

It didn't help that the wind seemed to be coming from all directions. Half the time, the powder I tossed just blew straight back in my face. I kept at it because the alternative was to go inside and endure more of Kelsey's silent treatment. Which was why I'd found any and every excuse to be outside since yesterday's... whatever the fuck it was.

Maybe the only thing more predictable than Kelsey Riggs was my own ability to screw everything up by opening my mouth.

Every time I get close to you, I remember what it felt like to lose everything.

Christ. Of all the ways I could have explained it, I'd chosen the worst possible combination of words. How had I fucked it up so badly? Might as well have told her she was a walking graveyard, that looking at her was like staring at Levi's headstone.

The look on her face—that quick flash of hurt before the walls slammed back into place, before she wrapped herself in the brittle armor she'd perfected in our last months together.

I'd watched it happen in real-time. The straightening of her spine, the careful neutrality that settled over her features, the way she'd stepped back and crossed her arms like she needed a physical barrier between us. Classic Kelsey.

In the window, I could just make out the outline of her head, a silhouette against the hazy afternoon light. I pictured her in the kitchen, jaw clenched, taking solace in control—maybe organizing the pantry, maybe scrubbing the stove even though it was already clean. That was what she did—fixed things. Tried to put the world back together with her bare hands.

I wasn't any better. I fixed stuff, too—engines, fences, even people, when they'd let me. But this wasn't a problem I could solve with a socket wrench. This was a wound that festered no matter how much whiskey I dumped on it.

I drove the shovel deeper, grunting with the effort. The driveway didn't need clearing—we weren't going anywhere until the plows came through. But I needed to move, needed to do something with the rage building in my chest. Not at her. Never at her. At myself for being such a goddamn idiot.

Another shovelful. Another. My breath came out in harsh clouds, immediately whipped away by the wind. Sweat froze at my temples, pulling at the skin with every movement.

My back ached, a steady throb radiating up my spine from laying my bike down back when I was young and stupid enough to think I was invincible. Good. Physical pain I could handle.

The cold, on the other hand, had moved past uncomfortable into that dangerous numbness where you stopped feeling anything at all.

Kind of like our marriage at the end. We'd both gone numb, unaware that we were bleeding out.

The memory of finding her in that crashed SUV hit me again—blood on her face, lips blue from cold, that horrible moment when I thought she was gone. My hands tightened on the shovel handle until the wood groaned in protest.

That was what I'd been trying to say. Getting close to her made me remember how it felt to almost lose her yesterday. Reminded me that I couldn't survive it happening.

Not wouldn't—couldn't. There was a difference.

But explaining feelings had never been my strong suit. Give me a transmission to rebuild or a custom bike, something I could fix with my hands, and I was golden. Ask me to explain the mess inside my head? Might as well hand me a scalpel and tell me to perform brain surgery.

The driveway was mostly clear, or as clear as it was going to get with snow still falling.

I finished another run, shoveling a path toward the road until my lower back was screaming and my bad shoulder locked up, refusing to lift the shovel one more damn time.

Back inside, the heat hit me like a wall, burning my frozen skin. I stomped the snow off my boots, hung my soaked jacket on the hook, and breathed in the familiar scent of her cooking.

The kitchen had been transformed into the set of one of those British cooking shows she used to love to watch. Three casserole dishes sat cooling on dishtowels. Nearby, another two waited on the stovetop for their turn in the oven. A pot of what smelled like my favorite beef stew bubbled away on the stove, mixing with the yeasty scent of bread dough. Sure enough, I spotted it rising in a covered bowl near the oven.

There was a time when the sight would have made me smile—coming home to the chaos, Kelsey in full general mode, barking at the kids to set the table or load the dishwasher. Now it was just her, alone, powering through. Like she could cook her way out of feeling anything.

Yesterday, she'd disappeared into one of the spare bedrooms for the remainder of the afternoon and evening, only coming out to grab a glass of water before fleeing again. But it was clear that she was back in Perfect Kelsey mode now.

When the world got too messy, when emotions got too complicated, she'd retreat into domestic goddess territory. Control what you can control. Feed everyone until they're too full to ask the hard questions.

I'd seen it a million times. After every fight, every family crisis, every time she was pissed. Our freezer would fill with labeled containers, the house would smell like a restaurant, and I'd wonder where in the hell she found the energy for it.

I planned to leave her to it. Take a hot shower and thaw out my frozen everything, giving her the space to work through whatever she needed to work through. That was our pattern—I'd retreat to the garage or the clubhouse, she'd retreat to the kitchen, and we'd orbit each other like suspicious planets until the immediate crisis passed.

I had just turned toward the hallway when she inhaled so sharply, I heard it over the rattling vent hood.

When I looked back, her shoulders were shaking. If I hadn't been paying attention. I would have missed it entirely. But I saw it. Saw the white-knuckle grip on the wooden spoon, saw the way she held herself too rigid, too controlled.

She wasn't pissed off.

She was hurt.

My feet moved before my brain caught up, crossing the kitchen in three strides. She didn't look up, even when my shadow fell across the counter.

I could have done the tough-guy thing and waited her out, arms crossed, pretending I'd come in for coffee. But there was something about the way she shook—like she was fighting it, trying not to let her body betray her—that reminded me too much of the days after we lost Levi, when I'd find her in the most random places. The pantry. Our closet. The laundry room. Every time, she'd offered a perfectly plausible explanation, but now I couldn't help but wonder if she'd been trying to hide her grief from me. Trying to be strong for everyone in the family.

I didn't say anything—my words had already fucked up enough between us in the past twenty-four hours. I just wrapped my arms around her from behind, pulled her back against my chest, and held on.

She resisted at first, but when I didn't let go, she stopped fighting. Her weight sagged back against me, her resistance crumbling as tears rolled silently down her face.

"I've got you," I murmured into her hair, tightening my arms when she started to shake harder. "You're safe, baby. I've got you."

One hand came up to brush the tears off her face while the other remained locked around her waist, keeping her upright when her knees began to buckle. She turned in my arms, burying her face against my chest, and I could feel the heat of her tears soaking through my cold shirt.

For a minute, all she did was cry. Silent, ugly, honest. The kind of sobbing that came out in quick gasps. I rocked her a little, just enough to remind her I was there.

"Been carrying this too long," I said, my voice rougher than I intended. "Too damn long, Kels."

The stew bubbled behind us, likely needing to be stirred, but I didn't move. Not when she was finally letting me hold her like this, finally letting me see the cracks in that perfect facade. Not when I finally had the chance to be something other than another source of pain in her life.

"I'm sorry," she whispered. "This is pathetic."

"It's just us. Let it out. I ain't going anywhere."

And I meant it. I wasn't sure when she'd stop shaking. But I knew I wouldn't let go until she did.

Her tears came harder now, followed by a low, keening sound. The kind of pain that had been building behind that perfect control for months, maybe years. I held her tighter, one hand stroking her hair while she soaked my shirt with two years' worth of suppressed grief.

"The girls," she choked out between sobs. "They're not coming, Teddy. Our daughters aren't coming for Christmas."

I'd been so focused on navigating whatever was happening between Kelsey and me that I hadn't fully processed that they weren't going to make it.

"And I can't even blame them," she continued, the words escaping in bursts between shuddering breaths. "Why would they want to come here? Watch their parents treat each other like enemies, or worse, strangers? Pretend everything's fine when nothing's been fine for years?"

"Kels—"

"I'm so damn tired of being angry at you." The admission came out broken, raw. "So tired of existing in the same space but never actually being together. And now I feel like I'm just—just a walking landmine."

I couldn't exactly argue. I'd been treating her like unexploded ordnance for years. Circling, never daring to dig beneath the surface. Now she'd finally detonated, and it felt like the only honest thing that had happened since Levi.

"I know I'm not Perfect Kelsey anymore." Her fingers twisted in my shirt, holding on like she expected me to pull away. "I know I fall apart at the worst times. That I say the wrong things and push when I should pull, and—God, I'm doing it right now. Falling apart on you when you probably just want me to get it together and—"

"Stop." I pulled back enough to look at her face, using my thumb to wipe away the tears that kept coming. "Just stop, baby."

Her eyes were red-rimmed and swollen, her nose running. Nothing perfect about her right now. But watching her finally let go, finally showing me the mess underneath all that control—something clicked into place in my chest.

How many fights could we have avoided if I'd just held her like this? If I hadn't retreated every time shit got complicated? If she hadn't hidden behind her picture-perfect facade?

We'd been so goddamn stubborn, both of us. So convinced we had to handle our grief alone, that showing weakness would somehow break us worse than we already were. But maybe the breaking was the point. Maybe we needed to shatter completely before we could figure out how to put the pieces back together.

"I'm sorry," she said, quieter this time. "I know I should be stronger."

"Who the fuck told you that?"

She laughed again, sharp and ugly. "You did. It's the only reason you married me, remember? 'Strong enough to handle your brand of crazy.'"

I'd said that a lifetime ago. Thought it was a compliment. "Yeah, well, I was an idiot," I muttered.

"Yeah, you are," she agreed with a sniff.

"You got it backward," I said, my voice rough. "About what I said yesterday…"

She blinked up at me in confusion, still crying but quieter now.

"You're not a reminder of what I lost." I had to look away, focus on the window where snow kept falling, because looking at her while I said what needed to be said might kill me. "You're a reminder that I can still lose things. That there's still something left that matters enough to be terrified of losing."

My throat closed, but I forced the words out anyway. She deserved to hear them. Deserved to know the truth, even if it made me sound like a pathetic bastard who'd failed in every way that mattered.

"We lost Levi," I said, pulling my lip between my teeth to keep it from shaking. "Couldn't save him. Couldn't fix it. Didn't see the signs right in front of me."

Kelsey's hand came up to my cheek, but I couldn't look at her yet. Needed to get it all out while I still had the balls to say it.

"I lost you. Watched you disappear into a version of yourself I didn't recognize. And instead of fighting for you, I just let you go. Signed those papers like they didn't mean I was signing away the only good thing I had left."

"But—"

"Then I lost myself trying to figure out how to live in a world where you weren't mine." My voice cracked, and I finally looked at her, let her see everything I'd been hiding.

"How's that working out?" she asked.

I huffed out a laugh. "Real shitty, actually, since I'm still buying your damn shampoo and body wash so I can pretend for five minutes that you're still here."

I gripped her face between my palms, probably too tight, but I needed her to understand this next part. Really understand it.

"When I found you in that car, I thought—" My voice broke completely, and I had to stop, swallow hard before trying again. "I thought that was it... that you were gone. And I couldn't—I couldn't survive losing you, Kels. I'd eat a bullet before I'd go through it."

She flinched, and I hated myself for saying it out loud, but it was the truth. Losing her would have been the end of me.

"I know it's fucked up. Know it's not fair to you. But I can't—don't know how to turn it off. Don't know how to stop caring about you. I'm not real good at the whole moving on thing, baby. Never have been."

Kelsey made a sound like she'd been hit in the gut, then pressed herself against me so hard it drove the breath from my lungs. Her arms went around the back of my neck, holding on like she was trying to crawl inside my skin.

"I don't want to fight anymore," she whispered against my throat. "I don't want to be angry. I want—" She pulled back to look at me, tears still streaming down her cheeks. But there was something softer in her eyes now. "Can we just call a truce? For Christmas? Can we try to make the best of this completely insane situation?"

A truce. Like we were warring countries instead of two people who'd once shared everything—dreams, fears, a bed, kids, thirty years of history that couldn't be erased no matter how hard we'd tried.

Outside, the snow continued falling, sealing us in together. Maybe that was what it would take—being forced into the same space with nowhere to run, no club to retreat to, no gym for her to disappear into. Just us and all the wreckage we'd left behind.

"Yeah," I said, my voice rough. "We can do that."

She sagged against me in relief, and I tightened my arms around her, breathing in a scent that meant home to me in a way nothing else did.

My stomach chose that exact moment to growl loud enough to

wake the dead, ripping through the emotional heaviness like a chainsaw.

Kelsey pulled back, a startled laugh escaping through the tears. "Was that you, or did a bear find its way inside?"

"Definitely a bear, although I wouldn't say no to an early dinner," I said, nodding to the spread covering every available surface, "seeing as you made enough to feed half of Colorado."

She wiped her face with the back of her hand, already shifting back into Martha Stewart mode. "Sit. I'll fix you a plate."

I caught her wrist gently. "You don't have to—"

"Theodore Riggs, you will sit your ass down and let me feed you, or so help me God, I'll use this wooden spoon on you."

I held up my hands in mock surrender, unable to keep the grin off my face. There she was—the woman I'd fallen in love with all those years ago, fierce and protective even when she was the one who needed taking care of. "Yes, ma'am."

She turned back to the stove, and I watched her move through the familiar motions—ladling stew into a bowl, cutting thick slices of the bread she'd somehow found time to bake, and arranging everything on a plate like it was going to be photographed for a magazine. Even when she was falling apart, she couldn't help but make everything look perfect.

"You know," I said, settling into the chair at the table, "Coulda just thrown a frozen pizza in the oven and called it a day."

Steam rose from the stew as she set everything in front of me, her eyebrows bunching together. "Why would I do that? You hate frozen pizza."

The fact that she still remembered—still cared enough to remember —did something uncomfortable to my chest. "Just meant you didn't have to go to all this trouble."

"It wasn't trouble." She brushed off the compliment, already turning back to check on whatever was in the oven. "I needed something to do with my hands."

I took a bite of the stew and immediately made an involuntary sound of pleasure that earned me a raised brow from across the kitchen. But it was exactly like I remembered. Tasted like home. Like

Sunday dinners when the kids were small, and the biggest crisis in our lives was Sky refusing to eat her vegetables.

Kelsey poured us both a cup of coffee before sitting down across from me at the table. "Better?" she asked, the side of her mouth lifting as she watched me sop up the last bit of stew with the bread.

"Getting there," I said, patting my stomach. "Might need to sample those casseroles—you know, to keep my strength up. Wouldn't want me wasting away to nothing."

She rolled her eyes but moved to fix me a plate, and just like that, we'd found our way back to something that felt almost normal.

Almost like us.

12

Two Days Until Christmas

teddy

THE HOT WATER from the shower eased some of the ache from my shoulders and back, but my body was still hellbent on reminding me I wasn't in my twenties anymore. I'd spent another morning outside, splitting wood until my back seized up before plowing the drive with the UTV, trying to work off my need to touch Kelsey. The storm had finally blown itself out, leaving behind a world buried in white and roads that would be impassable for days.

I toweled off and pulled on clean jeans and a black long-sleeved shirt, the fabric sticking to my damp skin. Christmas music drifted down the hall—Perry Como, from the sounds of it—singing about candy canes and holly. Like we needed reminding that it was beginning to look like Christmas after back-to-back blizzards.

After tying my wet hair back into a low knot, I made my way into the kitchen to find Kelsey bent over the island, rolling out gingerbread dough. She'd found another one of my flannel shirts, a green one that had always reminded me of the color of her eyes. Her hair was still damp from her own shower, leaving wet spots on the shoulders where it had dripped. Every time she leaned forward to reach the far edge of the dough, the hem rode up just enough to reveal the curve where her thigh met her ass, and I lost the ability to think straight. Nothing but smooth skin disappearing under worn flannel.

I cleared my throat before I did something stupid like drop to my knees right there in the doorway. "Need a hand?"

She glanced over her shoulder, one of her brows lifting in surprise. "You wanna help bake?"

"Hell, someone's gotta make sure you don't burn the first batch." I rolled up my sleeves and moved to the sink to wash my hands.

"Cookies only seem to burn when you're involved," she shot back, but I could hear the smile in her voice. "Or have you forgotten the time you set the smoke alarms off?"

"That was a fluke." I dried my hands, remembering exactly how those cookies had burned—because I'd had her bent over the deep freeze in the laundry room, my hand down the front of her pajama pants. "Can't expect a man to remember his own name, much less when the cookies need to come out of the oven, when you're making sounds like that."

Pink bloomed across her cheeks. She turned back to the dough, pressing her weight into the rolling pin. "Don't distract me."

"Distract you?" I moved closer, all innocence. "I would never."

"Right." She sprinkled some flour over the dough before dropping the bag back onto the counter, sending a puff of white into the air. "Because you've always been so good at keeping your hands to yourself when I'm trying to bake."

She wasn't wrong. Never had been able to resist her in the kitchen, something about the sight of her in an apron flipped all my switches. The concentration on her face when she measured. The way she'd bite her lip when reading a recipe. How her hips moved to the music she always seemed to have playing while she worked.

"I'll be good," I lied, already plotting.

"Sure you will," Kelsey replied with a snort, shooting me several skeptical glances as she continued rolling the dough. I waited until she was focused before making my first move—reaching around her to the drawer on her left, deliberately brushing against her hip.

The slight catch in her breathing made my pulse kick up. "Could have sworn the cookie cutters were in this drawer," I murmured. The layout of my kitchen was damn near identical to the one in the house we used to share. I could find my way around it with a blindfold on.

When I pulled away, she made a soft sound of frustration before reaching up to brush her hair back, leaving a smudge of floury dough across her forehead.

"You've got a little..." I gestured vaguely at her face, fighting a grin. When she tried and failed to get it, I stepped behind her properly, my hips pinning hers against the island before I tipped her head back. "Here, let me."

Kelsey didn't pull away as I swiped my thumb across the spot. Instead, she pressed back against me as I sucked the sweetness off my skin, just enough to let me know she felt it too. This electric current running between us, threatening to short-circuit what little self-control remained.

We'd been on our best behavior since calling a truce, not arguing... keeping our hands—and mouths—to ourselves. Acting like responsible adults who could coexist without it turning sexual. But the way she was looking at me now, green eyes homed in on my mouth like a heat-seeking missile, made it clear that particular ceasefire was about to end.

I didn't even have it in me to give a damn. I'd missed this. Missed the way her breathing changed when I touched her, the gentle tug-of-war between wanting to finish whatever task she'd set herself and wanting to give in to what I was offering.

We'd lost it somewhere along the way—first during the fertility treatments, when sex became clinical, scheduled around ovulation charts and injections. Every month that ended in disappointment added another layer of pressure until touching each other felt like work.

Then later, when Levi's struggles consumed everything. Therapy appointments, medication trials, the constant vigilance required to keep him safe—it all took precedence. We'd fall into bed exhausted, backs turned to each other, too drained to bridge the growing gap between us. Weeks would pass without anything more than accidental touches—months, toward the end.

Shannon Myers

But now, with her pressed against me, I remembered what we had before life got so complicated. When we couldn't keep our hands off each other. When the kids would catch us making out in the kitchen and complain about how gross we were.

"Teddy," she whispered, my name barely audible over Burl Ives's voice.

"What, baby?" I traced a line from her temple to her jaw before curving my fingers around her throat, loosely holding her in place. My other hand found her waist, thumb tracing over the flannel.

She shivered, goosebumps breaking out along her arms. "You said you'd be good."

"I am being good." I leaned down, my lips brushing her earlobe. "Haven't kissed you yet."

Yet.

Her breath came out in a little gasp, and she rocked back against me again, unconsciously seeking friction. My body responded instantly, blood rushing south so fast it left me lightheaded.

"Tell me how you want it," I said, my voice rougher than intended.

Her throat bobbed in a hard swallow beneath my palm. "Want what?"

"Like you don't know what I'm talking about," I murmured, pulling my lip between my teeth.

The pulse point in her neck thrummed. She abandoned any pretense of rolling, her hands gripping the counter. The flannel had ridden up in the back, confirming what I'd suspected when I walked in —she wasn't wearing a damn thing underneath.

"C'mon, Kels. You want it thick?" I asked, trying not to smile when she rubbed herself against the front of my jeans. "Thin? Cut into shapes?"

"Shapes?" She gave a strangled laugh. "Oh my God, you're talking about the cookies."

"What else would I be talking about?"

"You're the worst," she grumbled.

"Just trying to get this dough in the oven before it dries out. Not my fault your mind's in the gutter." I turned just enough to reach the

118

drawer behind me, grabbing the cookie cutters. "Looks like we've got a snowflake, a mitten, a tree, and a... dick?"

"It's a candy cane, Teddy."

"And what about the butt plug here?"

Kelsey took the cookie cutter from my hand and held it up for inspection, rotating it with a thoughtful frown. "I think it's supposed to be a Christmas light. Or maybe an ornament?"

The movement pressed us even closer together, and I had to bite back a groan at the feel of her soft curves against me and that shirt unbuttoned enough to tempt a saint.

"What?" she asked, tilting her head back to peer up at me.

"Nothing. Just waiting on you to tell me what we're doing here, sugar," I managed once my brain came back online.

The double meaning wasn't lost on either of us. Kelsey's tongue darted out to wet her bottom lip. I tracked it, keenly aware of all the things it could do.

Her smile was slow and lazy, the kind that used to flip my brain inside out when we were teenagers. "I thought it was obvious. We're making cookies. Now, are you gonna help or just stand there and stare at me?"

I loved this version of her, so different from the wounded, careful woman who walked on eggshells when we were together in Texas. Here she moved differently, like the pressure had been bled from her body by the altitude. Maybe it was because we were alone and relieved of the burden of putting on a front for our kids.

Or maybe it was just that I'd finally let myself be here this time, not halfway out the door.

We cut out the first two dozen cookies. She went for trees and snowflakes, all delicate points and perfection. Being the mature individual I was, I chose the butt plug and the candy cane cutters, cracking jokes like the shift of her hips wasn't actively torturing me. The flex of her shoulders, the little concentrated sounds she made while cutting out shapes.

Once they were arranged on the baking sheets to her liking, Kelsey bent over to place the first pan in the oven, causing the flannel to ride up. One look and my self-control snapped like a rubber band stretched too far.

With a low growl, I gripped her around the waist and hauled her up onto the island as soon as she finished setting the timer, flour puffing up around us like smoke.

Her thighs parted automatically to make room for me. I stepped between them, my hips settling against hers and erasing every coherent thought in my head.

I caught her mouth with mine, swallowing her little gasp of surprise. Her lips parted obediently under mine, and I took full advantage, deepening the kiss until we were both breathing hard.

This was what I'd been missing. Not just the physical contact, though God knew I'd been starving for that.

But the way she tasted. The way her hands fisted in my shirt, pulling me closer even as she made a sound that could have been a protest or a sign of encouragement. With her, it had always been hard to tell the difference.

My mouth moved to her jaw, tracing the line of it down to her throat. She tilted her head back, giving me access, and I took it greedily. The pulse point beneath my lips hammered against my tongue. I scraped my teeth over it gently, just enough pressure to make her shiver.

"Teddy," she breathed, my name coming out all broken and needy.

I hummed against her skin, working my way lower. She smelled like gingerbread and that expensive body oil she loved so damn much.

"Wait—we can't—"

I pulled back just enough to look at her. Her lips were swollen, pupils blown wide enough to eclipse the green. "Can't what?"

"This." She gestured vaguely between us, but her legs were still wrapped around my hips, holding me in place. "We can't—it won't fix anything. It never does. It just makes things more complicated."

As much as I wanted to show her I was still the man who could take her on the nearest flat surface, who never once left her wanting, she wasn't wrong.

Sex had been our go-to solution for every fight, every rough patch. A temporary fix that felt good in the moment but left us right back where we started once the high wore off. Sometimes worse off, because we'd relied on our bodies to say things we couldn't manage with words.

This was new ground. Fragile. And whatever we were trying to rebuild, I sure as hell didn't want to blitz it for a quick fuck in the kitchen.

"You're right," I said, tracing her hips through the flannel. "Can't fall back into the same old patterns."

Relief flickered across her face, followed immediately by something that looked a lot like disappointment. She started to push against my chest, already retreating into the careful distance she'd mastered over three decades of dealing with my shit.

I tightened my grip, keeping her right where she was. "But I'm not looking to fix anything right now, baby. Just wanna take the edge off for you."

Her breath hitched. "What?"

I slid one hand up her thigh, feeling her muscles tense under my palm. "Been wound tight since you got here. Hell, probably for a lot longer than that. And I'm good at this part, remember? Making you feel good. Letting you let go for a minute."

"Teddy—"

"Do you need to come for me, Kels?" I asked, my voice dropping lower. "Because I need to taste you again. Been dreaming about it for a long ass time."

Her eyes fluttered closed, and she bit down on her lower lip hard enough to leave marks. When she opened them again, they were glazed with want. She nodded, just once, but it was enough.

I started working the buttons on the flannel, taking my time with each one. Her breathing picked up with every inch of skin I revealed, her chest rising and falling faster. No bra underneath, just smooth skin and a flush that spread down from her throat when she was turned on. I'd mapped every variation of that flush over the years—knew exactly what shade meant she was close, what color meant she needed more.

This was somewhere in between. Interested but not desperate yet. I could work with that.

I undid the last button and pushed it off her shoulders, letting it pool behind her on the counter. Then I lowered my mouth to her collarbone, kissing my way across to her shoulder while my hands traced her sides.

I worked my way down to her perfect tits and greeted both nipples with my tongue, sucking one into my mouth while palming the other.

She arched into me, making soft sounds that went straight to my dick. I'd forgotten how responsive she was, how every touch seemed to light her up from the inside.

"That's it," I murmured, running my beard over the beaded pink tip. "Let me hear you, baby."

I moved to her other breast, giving it the same thorough attention. Kelsey was curvier now than she'd been in the months leading up to the divorce. I preferred the softer version over the lean, muscular woman who couldn't look me in the eye.

Her hips rolled forward, seeking friction, and I took another long, deep pull before releasing her breast with a soft pop. I kissed my way down her stomach, feeling her muscles jump under my lips. When I reached the island's edge, I dropped to my knees on the hardwood, knowing I'd pay for it later but too far gone to care in the moment.

The view damn near stopped my heart. Kelsey propped up on her elbows, chest heaving, thighs spread wide, and those pretty green eyes locked on me like she was afraid I might disappear if she blinked.

"Jesus, Kels." My voice came out rougher than I intended. "Look at you."

She shifted, self-conscious, and started to close her legs, but I caught her knees and spread them wider instead.

"Don't you fucking dare," I rasped, my mouth already watering at the sight of her pussy, bare and already glistening for me. "You're fucking beautiful. Always have been."

I pressed my lips to the inside of her thigh, smiling when her hips shifted restlessly against the counter.

"Please," she whispered.

"Please what, baby?" I asked, even though I knew exactly what she wanted. Needed to hear her say it.

She groaned in frustration. "You know what."

"Say it." I traced my fingers along the inside of her thigh, close enough to where she wanted me that she bucked against my hand. "Tell me what you need."

"I need—" She broke off, her face flushing darker.

"Need what?" I prompted, pressing my thumb against her inner thigh. "Need my mouth? My fingers? Both? Talk to me."

"Every—everything," she managed, her throat bobbing in a hard swallow.

And fuck if it didn't make me wanna pound my chest that she wanted this—wanted me, still, even after all the ways I'd let her down.

I flattened my hands on her hips and pulled her to the edge, close enough that I could lay her thighs over my shoulders before glancing back at the oven.

"Twelve minutes and—" I squinted, trying to make out the numbers on the timer without my glasses. "Twenty-nine seconds."

She blinked down at me with a dazed expression. "For what?"

"For you to come for me. Not letting you up until you do, so if you don't wanna burn the first batch..." I trailed off, grinning when her mouth twisted like she wanted to tell me to go fuck myself.

"You'd better get started," she finished, her brows arching in challenge. "I imagine you're a little out of—"

The rest of whatever she was going to say dissolved into a moan as I kissed my way up the soft skin of her inner thigh.

"Might have forgotten a few things as I've gotten older, sweetheart, but knowing how to make you come ain't one of 'em," I growled before licking a slow stripe from the base of her slit straight up to her swollen clit.

13

teddy

"OH, FUCK," she exhaled, her whole body jolting at the contact. One hand flew out to brace herself, sending the rolling pin tumbling to the floor with a clatter.

I flattened my tongue and alternated long, slow laps with tighter, back-and-forth flicks, working her open slowly and carefully, the way she liked best, even back then.

Kelsey was soaking wet, the taste of her taking me back to that first time, in my Bronco, out on some country road. I'd shoved her teal homecoming dress up around her waist and crouched just outside the open driver's side door, with no fucking clue what I was doing. I just remember trying to move my tongue like I'd seen guys at the clubhouse do with the club whores, using her sounds to guide me.

Her fingers threaded through the still-damp strands of my hair, roughly tugging it loose from the leather tie. The pain grounded me, reminded me this was real—not another dream where I woke up alone, reaching for someone who wasn't there.

I slipped two fingers inside her tight pussy, curling them up to find that spot that had always made her lose her mind. Her nails bit into my scalp as she pulled my face closer, her thighs snapping around my head like a vise.

She tried to bite down on the sounds she made, but the combination of my tongue and fingers coaxed little gasping moans from her throat.

"That's it, Kels. Been too fucking long since I heard you make that sound," I murmured, pulling back just enough to speak before diving back in.

The combination of my tongue and fingers had her riding my face, her hips moving in desperate little circles. Several times, I had to grip her leg with my free hand to keep her from sliding right off the island.

Less than a minute in, and her thighs were already shaking, the telltale tension a sign that she was close.

But I wanted to draw it out until she was desperate for it, until the counter beneath her was flooded. Until she knew without a doubt that she was the center of my whole world.

Always had been. Always would be.

I eased back, blowing a cool stream of air over the lips of her pussy, watching her jerk in response. Her fingers tightened in my hair, trying to guide me back, but I resisted, pressing soft kisses to her inner thighs instead.

"Teddy," she whimpered, and Christ, the desperation in her voice nearly undid me. "Please, I need—"

"I know what you need, baby." I traced lazy circles around her clit with my thumb, not quite giving her what she wanted. "But we're not rushing this like you do with everything else."

"I don't—" Her protest died when I dragged my tongue through her folds again before pulling back.

"You do," I insisted. "Always moving on to the next thing before you've finished the first. But not this time. This time, you're gonna take what I give you when I give it to you."

Kelsey growled in response, bucking her hips to try to chase the friction. I held her down with my forearm across her lower belly, keeping her pinned while I worked her with deliberate, maddening slowness.

"I hate you," she panted, but her fingers tightened in my hair, holding me exactly where she wanted me.

"No, you don't." I pumped a single finger into her before bringing it to my lips. "God, you taste so fucking good. Could keep you like this all afternoon. You'd love that, wouldn't you, baby?"

Instead of answering, she slid a hand up over her belly to cup her breast, hissing out a breath when her fingers closed around the peak of her nipple.

My dick throbbed painfully against my zipper, demanding attention I wasn't about to give it.

Not yet.

This was about her—about making her feel cherished, desired, worshipped in a way I'd failed to do for far too long.

"Whatcha doin', Kels?" I asked, palming myself through my jeans in an attempt to talk my dick down.

"Playing," she said innocently.

"Keep going," I rasped, my voice barely recognizable.

Her eyes met mine, heavy-lidded and glazed with lust, before she rolled her nipple between her thumb and index finger. A low moan spilled from her lips, vibrating through my entire body.

The need to kiss her again burned through me, but I held myself in check, content to watch as she touched herself for me.

If I'd had any lingering doubts about whether she still wanted me, the way she touched herself—open, unafraid, a little smug about it—obliterated them. Before the kids came along, she'd always liked putting on a show, knowing nothing brought me to my knees faster.

It didn't matter where we were, either. She'd once climbed onto my lap during a 4th of July cookout at the clubhouse under the guise of watching the fireworks. The woman had spread her pretty little gingham sundress across my lap and chatted away with some of the other Ol' Ladies seated nearby, all while working the head of my dick in and out of her pussy just to see how long I'd last.

I plunged three fingers back into her body, and she released a string of words, bucking wildly against my hand.

Nothing in the world quite like hearing your ex-wife, the woman who'd had you by the balls since high school, moaning your name.

My thumb circled her clit while my fingers kept up a rhythm I'd perfected over three decades of loving her,

"God, yes, Teddy—right there," she gasped, the wet sounds of my fingers pumping in and out her body mixing with her increasingly desperate whimpers and the soft strains of "Santa Baby" to form an erotic soundtrack I could listen to forever. "D-don't stop, please don't stop—"

Fat chance of that. I had no intention of stopping. I'd die between her thighs if she'd let me.

The taste of her, sweet and salty, fucked with my brain so hard that I almost lost the plot for a second—almost forgot that I was supposed to keep her on edge, not just get myself off on the needy sounds being ripped from her throat.

I doubled down, focused entirely on her pleasure, on giving her what she needed. My shoulder protested the angle of my hand, but I pushed past it.

"That's my girl."

Her breathing turned ragged, the little gasps coming faster now. I could read her body like a book I'd memorized cover to cover—knew she was right on the edge, just needed that final push.

I sucked her clit between my lips and hummed, the vibration sending her flying.

"Teddy—oh God, I'm—" Kelsey's body locked up before she began pulsing around my fingers in shuddering waves. She bit the back of her hand to try to silence her scream, but I caught it anyway, etching the sound into my memory for the inevitable moment she was gone again.

I kept going, drawing it out until she was shaking, trying to push my head away from oversensitivity. Only then did I pull back and let her catch her breath.

My knees cracked and popped when I finally stood, reminding me that I wasn't twenty anymore. Still, the sight of Kelsey sprawled across my kitchen island—flour in her hair, dough stuck to her elbow, a star-shaped cookie cutter somehow wedged under her left butt cheek—made every ounce of pain worth it.

For the first time in years, she looked wrecked—in a good way.

Satisfied, maybe even peaceful. For a split second, I let myself believe I could give her that steadiness again, that I could be the man who made her world safe instead of dangerous.

A full minute passed before sense returned to her eyes, and a slow grin spread across her lips. "You trying to kill me, Riggs?"

"Nah," I said, brushing flour from her shoulder as I helped her sit up. "Just helping you relax. Not to yank my own dick or anything, but I'm pretty good at it. I mean—" I waved my free hand over her body. "—the results clearly speak for themselves."

She rolled her eyes at the comment and pulled me down for a deep and dirty kiss. I let her taste herself on my tongue, let her hands drift under my shirt, let her feel every inch of me straining against my old Levi's.

"Speaking of your dick," she said, squeezing me through the denim.

I caught her wrist with a barely restrained groan. "This wasn't about me."

Her brow furrowed. "But—"

"Didn't do it to get something back, Kels," I insisted. "Shit, I get off on getting you off. Always have"

"I know you do," she whispered, her voice cracking like it did when she was about to cry. "But I wanna make you feel good."

"This was for you." I lifted her arm, pressing my lips to the inside of her wrist. "Just for you. You don't owe me anything."

I meant it, too. Needed her to understand this wasn't some transaction where she had to balance the books. "I wanted to do that. Wanted to watch you come apart. That's all I need."

Kelsey stared at me like I'd grown a second head, eyes narrowed in suspicion. "Since when does Theodore Riggs turn down a blow job?"

I held her gaze, my jaw working as I tried to find the right words. "Since I realized we've been using sex as a Band-Aid for years. And I'm trying real hard not to fall back into old habits."

Her expression shifted, something vulnerable flickering across her face before she shuttered it. "Right. Old habits."

"Not saying I don't want it," I added, my thumb stroking the inside of her wrist. "Christ, Kels, I'm so hard right now I can barely think straight. But I don't wanna go there unless it means something."

Not if it's just another way to avoid talking about the hard shit.

"Teddy—"

The timer came to the rescue once again, its shrill beeps saving us from whatever emotional minefield we'd been about to walk into.

I adjusted myself again and tried to think about literally anything other than how good her hand had felt for those few brief seconds. It would have been so easy to give in to what she was offering. Pretend it was just sex. Just two bodies remembering what they were good at.

But it wasn't that simple. Nothing between us ever had been.

Kelsey scrambled off the island, nearly taking me down with her when her knees buckled. I caught her around the waist, steadying her while she found her footing.

"How 'bout I get the cookies and you just stand here and look pretty?"

She shot me a look that was equal parts annoyed and satisfied. "This is your fault," she muttered, tugging the flannel back on with shaking fingers. "I think you broke me."

"Yeah?" I couldn't keep the grin off my face as I pulled the cookies out and set them on the stovetop before sliding the next pan in. "You complaining?"

She opened her mouth, probably to tell me exactly where I could shove my smugness but closed it again when she caught sight of the cookies. They were perfect—golden brown, edges crisp, centers still soft.

"Huh." She tilted her head, examining them. "Would you look at that. It's a Christmas miracle."

"Told you I wouldn't let them burn."

"No, you told me I had twelve minutes to come," she corrected, grabbing a spatula to transfer them. "Which, for the record, is an insane thing to say to someone."

"No, insane would have been seeing how many times I could make you come before the next batch was done." I waggled my eyebrows in the least mature way possible, and she snorted, a sound so familiar and sweet it almost hurt.

"A+ for confidence, but an F-minus for humility," she said, refusing to look at me. Not that it mattered. The flush creeping up her neck told me everything I needed to know.

I watched as she lined the cookies up in perfect rows on the cooling rack, trying to memorize every detail of the moment—my flannel shirt swallowing her frame, the bare skin of her thighs peeking out from below, her damp hair curling around her face like she'd just crawled out of bed after the best sex of her life.

"You're staring," Kelsey said without turning.

"Damn right I am." No point pretending otherwise. "It's been a long time since I got to see you like this. Let me look."

A beat passed. Her hands paused mid-cookie transfer, then slowly relaxed. She turned around, eyes searching my face. "You're really not going to make a move, huh?"

"Already made my move, baby," I said, dropping my voice to a rumble. "More than once. But I'm not pushing it." I crossed my arms, rooted to the tile so she could see I meant it. "This is fine."

Her laugh was bright and genuine, the sound filling up all the empty spaces in my chest I'd been trying to ignore. "Who the hell are you, and what have you done with my ex-husband?"

My smile faded. "Trying to do it different. That's all."

This time, when her eyes met mine, there was something like tenderness in the way she looked at me—as if she was seeing through to the inside, to the scared asshole who just wanted to keep her safe and close and happy, even if he didn't know how.

"You're right," she murmured, toying with a button on her shirt. "We've got at least seven more batches to go. Better pace yourself, Riggs. You're not as young as you once were, and I'd hate for you to start something you can't finish."

I crossed the kitchen in three strides, caging her against a cabinet. "You questioning my stamina, sweetheart?"

"Maybe I am." She tilted her chin up, defiant even in surrender. "What are you gonna do about it?"

I cracked my neck from side to side and rolled my shoulders before dropping back to my knees between her spread legs. "Oh, darlin'. I'm gonna prove you wrong."

❄

The fire crackled as I tossed another log in, sending sparks spiraling up the chimney like tiny orange stars. The whole cabin still smelled like gingerbread—a scent that would forever remind me of Kelsey on my tongue, of her coming apart in my kitchen. Repeatedly.

I dusted off my hands and turned to find her curled up on the couch in yet another shirt she'd claimed as her own, remote in hand, scrolling through my streaming options with the kind of intense focus most people reserved for major life decisions.

"*The Muppet Christmas Carol*?" I asked, unable to keep the grin off my face when I saw her selection. "Really?"

She shot me a look. "You love this movie."

"I tolerate this movie," I corrected.

"Well, too bad because it's tradition, mister," she said, which wasn't all that far from the truth. It had been Addie's favorite since she was five, and she'd demanded we watch it every Christmas Eve until it became as much a tradition as hanging stockings or leaving cookies for Santa.

I flicked off the overhead lights, leaving just the tree and fireplace to illuminate the room. The shadows softened everything, made it easier to pretend this was just another December night from before. When movie night was sacred, when all three kids would pile on the couch between us, back when everything made sense.

"Wouldn't be Christmas without Gonzo narrating Dickens, I guess," I conceded.

"Exactly." Kelsey patted the cushion beside her. "Now get your ass over here before I start it without you."

"Fine," I said, dropping onto the couch beside her. "But if I hear one word about how Michael Caine was the only actor who took his Muppet role seriously, I'm putting on *Die Hard*."

She curled into my side immediately, the same way she'd done for thousands of movie nights before. Head on my chest, arm draped across my stomach, legs tucked up beneath her. My arm went around her shoulders automatically, pulling her closer. Muscle memory. That, or maybe she'd just been made to fit there.

The opening credits rolled with Scrooge scowling his way through Victorian London as Muppets sang about what a prick he was. Kelsey nudged me when Rizzo and Gonzo showed up outside Scrooge's counting house, doing their vaudeville routine. "This is your favorite part," she murmured.

"My favorite part is when it's over," I lied.

She snorted, the sound vibrating through my chest. "You cried last time we watched it."

"Did not."

"Did too. When Tiny Tim died. I saw you."

"Had something in my eye," I muttered, but she was right. Something about that little puppet and his father's grief always got me, especially after—

I shut the thought down before it could take root. Not tonight.

My hand moved to her shoulder, fingers tracing absent circles. This had been my move since we were teenagers—the mindless touching that said I'm here without requiring words. She relaxed into it, her breaths evening out as the Ghost of Christmas Past appeared on screen in a beam of light.

"I love this part," Kelsey whispered as the ghost took Scrooge back to see his younger self, before life had turned him hard and bitter. "When he remembers who he used to be."

I studied Scrooge's face—the wonder and pain of seeing his past self, of remembering the boy he'd been before everything went wrong. Maybe that was why Kelsey loved it. We'd both been different people once. Softer. Less broken. The kind of people who believed love was enough to fix anything.

Her hand had started moving under my shirt at some point, fingers tracing the line of hair on my stomach in lazy patterns that made it hard to focus on the movie. Not sexual, exactly. More like she needed to touch, to confirm I was solid and real beneath her palm.

I caught her hand, pressing it flat against my stomach, and she nuzzled against my chest. We stayed like that through the Ghost of Christmas Present—the spirit of generosity and abundance, showing Scrooge all the love and warmth he was missing by shutting himself away.

Then the third spirit appeared.

The Ghost of Christmas Yet to Come—the silent, hooded figure that even the Muppets couldn't make less ominous—pointing at a future Scrooge hadn't chosen yet but was hurtling toward anyway.

On screen, Scrooge begged to know if these shadows were what would be, or what might be if he didn't change his ways, and I couldn't help but think about my own future.

What would my ghost show? More empty Christmases in this cabin, trying to pretend the half-decorated tree wasn't a metaphor for my half-lived life? More nights buying Kelsey's expensive shampoo just to breathe in the memory of her? More years of going through the motions while the best part of my life existed five hundred miles away, building a new future that didn't include me?

Or worse—regret. The kind that ate you alive. The kind that came from having one last chance to say something real, to have the hard conversations, but choosing to stay silent. Letting her walk away again because I was too scared to admit I'd never stopped wanting her in every way that mattered.

Kelsey must have felt me tense because she shifted, turning to look up at me. "You okay?" she asked softly.

"Yeah." The lie came automatically, but she saw through it.

On screen, Scrooge was promising to change, to honor Christmas in his heart and try to keep it all year round. But that was the thing about promises made in the dark—morning always came, reality always intruded, and most of us went back to being exactly who we were before.

Without a word, Kelsey moved, swinging one leg over to straddle my lap, the movie forgotten behind her.

"Hey," she whispered, cupping my face between her palms. "Where'd you go?"

"Nowhere." I gripped her hips, pulling her closer until there was no space between us. "Just thinking about what happens when—"

She kissed me before I could finish, deep and desperate, like she could swallow the words before they poisoned the air between us.

When she pulled back, her lips were swollen, her breathing ragged.

She kissed along my jaw, down to my throat, her teeth grazing a spot on my ear that made me groan.

"I'm gonna take care of you now," she whispered against my skin. "Don't think about tomorrow. Just be here with me tonight. Please." The words came out in a rush, her cheeks darkening even in the firelight.

Every rational part of my brain screamed that it was a bad idea. That every act of intimacy we shared would make it harder when she inevitably went back to Texas, back to her life without me.

And I'd be here, even more broken than before, with new memories to torture myself with during the long Colorado nights.

I'd lie awake wondering if she'd met someone else—someone who made her happy, who didn't retreat to the clubhouse when shit got complicated, who knew how to say the right words instead of hiding behind silence and distance.

But who was I to deny her anything when she looked at me like that? When she said please in a tone that had always been my undoing?

"Yeah," I breathed, lifting my hips so she could tug my jeans down. "Yeah, okay, baby."

She smiled—soft and real and tinged with the same melancholy I felt—before sliding off my lap and settling between my knees.

It was most definitely a mistake. Hell, everything about the past three days had been a mistake. But when her mouth closed around me, hot and perfect and familiar, I couldn't bring myself to care.

The movie played on behind her—Scrooge learning his lessons about love and redemption and second chances—while I raked my fingers through her hair and tried not to think about how this was just another Ghost of Christmas Past we were creating. Another memory that would haunt me through all the Christmases yet to come.

But for now, I let myself have it. Let myself pretend that redemption was possible, that second chances weren't just fiction, that the woman I'd loved since I was seventeen might somehow find her way back to loving me, too.

Even if it was just for tonight.

14

kelsey

THE STRANGLED SOUND that tore me from sleep wasn't human. It came from somewhere deep and primal, the kind of noise wounded animals made in the throes of death. My body knew before my brain caught up—muscles locking, lungs seizing, adrenaline flooding my veins.

Beside me, Teddy thrashed against the sheets, his breathing ragged and broken. Moonlight reflected off the snow-covered ground beyond the windows, enough for me to see his familiar features twisted into something haunted. His lips moved, forming words I couldn't quite—

"Levi. No, no, please—"

My entire body went rigid.

This wasn't a medical emergency. It wasn't a heart attack or stroke or any of the things my sleep-addled brain had initially supplied. This was worse—something I recognized with the kind of bone-deep knowing that came from having lived through it once already.

It was the same dream that had plagued me for the past two and a half years. The nightmare that had broken everything beyond repair. The weight of our son's body in Teddy's arms. The paramedics who

Shannon Myers

wouldn't meet our eyes. The terrible finality of hospital doors closing, of time running out, of all the words we'd never get to say.

My hand hovered in the air between us, fingers trembling. I should touch him—should pull him out of whatever hell his subconscious had dragged him into. But I couldn't make myself move, couldn't bridge those final inches.

"Teddy," I managed, though it came out small and scared, nothing like the comforting, steady tone I'd been aiming for.

He didn't respond, lost in whatever horror was playing out behind his eyelids. His chest heaved with each labored breath, sweat beading on his forehead despite the December chill seeping through the windows.

I forced myself to reach out, my fingers barely grazing his arm. "Teddy, wake up."

He lurched upright so violently I nearly fell off the bed. His eyes— wild, unseeing—stared right through me, the same way they had that night. Like I wasn't really there. Like maybe I'd never been there at all.

My ribcage tightened around my lungs, squeezing until each breath became a conscious effort. The room seemed to tilt on its axis, walls pressing closer while simultaneously stretching away. My ears filled with a roaring sound that had nothing to do with the wind outside.

No. Not now. Not here.

I slid from the mattress on legs that felt disconnected from my body, my hands already moving to smooth the rumpled sheets.

Fix it. Make it neat. Make it right.

If I could just get the corners tucked properly, if I could just straighten the comforter, maybe everything would stop spinning.

"Kels?" Teddy called out, his voice still rough with sleep.

I couldn't look at him. Couldn't risk seeing that devastation on his face again. Instead, I focused on the pillows, fluffing each one before positioning them against the headboard. One task, then another. That was how you survived. That was how you kept going when your body forgot how to work.

"Don't." There was something broken in the way he said it, making my hands still. "Don't go quiet on me. Not now."

The click of the bedside lamp made me flinch. Soft yellow light

138

flooded the room, chasing away the shadows but somehow making everything feel more exposed. More raw.

I kept my back to him, continuing to adjust the already-perfect pillows. "You were just having a nightmare. It's—it happens. I can make some tea or get you a glass of—"

"Kelsey," he pleaded. "Baby, look at me."

I couldn't. If I looked at him, if I saw what I knew would be written across his face, the careful control I'd managed to maintain for the past three days would shatter. And once it broke, I wasn't sure I'd be able to piece it back together again.

His hand caught my wrist as I reached for another pillow, gentle but insistent. "Please."

The contact sent electricity shooting up my arm, not desire but something closer to panic. I jerked away, the movement too sharp, too telling.

"Christ," he muttered, dragging both hands down his face. "We're right back there, aren't we? Back to you shutting down, and me not knowing how to reach you."

Twelve seconds of silence.

Then twelve more.

The distance between us was growing with every breath I didn't take, every word I didn't say.

Twelve seconds would stretch into twelve minutes and then twelve miles—the same progression that had destroyed us the first time around.

The terrible arithmetic of loss, multiplying the space between us until we were strangers again. Maybe we were doomed to fall back into the same patterns as before, cursed to drift apart, no matter how hard we tried to hold it together.

"I'm not shutting down," I said in a monotone. My hands had resumed their nervous movements, straightening things that didn't need straightening, creating order where none existed.

"Then what do you call this? Because from where I'm sitting, looks like every other time you've—"

"Every other time I've what?" The words came out sharper than intended, defensive. "Every other time I've tried to help? Tried to make things better?"

"Every other time you've disappeared on me while being right fucking here."

The accusation was too accurate to deny. I was falling back into old habits, retreating behind tasks and efficiency, using motion as armor against feeling. But knowing it and stopping it were two different things.

"Don't shut me out," he said, quieter now but no less desperate. "Not tonight. Not after everything we've—please, Kels. Just... sit. Talk to me. Anything but this."

My throat closed around whatever response I might have made. Because what could I say? That watching him relive our son's death had triggered every carefully buried instinct to run? That I was drowning in guilt and shame so thick I could taste it? That if I stopped moving, stopped fixing, stopped pretending to be useful, he'd realize that the real Kelsey was just like that reindeer with the wonky antler back at the other cabin?

Not worth repairing. Not worth saving. Not worth loving.

The sheets were perfect now—corners sharp enough to please a drill sergeant.

"I'll get you some water," I said, already turning toward the door, desperate for even a thirty-second reprieve from the weight of his gaze.

I made it approximately two steps before he was up, his hands catching my shoulders, spinning me back to face him. Not rough, but insistent. Determined.

"No," he said, and there was something wild in his eyes now, pain manifesting as frustration. "Watched you run this exact same play a hundred fucking times before, and I'm not letting you run away. We're gonna stand right here and actually talk for once in our goddamn lives."

"Let go of me," I croaked, my stomach churning with dread.

"Not until you tell me why you do this. Why you always—" He stopped, jaw clenching like he was trying to crush the words into something less devastating. "After Levi died, you wouldn't even look at me."

"That's not—"

"It is," he cut me off, years of hurt finally spilling over. "You stopped saying his name! Our son's name, Kels. Like, if we didn't talk about him, it wouldn't be real. And when I tried—Christ, when I tried to bring him up, you'd shut down. Go reorganize the pantry or scrub the baseboards or bake another fucking casserole nobody wanted to eat."

My shoulders tensed beneath his hands because once again, Teddy was right. I had done all those things. Was still doing them.

"But I never stopped—" He broke off and cleared his throat, his grip on my shoulders loosening but not releasing. When he spoke again, his voice was thick with the emotions he was struggling to hold back. "I never stopped wanting you. Even when you pulled away from me, like you couldn't stand the thought of me touching you. Even when you were at that gym seven days a week, changing everything about yourself like you were trying to become someone else entirely. I still wanted you. Still loved you. Still do, if I'm being honest."

My throat burned with unshed tears, but he wasn't done yet. The dam that had broken, and everything we'd carefully avoided for years, came pouring out.

"I didn't just lose Levi that night. Lost you, too. Watched you slip away piece by piece and blamed myself. Every fucking day, I blamed myself for not waking up sooner. For not being able to save him. And I thought—I thought you blamed me too."

"So you ran to the club," I said with a brittle laugh, needing to push back against the version of truth he was serving. "Where everything's sunshine and rainbows, and the women are always happy to see you."

"What women?" he asked, his voice deadly calm.

"Oh, please. You can drop the act. We're divorced now, no sense in acting like you weren't getting your dick wet—"

Teddy pressed me against the door, his hand locking around my jaw to hold me in place.

I'd gone too far, struck too close to something raw.

"Told you before, I never cheated on you," he said, adopting a carefully controlled tone.

I searched his hazel eyes for signs of deception but found only raw honesty and a pain that mirrored my own.

"One woman," he growled, baring his teeth. "Been with one woman my entire life, baby. You. Never touched anyone else, never wanted to. Even after the papers were signed, even when I couldn't stand to be in the same state as you because it hurt too fucking much—there was only you."

"But you were always gone," I whispered, hating how meek my voice sounded. "Every night. Sometimes you wouldn't come home until—"

"Because I couldn't stand being in that house," he admitted, his thumb brushing away a tear I hadn't realized had escaped. "There were reminders of him everywhere—his backpack still lying on the bench in the mudroom where he left it, the hamper of dirty clothes in the laundry room. And you—Jesus, Kels, you were like a ghost. There, but not there. Going through the motions on fucking autopilot."

As much as I tried to convince myself things had gotten better since the divorce, a part of me still felt like a ghost, haunting an empty house that once held happy memories but was now nothing but a tomb for the family and marriage I'd lost.

"I thought if I gave you space, you'd come back to me." Teddy pinched the bridge of his nose with his free hand and exhaled slowly before forcing himself to continue. "Thought maybe you needed time to grieve without me hovering. But the space just kept growing until I couldn't reach you anymore."

"I couldn't—" The admission caught in my chest, fighting against years of carefully constructed walls. "I couldn't let you see me fall apart."

"Why? You think I couldn't handle it?" Teddy's voice came out strangled. "Jesus Christ, Kelsey. You think I was that weak? That selfish?"

I wanted to pull away, to retreat into myself where it was safe, where the ugly truth couldn't hurt anyone but me. But his body caged me against the door, and there was nowhere to run. Nowhere to hide.

"Say something," he demanded when the silence stretched too long. "Anything."

"I can't," I whispered.

"Can't what?" He released my jaw to drag a hand through his hair, the movement sharp with frustration. "Can't talk to me? Can't be honest for once in your life?"

My head shook. A tiny movement, barely perceptible, but it was all I could manage. "I can't tell you what you want to hear."

"Don't want you to tell me what I want to hear," he snapped. "I just want the truth. However bad it is, just… tell me you hate me. Tell me you've moved on. Tell me what we've been doing these past few days means nothing. Whatever it is, Kels, just say it. We've already lost everything once. What's left to lose?"

Everything, I wanted to scream. Because we'd found something in this blizzard. Something fragile and tentative, but real. And I was about to destroy it with the truth I'd been carrying like a stone in my chest since the night our son died.

"You want the truth?" I asked, hearing the hysteria bleeding into my voice. "Fine. You're right. I pulled away. I shut you out. But it wasn't because I blamed you."

"Then why—"

"Because I blamed myself!" The admission ripped from my throat, raw and ugly. "Because I was the one who was supposed to be watching him that night. I was the one who should have checked on him. Should have known something was wrong."

Teddy's face went pale. "Kels—"

"No, you wanted honesty, and you're gonna get it." I was shaking now as if my body was revolting against my sudden decision to be transparent.

"I spent years being hypervigilant. Checking his meds, monitoring his moods, terrified that if I looked away for even a second—" A sob built in my throat, and I slapped my palm over my mouth, physically trying to hold back the confession. But it was too late. The truth I'd buried so deep was clawing its way out, demanding to be heard.

"I was so tired. So fucking tired of checking on him every hour. Of hiding the knives. Of counting his pills—"

"Stop." His hands came up to frame my face, thumbs brushing away tears I hadn't realized were falling. "Baby, stop."

But I couldn't.

"I can't stop," I croaked, sobbing so hard my ribs ached. "I keep seeing it, over and over. He was so upset about that girl he had a crush on turning him down at the dance, and I remember telling him it was her loss. The way he looked at me before he went upstairs. It was like he knew. Like he knew I couldn't save him. Couldn't fix what was broken inside him.

"I was his mother. I should have wanted to keep fighting for him forever. It was my job. But when it ended, when the doctor came out and told us there was nothing more they could do, all I felt was—"

My legs gave out, and I would have hit the floor if Teddy hadn't caught me, his strong arms banding around me as I broke myself wide open.

"The only thing I felt was relief," I sobbed. "Relief that I wouldn't have to live like that anymore. Relief that I could finally go to bed without being afraid to wake up. That maybe, finally, you and the girls could have more of me than just the exhausted scraps left over after managing his illness. That maybe we could be normal again, not constantly walking on eggshells, terrified of saying the wrong thing or missing a warning sign—"

Tears streamed down my face, hot and shameful, but the words kept coming in breathless rushes.

"And I hated myself for it," I gasped against his chest. "Hated myself so much that I couldn't imagine you ever wanting me again if you knew the truth. Because what kind of mother feels relieved when her child dies? How could you love someone like that?"

I pulled back, still unable to meet his eyes. "So I made it easy for you. I ended our marriage before you could. Before you could look at me and see what I really was. Before you could realize you'd married a monster."

My voice broke completely, shoulders curling inward like I could make myself small enough to disappear. Like I could fold in on myself until the shame couldn't find me anymore.

"Jesus, Kels," Teddy said softly, and I waited for him to pull away in disgust, to confirm every horrible thing I believed about myself.

But instead, he just held me tighter, his big hands spanning my back, his body trembling as hard as mine.

"You think you're a monster?" he rasped, dropping his cheek to rest against the top of my head. "I pleaded with God to take me that night. But even in the middle of doing CPR and begging Levi to breathe... some part of me already knew it was too late. We'd lost him long before that night, maybe years before. And when they told us he was gone, I felt it, too, Kels."

He rocked us both as he talked, steady and slow, like he was trying to put me to sleep. Like he had with our kids when they were babies.

His chest hitched. "There was this sick sense of relief that it was finally over. Wouldn't have to spend the rest of my life terrified every time my phone rang, wondering if this was it. Wouldn't have to watch him suffer anymore, battling demons none of us could see or understand. It was like I'd been holding my breath for thirteen goddamn years, and I could finally breathe again."

I stared at him, unable to process what he'd just said. The words didn't make sense. Couldn't make sense. Because Teddy was supposed to be the good parent. The one who'd never given up hope, who'd fought for Levi when I'd wanted to run. The one who deserved to keep his memories pure and untainted by the ugliness that lived inside me.

"No," I whispered, shaking my head. "You don't get to—you can't just say that to make me feel better."

"I'm not," he said, his voice breaking. I looked up to find his face wet with tears. "You think I'd lie about this? That I'd make up something so fucked up just to—"

"But you tried to save him," I said desperately, needing him to take it back. Needing to be the only villain in this story. "You were trying to save him. You knew exactly what to do, no hesitation. You—"

"Every compression felt like my body just doing what it was trained to do," he interjected, jaw clenching so tight I could see the muscle jumping beneath his skin, "but my brain had already accepted what was coming. I kept thinking—fuck, I kept thinking that at least he wasn't hurting anymore."

He dragged in a shuddering breath, his hands tightening on my back like he was afraid I'd pull away.

"Felt like a fucking monster, too," he continued, the words coming faster now, like he couldn't hold them back any longer. "Every time I looked at you, all I could see was my failure. And I convinced myself you blamed me for not doing more to bring him back. Thought you'd finally seen what kind of man I really was, and that's why you couldn't stand to let me touch you anymore."

All this time, I'd thought I was the only one drowning in shame. The only one who'd felt that terrible, shameful sense of relief. But he'd been carrying the same burden, believing the same lies about himself.

"I didn't know," I whispered, reaching up to trace the lines time and grief had etched into his skin. "I never knew you blamed yourself."

"Because I couldn't tell you." He exhaled a soft laugh. "Couldn't let you see what kind of man I really was. Thought if you knew the truth, you'd leave. So I just—I let you go instead. Signed those divorce papers like it didn't rip me to fucking shreds, because at least that way, I got to pretend it was my choice."

We stood together in the darkness, clinging to each other like survivors of a shipwreck. Outside, the wind had finally died down, leaving behind an eerie stillness that made the cabin feel even more isolated. Cut off from the rest of the world.

Maybe that was what we'd needed all along. To be forced into the same space with nowhere to run, no distractions to hide behind. Just the two of us and all the ugly truths we'd been avoiding.

"We're so damn stubborn," I finally said, half-laughing, half-sobbing against his chest. "If we'd just talked about it…"

"I know." Teddy exhaled a long sigh, one hand coming up to cradle the back of my head. "But we didn't know how. Least, I sure as hell didn't. Every time I tried to bring him up, you'd get this look on your face like I was hurting you just by saying his name."

"Because it did—it does…" I trailed off, trying to figure out how to put it into words. "It's like when someone asks how many kids I have, and I immediately say three. Then, I remember, and it's like losing him all over again. But not talking about him was worse. Just like the ornaments, he was part of our story. Good or bad, he was ours," I finished, hiccupping on another sob.

It felt inadequate, but there would never be enough words to convey the enormity of losing a child.

"He'll always be our boy. Never gonna forget him," Teddy said fiercely. "Not for one goddamn second. But we were so busy trying to protect each other that we just—"

"Broke," I finished. "We broke, Teddy. Shattered into so many pieces, I didn't think we'd ever find our way back."

His hand moved to the back of my neck, his thumb stroking the sensitive skin there. "You think we can? Find our way back?"

The question hung between us, heavy with possibility and fear in equal measure. I wanted to say yes. Wanted to believe that this—whatever this was—could be more than just a temporary truce born of proximity and nostalgia.

But that felt too much like hope, and I'd learned not to trust hope.

"I don't know," I answered honestly. Because we hadn't broken all at once. Between fertility treatments, raising three kids, Levi's issues, and the shit that went down with the club, it just felt like we could never find our footing.

"We were always off-balance, and by the time we noticed the cracks, we were so tired, Teddy. So worn down. I didn't know how to fix it then, and I don't know where to begin to undo it all now."

Teddy hummed in agreement. "Me neither. But maybe we don't have to fix it all at once. Maybe we just take it one day at a time. One conversation at a time."

I nodded against his chest, bone-deep exhaustion crashing over me like a wave. He must have felt it because he guided me back to the bed, pulling me down beside him. We didn't bother getting under the covers. Just curled around each other, my face buried in his neck, his arms wrapped around me so tightly I could barely breathe.

"I've got you," he murmured, turning his head to press his lips to my hair. "I'm right here, baby. Not going anywhere."

Something in me that had been wound impossibly tight for years finally loosened, and I relaxed against him, letting the exhaustion pull me under into something that felt almost like peace.

15

Christmas Eve

kelsey

I WOKE to the weight of Teddy's arm draped over me and the warmth of his chest against my back. With his fingers curved protectively around my hip, I could almost believe the past two years had been nothing but a particularly vivid nightmare.

Blue-gray early morning light filtered through the floor-to-ceiling windows, casting the snow-covered world outside in shades of shimmering silver and pearl. It was as though someone had taken an eraser to the earth, wiping away all the messy parts and leaving nothing but clean, white possibility.

For several minutes, I lay there, watching the icy sun creep up over the ridgeline, letting myself pretend this was my life... my home. Pretending I would wake every winter morning to the feel of Teddy's breath against the back of my neck, our bodies pressed so close together that I couldn't tell where his ended and mine began.

But then reality, relentless bitch that she was, intruded to remind me that nothing was permanent. Everything had an expiration date. Even peace.

If I shifted even an inch, the whole arrangement would collapse—

Teddy's arm would tighten, or I'd startle him awake. We'd have to look at each other and acknowledge the emotional wreckage scattered across the sheets between us. The things we'd said and couldn't take back. The absolution I still wasn't sure I deserved.

So, I stayed right where I was, holding onto the fantasy in my mind until my bladder demanded I get up. I began the delicate process of extracting myself without waking him. One careful inch at a time, I eased my body away from his, sucking in a breath when his arm tightened momentarily before going slack again.

I grabbed the flannel shirt from where I'd left it draped over the chair and pulled it on over my pajamas.

Teddy stirred in his sleep, his fingers instinctively reaching for the empty space I'd left behind. The lines around his eyes appeared softer, the perpetual tension in his jaw released. He looked younger. Not young—we'd never be young again—but unburdened. Less like the hardened biker he projected to the world and more like the boy who'd taught me to ride a motorcycle when I was eighteen. The boy who'd anxiously pressed his lips to my throat and apologized for hurting me the first time we made love.

God, we'd been so naïve then. So certain that love would be enough to carry us through anything life threw at us. I turned away before the dull ache in my chest could grow teeth and rip me open all over again.

After using the bathroom, I splashed cold water on my face, carefully avoiding my reflection in the mirror. I didn't need to see the evidence of last night's emotional bloodletting. I felt it in every cell of my body. Like I'd been turned inside out and put back together slightly wrong.

The coffee maker beckoned from the kitchen, and I moved toward it on autopilot, my body remembering the ritual even as my mind stayed foggy. It was strange, being in someone else's kitchen and knowing exactly where everything was. Teddy's cabinets were organized the same as the ones in our old house.

While the coffee brewed, I drifted toward the living room. The fire had burned down to gray ash, all except for a few stubborn embers still glowing orange near the center. The tree stood in the corner, fully decorated, golden lights twinkling softly. Evidence of our tentative truce, our fumbling attempts to be something other than two people who'd destroyed each other.

My eyes drifted to the hook by the door where Teddy's kutte hung, the same one he'd had since he patched in at eighteen. The leather was worn soft from years of use, shoulders creased from where it had molded to his body. I'd washed blood from it more times than I cared to remember. Had even helped him patch a bullet hole in it once, my hands shaking as I worked the needle through the leather and tried not to think about how close I'd been to becoming a widow. It was as much a part of him as his wedding ring had once been. Maybe even more so.

In the chaos of the blizzard, my accident, and everything that had followed, I hadn't really looked at it. Now I couldn't seem to look away. I moved closer, drawn by the same masochistic impulse that made you press on a bruise just to see if it still hurt.

The top rocker sewn onto the back still read "Silent Phoenix"—the club his father had founded, the legacy that had defined our life together. Beneath it, a blazing phoenix emerged from flames, wings spread wide.

My fingers drifted lower, to the bottom rocker that had read "Texas" for the entirety of our marriage, and everything inside me went still.

"Colorado."

I blinked at the weathered stitching, confirming what my eyes were telling me even as my brain scrambled to reject it.

No. No, that couldn't be right. In the middle of our divorce, he'd gone nomad. He'd told me as much when we signed the papers. And months later, when Addie slipped up and mentioned he was living in Colorado, I assumed he'd retreated here to lick his wounds while helping the chapter.

Nomad meant temporary. Nomad meant he was still figuring it out, still floating, still possibly open to—

To what, exactly? Coming back to Texas? Coming back to me?

I turned the kutte around with shaking hands, needing to see the rest, even though some part of me already knew what I'd find. There, over the left breast, was the same patch his father had once worn on his own kutte.

"President."

The man who led the chapter, who made the calls, who carried the weight of every brother's life on his shoulders. The man who couldn't just walk away when things got complicated.

The kitchen suddenly felt too small, the walls pressing in on me like a vise. I'd known, logically, that he was here. That he'd bought this cabin and the other. But knowing it and understanding what it meant were two different things. And standing here, holding the evidence of his commitment—the same way I'd once held his hand when he made vows to me—drove it home in a way nothing else had.

While I'd stayed in our old house, surrounded by bad memories and empty rooms, he'd been here. While I convinced myself he was miserable without me and that we'd find our way back to each other, he'd been building something new from the ashes of the marriage we'd torched. Something permanent. Something that had nothing to do with me or the life we'd once shared.

This place wasn't a retreat or an escape—it was his home. This chapter wasn't a distraction—it was his purpose. Colorado wasn't a temporary solution—it was his answer to the question of how to keep going when everything fell apart.

And that answer didn't include me. I wasn't even a part of the equation.

President. The word might as well have been "goodbye" for how final it felt.

That was the problem with temporary ceasefires and forced proximity—they created the illusion that everything could go back to how it was. I'd been so busy thinking about all we'd confessed last night, about the beautiful, terrible truths we'd shared, that I'd forgotten the most basic truth of all: geography didn't care about feelings. Distance didn't shrink because you had a breakthrough.

He'd put down roots somewhere I wasn't, and I'd stayed in the place he'd left behind.

Both choices were valid. Both were necessary, maybe. But they led to different futures, different paths that ran parallel but never quite touched.

And last night hadn't changed a damn thing about that.

We were still five hundred miles apart, with separate lives that only intersected in the past.

My throat tightened with fresh tears, but I was too exhausted to let them fall. What was the point? We'd already cried ourselves empty, confessed our worst secrets, forgiven the unforgivable. We'd found our way back to honesty, to seeing each other instead of just our own reflections of guilt and failure—doing the work, as my therapist would say.

But that didn't mean we'd found our way back to each other.

Not really.

The coffee maker beeped, startling me back to the present, but I couldn't let go of the kutte. Couldn't stop staring at the patches that rewrote everything I thought I knew about where we stood.

It felt like a door was closing between us.

Or maybe it had been closed all along, and I'd just been too desperate to notice. I'd gotten caught up in playing house and being the center of his world again that I failed to see the signs in front of me.

Behind me, I heard movement as Teddy approached. But I stood paralyzed, kutte still clutched in my hands as the second chance I hadn't dared to hope for crumbled before it had even begun.

"Mornin'," he said, his voice still rough with sleep. "You're up early." The floorboards creaked as he moved closer, stopping just behind me. Close enough to touch but not touching.

My fingers tightened on the leather until my knuckles went white. "Couldn't sleep."

"Kels?" There was a question in the way he said it, a wariness that told me he'd already clocked what I was holding. "What are you doing?"

"Nothing. Just—" I cleared my throat. Perfect Kelsey mode, already sliding back into place like a mask I couldn't stop wearing. "Just looking."

I couldn't tell if the sudden tension crackling between us was left over from last night's confessions or something new—something charged by the discovery of what his life had become without me.

His hand came to rest on my shoulder, squeezing gently. "C'mon, Kels. Talk to me."

I turned around to find Teddy in nothing but the sweatpants he'd gone to bed in, his long hair falling in loose waves around his shoulders. Even now—furious and hurt and feeling like the world's biggest idiot—I couldn't help but notice how beautiful he was. Couldn't help but notice the swirls of ink covering his skin, my name scarred over his heart.

Teddy's attention went from my face to the kutte and back again. Whatever he saw made him take a step forward, mouth opening to say something I wasn't ready to hear.

Before he could speak, his phone erupted from somewhere nearby, the buzzing aggressive and insistent.

He located it on the coffee table and glanced at the screen before silencing it. "My mom. I'll call her back later."

The phone immediately started vibrating again.

"Jesus," Teddy muttered, pinching the bridge of his nose.

A cold knot formed in my stomach. Lucy Riggs had nerves of steel —she'd raised four boys in the MC, held down the fort when Paul was locked up in the eighties, survived raids and lockdowns, and God knew what else. She wouldn't be calling unless something was wrong. I'd learned that over the past 30-plus years of being part of the family. Or formerly part of the family.

Whatever the hell I was now.

"You should get that," I said, my voice coming out steadier than I felt. Anything to delay the inevitable. Anything to give me time to reassemble the careful walls that had crumbled so spectacularly last night.

I moved to hang the kutte back on its hook, trying to make it seem like I hadn't been standing there memorizing every patch like they were tea leaves that could tell me our future. "Just answer it. It could be important."

He hesitated, his gaze flicking between me and the phone like he was trying to decide which crisis to handle first. The phone buzzed again, more insistent somehow.

"Sorry." Teddy sighed, running a hand through his hair. "Just... give me a minute. If I don't answer, she'll just keep calling until I do."

I nodded, and he grabbed the phone before disappearing back into the bedroom. "Timing is impeccable as usual, Ma," he drawled, closing the door behind him with a soft click.

Alone again, I smoothed my fingers over the leather one final time before forcing myself to step away. The smart thing would be to leave it alone. To pretend I hadn't seen it, hadn't understood what it meant. To finish out the remainder of my stay with grace and dignity, and all the other things I was supposedly good at.

With that in mind, I knelt in front of the hearth and worked on coaxing the fire back to life, eager to have something to focus on besides the weird fluttery feeling in my chest that, for once, I couldn't blame on AFib.

Through the bedroom door, I could hear the low rumble of Teddy's voice—too muffled to make out what he was saying, but his tone was reassuring. Seemed whatever crisis Lucy had called about wasn't much of a crisis at all.

Once the fire was blazing again, I moved into the kitchen and poured myself a cup of coffee, doctoring it with cream and sugar before taking a careful sip.

The rational part of my brain—the part that had gotten me through the past two years—knew I should be happy for him. Proud, even. But the rest of me—the messy, irrational, still-in-love-with-him part—felt like I'd been gutted.

My phone chimed on the counter where I'd left it last night. I wiped my hands on a towel before reaching for it, unsurprised to see a string of messages from Addie and Sky.

The girls were not early risers. Never had been. During breaks from school, they kept what Teddy had always referred to as 'brunch hours'—lounging around in bed until ten or eleven o'clock in the morning.

But when faced with the possibility of reuniting their divorced parents, they had no trouble getting up before the sun and texting the next phase in the Parent Trap Playbook they'd been running all week.

Sky
morning mama!!
how are things going??

Addie
How'd those gingerbread cookies turn out?

Sky
did dad help?

My fingers hovered over the screen as I tried to figure out what to say. I typed out a response, deleted it, tried again.

Me
They came out great. Your dad's been a huge help.

Technically, it wasn't a lie. The cookies had turned out perfectly. And their father had helped me. Multiple times, in fact.

Addie
Did y'all watch The Muppet Christmas Carol like I suggested?

Sky
did dad cry during it???

My face heated, and I nearly dropped my phone at the memory of kneeling before Teddy while Scrooge faced a bleak future with the Ghost of Christmas Future on the TV behind me. The way he'd groaned my name and dragged his fingers through my hair. Hardly a story I'd share with my daughters, though I suspected it was exactly what they were after.

Me
He handled it like a champ.

My traitorous brain helpfully supplied the image of Teddy, head tipped back, eyes closed, shuddering with pleasure as I swallowed him down.

Sky

not buying it.

dad's a secret softie, and nothing will convince me otherwise

Addie

Looks like the storm's in Minnesota now. How are the roads?

Me

Roads haven't been plowed yet, and it's still pretty icy, so looks like we'll be here through Christmas. How are things with you two?

Addie

Things are good here.

Sky

we're at the bakery, helping piper make all the things!

she said to tell you hi

can you believe bakers have to be at work when it's still dark out? 💀

Addie

There's enough here to feed the entire MC.

Sky

Or dane for a couple of days.

ANYWAYYYY

how are things with dad going?

have y'all talked about what happens after Xmas?? 🙄

Addie

Maybe you could extend your stay.

If the roads are still bad, I mean.

Sky

yeah!! and you could do new years together

> I heard summit ridge does this huge thing with
> fireworks and food trucks

The messages kept coming, each one landing like a tiny knife between my ribs. They were so excited, so certain that their plan was working. That forcing their parents into close quarters had somehow fixed everything that had broken between us.

> **Me**
> We'll see.

My default was always to say yes. Even if the answer was ninety percent no, I'd perform some kind of emotional sleight of hand—placating them temporarily while hiding the bigger picture. I stared at the screen a moment longer before starting a new message—a longer one, one that would burst their bubble but felt necessary. They needed to understand the reality of the situation.

> I know you girls meant well with this whole plan,
> but I need you to understand—

I stopped. Deleted it. Started again.

> Your dad and I can be friendly, but that doesn't
> mean—

Deleted again. The blinking cursor mocked me with its incompleteness, its inability to capture the impossible situation we'd found ourselves in.

What was I trying to say? That I'd spent two years unsuccessfully trying to figure out who I was without Teddy, only to realize I'd never truly stopped loving him the second I saw his Bronco in the driveway? That I was standing in his kitchen wearing his shirt and drinking his coffee and already grieving the loss of something I'd never actually had? That I just learned that while I'd been treading water in Texas, their father had been building a kingdom in Colorado? That we'd finally, finally talked about Levi, but somehow it had only highlighted everything else we'd never addressed.

The truth was, I didn't know what to tell the girls. Didn't know how to explain that their parent trap had worked too well, in that it had forced us to finally face each other, finally be honest, finally remember what we'd been before grief and exhaustion and all our failures had turned us into strangers.

And none of it mattered.

Because in four days, I was going home.

16

kelsey

Me

Your dad's built a life here. He's the president of
the Colorado chapter. We can't just pretend that
doesn't change everything. We're not the same
people anymore, and I'm just not sure there's
room for—

"EVERYTHING OKAY?"

I jumped, my thumb hitting send before I could stop it, before I could delete the rambling thought that would definitely cause my daughters to panic. Teddy stood behind me, still shirtless because apparently he was trying to kill me, his expression guarded in that way that meant he'd been standing behind me for longer than I'd realized.

My phone vibrated against my palm. Definitely Addie, reading my half-finished text and drawing conclusions that would require damage control I didn't have energy for. But I didn't dare flip it over to check. Not with Teddy standing so close, watching me with a look I couldn't decipher. Maybe he was waiting for me to discuss the text or

161

acknowledge what I'd seen on the kutte. Or maybe he was just hungry and wondering why I hadn't started breakfast yet.

"Hey," he said cautiously. "Wanna tell me what's going on?"

"Nothing." The word came out clipped, a little too high-pitched to be believable. "Just the girls seeing how we are."

I forced a smile so stiff it felt like it might crack my face in half, really trying to drive home how absolutely unbothered I was.

His silence told me he wasn't buying it. I could feel his eyes on me —eyes that had always seen straight through my bullshit, even when I'd perfected the performance for everyone else in my life.

I cleared my throat, scrambling for safer ground. "What did your mom want? Everything okay?"

"Yeah, she was just calling to 'check in,'" he said with an eyeroll. "Pretty sure she'd recruited Piper to her cause. They were trying like hell to get Avery to say Aunt Kelsey."

"Piper's there? Like, right now?" I asked with a frown.

Teddy nodded. "Yeah, guess her blood pressure's been elevated, and Dane didn't want her on her feet or trying to keep up with an almost two-year-old this close to her due date, so they're hanging out over there."

"But the girls just texted that they were at the bakery with Piper," I argued, the lack of sleep making me doubt myself.

"When'd they text you that?" he asked, confusion flickering across his face.

"Just now. Like, two minutes ago." After scrolling up enough to hide my last text and all the ones sent in response, I held the phone up as if the timestamp would somehow clear things up.

Teddy's brow furrowed as he read the texts. "Huh. Ma said the girls were up at the bakery with Dane when I asked to talk to them. Sounds like he's got them managing the pick-up orders. Maybe they just wanted it to sound more exciting than it is."

Piper was with Lucy. The girls were helping at the bakery. Everything was fine. Completely normal, everyday stuff that had nothing to do with whatever Teddy and I were currently navigating.

"That's good. Make 'em earn their keep." I forced a chuckle before falling back into the role I knew how to play best. "I'll grab you some coffee."

Because that was what I did, I took care of things. Made everything look perfect on the outside, so I could convince myself I wasn't falling apart inside.

Maybe if I tried hard enough, I could pretend that the separate lives we'd built still had room for each other. That the miles between Texas and Colorado could shrink to nothing. That a President's patch didn't mean what I knew it meant.

When I tried to step around him, Teddy moved into my path, blocking any escape route.

"You wanna tell me what's really going on? You've been as jittery as a June bug since I walked out here."

My spine stiffened. "I don't know what you're talking about."

Teddy sighed. "Back to the same fucking song and dance as before."

I opened my mouth to protest, to offer some deflection about the weather or about needing to start breakfast, but he cut me off.

"How 'bout this? I'll start it off. You were holding my kutte."

There it was. The conversation I'd been trying to avoid since the moment I'd seen the patches.

"I was just hanging it up. It must have fallen."

Except it hadn't fallen. We both knew that.

"You saw the patches."

It wasn't a question. I met his eyes, seeing the resignation there, the same inevitability I'd been feeling since I'd read that word. President.

I could pretend I didn't know what he meant. Could play dumb, retreat, rinse and repeat. But I was so tired of running. So tired of pretending.

"Yeah," I said quietly. "I saw them."

The silence between us was so thick it was almost suffocating. Through the windows, the morning sun was turning the snow-covered landscape into something almost painfully bright. Beautiful and cold and so far removed from the messy reality of two people trying to figure out if there was anything left to salvage.

"Say something," Teddy urged, his jaw flexing and tightening beneath his beard. "Anything. Yell at me. Tell me I should have mentioned it sooner. Just—don't go quiet on me again."

But what was there to say? That I'd been stupid enough to think these few days meant something? That I'd let myself hope for a future that geography made impossible?

"I should've seen it the first night," I admitted, tracing a fingernail with the edge of my thumb. "When you showed up at the cabin expecting the girls. But I think I was too busy being mortified about the whole situation to really notice. And I guess I always assumed…"

I trailed off, unsure how to finish my sentence without revealing exactly how pathetic I'd been. How I'd been clinging to the fantasy that he was still adrift, still figuring things out, still possibly open to coming back to Texas. To me.

"Assumed what?" he asked quietly.

"I thought—" I stopped, swallowing hard against the lump forming in my throat. "When Addie mentioned you were in Colorado, I thought you were just helping out the chapter. I thought it was temporary."

"And now?"

"Now I know it's not temporary." The words came out barely above a whisper. "You're not just passing through. You're… you're president," I said finally, the words tasting like ash in my mouth. "That's not exactly a position you can just walk away from."

"No," he agreed, his tone carefully neutral. "It ain't."

"That's good, though," I heard myself saying, the words automatic, rehearsed. The same voice I'd used when the girls had gotten into their first-choice colleges, and I'd been dying at the thought of them leaving. "You always wanted to follow in Wolverine's footsteps. Run your own chapter."

"Don't do that." His hand came up like he was going to touch my face, then dropped. "Don't go all fucking polite on me now."

"What? I can't be supportive? I can't tell you that you deserve a fresh start somewhere that doesn't—" I mashed my lips together, trying to mask the sudden quiver.

"Somewhere that doesn't what?" His eyes searched mine, looking for something I wasn't sure I could give him.

"Somewhere that doesn't remind you of everything we lost," I whispered.

Teddy rubbed the back of his neck like he was about to say something terrible and probably necessary and wanted to avoid it. "That what you think this is? That I chose Colorado over you? That I left to get away from everything we had in Texas?"

"Isn't it?" I wrapped my arms around myself, suddenly cold despite the flannel and the fire crackling behind me.

"Hell no." He stepped closer, close enough that I had to tilt my head back to maintain eye contact. "Colorado chapter was damn near wiped out after that shit with the Sons of Death MC, remember?"

I nodded. How could I forget a war that had lasted almost two decades? A war that had put a target on not just the back of every SPMC biker, but family members as well. The Sons of Death had ruthlessly gunned down Ol' Ladies and children in their front yards, decimating entire clubs before moving onto the next like a fucking plague.

I'd homeschooled the kids for over a year, sick to my stomach every time the phone rang. Had every club in the country not banded together in the eleventh hour, Teddy and his entire family would have been wiped out.

"Bear and I made a few runs up here, helping them rebuild. Liked the mountains. Liked the club. Irish—the pres at the time— offered me a spot right after..." He trailed off, but I could fill in the blanks.

Right after everything went to hell.

"Thought—Christ, Kels, I thought maybe we could start over here. Away from the house, from the memories, from everything that hurt too much to look at. Came out here to get things ready. Was gonna surprise you with it, this whole new life where we could be different. Where we could heal."

"But I asked for a divorce before you could tell me."

"Yeah." His voice was rough, like the word was being dragged across gravel. "After that, went nomad for a while. Couldn't settle anywhere. Kept riding, hoping maybe if I went far enough, fast enough, I could outrun it all."

But you couldn't outrun grief. I had the gym membership to prove it.

"Irish didn't give up easily. Chapter needed stability, needed someone who understood both the old ways and the new direction the MC was heading when he decided to step down. So I came back. Took over. Built something here because..." He paused, his Adam's apple bobbing in a hard swallow. "Because there was nothing left for me in Texas."

Nothing left. The words cut deep, even though I knew he didn't mean them the way they sounded. He meant the house, the town, the life we'd built. Not me. At least, I hoped that was what he meant.

My phone buzzed again on the counter, and I snatched it up, desperate for the distraction.

Addie
Will you please tell us what's going on?
Did you have a fight?

Sky
room for WHAT??
are you two ok???

Addie
Why won't you answer???

Sky
mom!
mother!
madre!
talk to us!!!!!!!!!!!!!!!!!!

Addie
You're not giving up, are you?

For a moment, the edges of the screen blurred, the letters swimming.

Teddy cleared his throat, voice soft. "You wanna talk about it?"

No, I didn't want to talk about it. I wanted to go back to the person

I was before I got out of bed, someone who looked at snow and saw a metaphor for fresh starts and second chances.

But a fresh start required knowing what you wanted to start fresh toward. And I had no idea what that looked like with five hundred miles and a whole ass club between us.

I shook my head, just once. "No," I whispered, because what I wanted to say would sound insane out loud.

It feels like every part of you that's thriving in Colorado is another part that has no use for me.

I'm so proud of you, it hurts.

I want you to ask me to stay.

But that wasn't how any of this worked. It wasn't how we'd ever worked.

That was the price of admission—what I'd signed up for when I fell in love with him at fifteen. Being with Teddy Riggs meant always coming second to the club, always being kept at arm's length from the parts of his life that really mattered.

I'd just forgotten during the past few days.

I took a shaky breath and tried to steady my voice. "I'm happy for you," I said. "I am. You finally got your own club. Your own life. I hope you—" My voice cracked. "I hope you get everything you want."

He frowned, like I'd said something in another language. "Then why do you sound like you're about to cry?"

Maybe it was because I'd always thought that if he ever found happiness, it would be with me. Maybe it was because the thought of him moving on without me felt like losing Levi all over again.

A different kind of grief, but just as sharp. Just as permanent.

I couldn't answer. Couldn't find the words to explain that watching him build a beautiful, full life felt like proof of what I'd long suspected —that he was better off without me dragging him down.

17

teddy

"HEY," I said softly, reaching out to tuck a strand of hair behind her ear, needing to touch her even if it felt like she already had one foot out the door. "Look at me."

Kelsey kept her eyes down, shoulders curling forward like she was trying to shield herself from whatever came next.

I tilted her chin up with two fingers, gentle but insistent, until her tear-filled eyes met mine. Seeing the proof that I'd managed to hurt her yet again fucking gutted me.

"C'mon. Don't do that," I warned, my voice rough. "Don't you dare shut down on me again. And don't—" I had to swallow hard, fighting the urge to shake her until she understood. "Don't congratulate me like I'm a fucking acquaintance you ran into at the grocery store. Not after everything we've been through this week."

Her jaw tightened, and she jutted her chin up at me, that stubborn streak flaring to life. "You built something good here, Teddy. The club needs—"

"Stop. Just fucking stop," I bit out, and she shrank back at the heat in my voice, bringing her elbows in close to her body. I released her to drag both hands through my hair, trying to find the right words. "Yeah, I built something. And yeah, it's good. Got brothers I'd die for, a chapter that's thriving. And you know what? None of it means shit."

"You don't mean that—"

"Yes, I fucking do. Spent the past one year and ten months feeling like half my goddamn heart got ripped out of my chest," I snapped, forcing the words past the anvil lodged in my throat. "Walking around pretending I'm whole when really I'm just—I'm mailing it in. Every single day."

She tried to step back, a familiar move I'd been on the receiving end of one too many times. But I wasn't having it. Not this time. My hands found her hips, holding her firmly in place.

"No, you don't. Been carrying it too fucking long, and you're gonna let me get this out." I searched her face before continuing. "Took over because I needed something to care about after I lost everything else that mattered. Needed a reason to get up in the morning."

My grip tightened on her hips. "You think putting five hundred miles between us made a damn bit of difference? You think I just forgot about you because I'm in Colorado and you're in Texas? Baby, I wake up every goddamn morning, reaching for you before I remember you're not there. I cook every meal for two. At night, when I'm lying in bed, I remember how you used to press your cold ass feet against my legs to warm them up."

"Please," she whispered, her palms pushing weakly at my chest.

"Please what?" I released her hip to cup her cheek, needing her to understand. "Please stop telling you the truth? Please let you walk away again without a fight? Not fucking happening, baby. Not this time."

"But it hurts too much," she choked out. "Hearing this, knowing it doesn't change anything—"

"It changes everything." I dropped my forehead to hers. "You think I decorated that rental cabin for the girls, baby? Did it because it made me feel close to you. Made me remember what it was like when we were happy."

She hiccupped through another ragged breath, her hands coming up to grip my biceps, squeezing me tightly.

"Those ornaments we put on that tree over there—" I gestured toward the living room. "They're us, Kels. Every Girl Scout ornament Addie made, all the glittery ones Sky brought home from school, even that weird one Levi made with Santa riding a tornado—they remind me of all the Christmases we spent together. Of you corralling the kids while I tried to get the lights on the house. Of staying up till two in the morning, putting together bikes and dollhouses. They're a reminder that we were good once. That we had something worth fighting for."

"We were good," she agreed, tears flowing freely now. "But that doesn't mean—"

"These past few days," I interrupted, needing her to hear what I was about to say. "Being here with you, waking up next to you, watching movies and baking cookies and doing all the normal shit we used to do—it's the most alive I've felt since I signed those fucking papers."

I pulled back just enough to look her in the eye, making sure she could see every bit of truth written across my face.

"So I'm gonna ask you again, and I need you to be honest with me, darlin'." I gripped her face in my hands, drying her tears with my thumbs. "Do you feel it too? Or am I standing here bleeding all over your feet for nothing?"

Because everything I was, everything I'd built, everything I'd become—none of it meant a goddamn thing if she didn't feel it too.

Outside, the morning sun climbed higher into the sky, but all I could see was her—the woman I'd loved since I was seventeen, the mother of my children, the only person who'd ever made me want to be better than I was.

"Of course I do," she blurted, and for a second, hope flared so bright in my chest it hurt. Then she kept talking. "But it doesn't change anything, Teddy. I live in Texas. You live here. You have a whole chapter depending on you, and I'd—I'd ruin it."

Ruin it.

I recoiled at the statement, taking a step back to process. Like she was one of the natural disasters our son had always been so fascinated by, and not the only thing that had ever made any of it worthwhile.

Something must have shown on my face because she immediately tried to soften it.

"You know what I mean. You have responsibilities—"

"No," I said, moving back into her space before she could blink. My hands found the counter on either side of her hips, caging her against the island. "Fuck my responsibilities."

"But you've worked so hard for..." she trailed off, and I leaned in close enough that she had to tilt her head back to maintain eye contact.

"For what?" I demanded. "A title? So I could prove to my old man I'm as good a leader as he was? Told you, none of it means shit without you, Kels."

She opened her mouth, probably to argue, to tell me I was being irrational or making decisions based on emotion instead of logic. All the reasonable things that made perfect sense on paper but crumbled to dust when held up against the reality of how much I needed her.

I didn't give her the chance.

"Remember the first time I saw you?" I asked, my voice dropping lower. "You were fifteen, walking down the hallway at school with your friend—what was her name? Doesn't matter. Point is, I couldn't take my eyes off you. You were wearing a dress—yellow with white flowers—laughing at something, and I swear to God, Kels, it was like everything else just fell away.

"Took me three weeks to work up the balls to talk to you. Three weeks of finding excuses to walk past your locker, to sit where I could see you in the cafeteria. My boys gave me so much shit about it. Big bad biker's son, tongue-tied over some sophomore."

A small, watery smile tugged at her lips. "You asked me if I knew where the library was when you were standing right in front of it. Idiot."

"Yeah, well." I huffed out a laugh. "Cut me some slack. You were the most beautiful thing I'd ever seen... my brain stopped working."

I traced the line of her jaw with my thumb before continuing, "Remember when you asked me to the homecoming dance. Just marched right up to me in the parking lot, all five-foot-nothing of you. I fucking hated school dances. Hated the music, the crowded gym, the teachers watching everyone like hawks. But you wanted to go, so I showed up, in a suit and everything."

"Your dad's suit," she said, the smile widening. "It was too big in the shoulders."

"Wasn't exactly focused on fashion." I shifted closer, my hips pressing against hers. "I was too busy trying not to stare at you in that dress. Teal, with thin straps that kept sliding down your shoulders. Every time I'd fix one, you'd smile at me, and I damn near forgot my own name."

I could still see the mum I'd bought her—some black and gold monstrosity that had cost me a week's pay from my part-time job working in Phantom's garage.

"We left early," I continued, my voice taking on a wistful tone. "Planned on driving you home, but what'd you say?"

Pink bloomed across her cheeks, but she held my gaze. "I said I didn't want to wait anymore."

"Said you didn't want to wait anymore," I repeated. "And I tried to be responsible, tried to tell you we should slow down, that you deserved better than the inside of my Bronco next to an old oil well for your first time."

"I didn't want better. I just wanted my first time to be with you," she said, her voice barely above a whisper.

My lips curved into a smile at the memory. "Only you didn't know it was my first time, too. I was so fucking terrified of doing it wrong, of hurting you. But you just kept touching me, kept pulling me closer, and when it was over—" I had to stop, clear my throat. "When it was over, you curled into my side and told me you loved me. First person who ever said that to me who wasn't blood."

Kelsey blinked rapidly, trying to dispel the tears building in her eyes.

"Knew right then," I said fiercely. "Seventeen years old, and I knew you were it for me. The only woman I'd ever want. Had two dreams back then, Kels. To marry you and run a chapter like my old man. That's it. That's all I wanted."

"And you got both," she whispered, her chest heaving with a sob.

"Yeah, I did. For a while, anyway." I pulled back to look at her. "You know how I earned my three-piece?"

Her brows scrunched together. "Your dad sponsored you?"

"Not what I'm asking, baby." I rubbed at the back of my neck. "I'm asking if you know what I did to earn it. What I had to do to prove I was worthy of wearing the colors."

Understanding dawned on her face, closely followed by a flash of fear. "In by blood, out by blood," she said, softly reciting the club mantra.

"See, there was a guy," I said, my voice going flat the way it always seemed to when I talked about the darker parts of club life. "Forty-something. Had been following you around for weeks. Showed up outside your house, outside school, at the fucking mall where you worked. Remember?"

She nodded slowly. "He said he was a security guard or something, but he always gave me the creeps."

"I remember," I ground out through clenched teeth. "My old man had some guys from the club do a little digging; found out the guy had a record. Assault, kidnapping, rape—victims refused to cooperate with police, so the charges were all eventually dropped. Asshole had a whole system worked out. He'd watch his victims, learn their routines, wait for the perfect moment to grab them."

Kelsey's face had gone pale, but she didn't pull away.

"Pops and I did a little recon and found drawings in his trailer," I continued, each word tasting like metal on my tongue. "Detailed plans for what he wanted to do to you. Where he'd take you. How long he'd keep you before—" I stopped myself, my throat closing around shit too sick to ever say aloud. Not to her.

"I volunteered for the job. Told the club I wanted to handle it myself—my first kill. Should have been nervous about taking a life, but I thought about what he wanted to do to you. About how I'd feel if I let someone else handle it and he somehow got away, came back for you—" I shook my head.

"Didn't feel a damn thing except relief when I sent that motherfucker to the Reaper. Need you to understand. Everything I've ever done, every choice I've ever made, it all comes back to you."

I pulled her up against my chest, her jaw slack and eyes wide with shock. "I'd do it again, Kels. In a heartbeat. I'd do it a thousand times over if it meant keeping you safe. The club, the chapter, all of it—it only matters because it gave me a way to protect you, to provide for you and our kids. And I know none of it turned out how we planned. Know there's been more pain than I ever wanted you to feel. But if someone came to me right now, told me I could go back and choose a different path—one where I never met you, never fell in love with you, never had to go through any of this—I'd tell them to go fuck themselves."

She swayed against me, a choking sob slipping past her lips.

"Because even with all the heartbreak, even with all the ways we broke each other, I'd still choose you," I managed, nostrils flaring with each measured exhale as I tried and failed to rein in my emotions. "Every single time. I'd go through it all again—the pain, the loss, the two years without you—if it meant having you in my life at all. You're it for me, Kelsey Dawn Riggs. Always have been."

Her response came out so quiet I almost missed it, even with mere inches between us. "You're it for me, too," she whispered. "And no matter what came after. No matter how much it hurt. I'd still choose you."

Something in my chest cracked wide open, flooding me with a relief so intense it made my knees weak. I hadn't realized how much I'd needed to hear those words until they were hanging in the air between us, real and solid and impossible to take back.

"Then let me make this easy," I said, already making the decision before my brain could catch up with my mouth. "I'll step down as president. Irish can take the chapter back, or one of the others."

"What?" she gasped, jerking her head up in surprise.

I'll move back," I continued, the words coming faster now that I'd started. "To Lubbock. To the house. To wherever you need me to be. You wanna stay in Texas? Fine. I'll figure out the rest. But you come first, Kels. You've always come first, even when I was too stupid to show it."

She shook her head, looking dazed. "I'd never ask you to do that, Teddy. The club is your life—"

"You're my life, goddammit," I growled, my heart hammering against my ribs like a jackhammer. "The club's in my blood. It's a part of me, but it ain't everything. You think this is new, baby? Been willing to give up everything for you since the day we met. So, if your future's in Texas, then that's where I'll be. Simple as that."

"I don't want to go back to the way things were," Kelsey confessed, chewing the corner of her lip.

My stomach dropped. Here it was—the gentle letdown, the 'it's not you, it's me' speech I'd been dreading.

I started to pull away, needing a minute to shove my feelings down deep before I did something truly pathetic like beg. "Okay. Okay, I understand—"

She grabbed at my arm. "No, wait. I mean, I-I don't want to go back to our old lives. I hate that house!"

I frowned, trying to make sense of what she was saying.

"I've been pretending I'm fine there, but I'm not. It's like living in a haunted house. I only stayed because I didn't know where else to go." She angrily swiped at the tears on her cheeks, hiccupping as she tried to get her breathing under control. "Because leaving felt like I was abandoning our memories, even the painful ones. But if I'm being honest, I—" She stopped, biting her lip again like she was afraid to finish the thought.

"You what?" I prompted gently. I needed her to say it. Needed to hear what she really wanted, not what she thought I wanted to hear.

"I wouldn't mind getting away from the desert heat," Kelsey said, her voice so quiet I almost missed it. "Living somewhere with four seasons. Somewhere I could—" Her eyes widened with alarm, like she hadn't meant to say the last bit out loud.

"Not that I'm—I mean, I know you're not asking me to move in or anything," she backtracked quickly, her cheeks flushing. "I'm not trying to invite myself or assume you want me here permanently. I just meant that theoretically, I wouldn't be opposed to the idea of possibly considering—"

"Move in with me," I interrupted, unable to listen to her stumble over herself for another second.

Her mouth opened, closed, then opened again. "What?"

"Move in with me," I repeated with a low chuckle. "Here. This cabin or the other one. We'll bring whatever you want from Texas and leave the rest."

"Teddy, we can't just—"

"Why not?" I challenged. "You just said you hate that house. Said you want out of Texas. And I just told you I'd give up the presidency and move back if that's what you needed. So why can't I ask you to come here instead?"

"Because it's—" She fumbled for words, her breath coming faster. "It's too fast. Too soon. We've only been around each other for, like, five days—"

I ran my tongue over my teeth, fighting the urge to laugh again. "Been together for thirty years, baby. Five days, five decades—ain't gonna change how I feel about you. But if you need time to think about it, I get that. Just don't say no because you think I'm not sure. I've never been more sure of anything in my life."

"But what would I even do here?" she asked, voice small.

"Whatever you want. Take a pottery class like you always talked about. Teach yoga. Run your business. Hell, I'm sure there are hundreds of old people around here just waiting for you to adopt them," I teased.

"I'm a senior transition specialist, Teddy," she corrected sternly, but there was a little twitch at the corner of her mouth that meant she was trying not to smile.

"Point is," I continued, "you could do anything. Or nothing. Just be here. With me."

She searched my face, and I could see the war playing out behind her eyes. The practical Kelsey, who made lists and planned everything, versus the woman who'd been brave enough to ask a seventeen-year-old biker's son to a high school dance because she wanted him.

"This is crazy," she whispered.

The corner of my mouth lifted in a grin. "Riggs' men ain't exactly known for being rational when it comes to their women, baby. Ask Dane and my old man about that. Besides, we did the sane, reasonable thing for decades, and look where it got us. Maybe it's time to try crazy."

"Oh my God. My therapist would have a field day with this," she muttered.

"Killing me here, Kels," I said, my voice dropping low. "Yes or no."

She stared up at me, those green eyes searching mine like she was looking for the catch, the fine print, the reason this couldn't possibly be real.

But then something shifted in her expression—a letting go, a surrender to whatever this was between us.

"Yes."

"Yeah?"

"Yes, Teddy," she breathed, and the smile that broke across her face damn near brought me to my knees. "I'll move in with you."

18

teddy

I KISSED her before she could second-guess her decision or talk herself out of it. Before the doubts could creep back in. Before reality had a chance to remind us of all the reasons this was reckless and impulsive and probably destined to blow up in our faces.

She melted against me, her hands climbing up my chest to tangle in my hair. The small bite of pain only made me pull her closer, needing to eliminate every inch of space between us.

"Need you to know something," I panted against her lips. "I'm gonna fuck this up sometimes. Gonna say the wrong thing or handle shit badly. But I'm not walking away again, Kels. Not for the club, not for anything. You're stuck with me now."

"I'm counting on it," she whispered before sucking my bottom lip between her teeth.

My hands dipped lower, kneading the curve of her ass. "Fuck," I growled. "Never been able to take it slow with you. Don't see any reason to practice restraint now."

Kelsey gasped as I hauled her up into my arms, her legs instinctively wrapping around my waist. "But your back—"

"Is fine," I argued as I carried her down the hall. "Everything's fucking fine now that you're staying."

I kicked the bedroom door open, not bothering to be gentle about it. We'd been gentle long enough. Careful. Tiptoeing around each other for years when what we'd really needed was this—raw, honest, desperate.

I lay her down in the center of the bed, taking a moment to just look at her—hair fanned out across my pillow, lips swollen from my mouth, chest heaving beneath the flannel she'd claimed as her own.

Christ. Fifty-one years old, and she still took my breath away like she had when we were kids. Still had the power to turn me into a bumbling seventeen-year-old kid again with more hunger than sense.

"Teddy, come here," she whimpered softly, reaching for me.

"Patience, baby." I caught her wrists and pinned them gently above her head. "Gonna take my time with you."

She nodded, and I released her to peel my shirt off her shoulders. The pajamas underneath came off next, revealing inch after inch of soft skin.

When I tossed the fabric aside, exposing her to the morning light streaming through the windows, she tried to cover herself.

"Don't," I warned, letting a little roughness seep into my tone. "You're fucking beautiful, Kels. Don't hide from me."

"But the windows..."

I cocked a brow, and she trailed off like she'd lost her train of thought. A fraction of a second later, her hands fell away from her body, moving up to rest against the pillow behind her head.

"I like Bossy Teddy," she murmured, sucking in a breath as my hand traced the curve of her collarbone, the swell of her breasts, the faint stretch marks on her belly from carrying our children.

"Like it when you let me take care of you, darlin'," I rasped, watching the goosebumps breaking out across her skin before lowering my mouth to follow the path my fingers had just taken.

She arched up off the mattress with a whimper when I reached her nipples, already hard and begging for attention. I smiled against her skin before drawing one into my mouth, sucking gently before grazing it with my teeth.

Every one of her sounds went straight to my dick. I was so hard it hurt, straining against my sweatpants, but I ignored it.

This was about Kelsey.

About showing her how much she meant to me, what she'd always meant to me.

I worked my way down her body, taking my time despite the urgent need thrumming through my veins. Teased her nipples until they were pink and puffy, kissed the soft curve of her stomach, the jut of her hipbone.

By the time I settled between her legs, my shoulders spreading her wide, Kelsey was squirming restlessly. Still, she kept her hands locked above her head. Because even though it had been ages since we'd been together like this, my girl still remembered the rules.

Kelsey was a control freak in every area of her life except one—the bedroom. In here, she was mine to command. I owned her pleasure, her worries, her stress. Her only job was to let go and let me give her what she needed.

Her pussy was already slick and swollen, and I hadn't even laid a finger on her yet. Not that she'd ever needed help in that department.

"Spread for me, Kels," I ordered, voice low and shaky, but she didn't hesitate. Just let her knees fall apart until I could see every perfect detail.

"That's my good girl," I murmured, my breath ghosting over her clit.

A moan escaped her throat at the praise, her pussy clenching around nothing. I'd forgotten how responsive she was to those words —how easily they could make her come apart.

"Touch me. I need—"

"I know what you need, baby." I pressed open-mouthed kisses to the inside of her knee and the soft skin of her inner thighs, everywhere but where she wanted me most.

She growled in frustration, and I couldn't help but grin against her skin. The playful push-and-pull had always defined us in the bedroom. Before grief had stolen it. Before wanting each other came with so much damn responsibility.

With one hand splayed flat on her belly and the other digging into the meat of her thigh to keep her pinned open, I drew out my torture, teasing her with light, flicking passes of my tongue, never quite close enough to get the job done.

"Please, Teddy," she begged, a broken sound clawing its way out of her throat. "Please."

"There's the magic word," I whispered up to her with a grin before dragging my tongue up her slit.

She eagerly ground her pussy against my face as I sucked her clit, gentle at first, then harder, alternating with soft laps and tight little circles. I slipped a finger inside, twisting just so until she let out a sound that belonged in a goddamn porno.

"That's it, Kels. Let go for me," I commanded, my voice gone hoarse from need. I added a second finger, stroking in and out slowly, using every trick I'd learned since my Bronco days. I kept my focus on her face as I did it. Watched the way her eyebrows pinched together, mouth slack and wet, eyes glazed with want.

She bit her lip hard, stifling another moan. "I—fuck, I'm close," she warned, like I'd ever let her come before I was ready.

I eased up for a second, just to drive her insane, and looked up the length of her body. "Not yet. Stay with me."

She fisted the pillow with a mewling whimper, clinging to control like she could will herself not to fall apart. I went back to work, relentless, tongue and fingers together until her whole body bowed off the bed.

"Come for me," I growled, and that was all it took. She broke, cried my name as her walls pulsed around my fingers, wetness flooding my hand. I kept going until she was spent and boneless on the sheets, chest heaving, limbs shaking.

I quickly shucked my sweatpants, letting them fall to the floor before hooking my fingers under her knees and dragging her to the edge of the mattress.

Kelsey looked up at me with a drowsy smile, green eyes widening slightly when they landed on my cock—already hard enough to pound nails.

"Need a minute?"

Shaking her head, she reached for me before catching herself. "Can I touch you—please?" she asked, her voice gone small and sweet and so unlike the woman who commanded every room she walked into.

That fucking did me in. "Yeah, sugar. You can touch me," I said, groaning as her palm wrapped around my shaft.

She stroked me from root to tip, her fingers reverently tracing the veins and ridges as she guided me forward. My cock brushed against the inside of her thigh, leaving a streak of precum across her skin. Without missing a beat, she swiped it up with her index finger before bringing it to her lips.

The sight of my girl tasting me—so fucking unashamed, so in control of her own want—damn near pushed me over the edge.

"Missed this side of you, Kels," I growled, bracing myself before nudging the head of my cock inside her. She always ran tight after she came and now was no exception.

Kelsey sucked in a sharp breath, her nails sinking into my shoulders. "God, Teddy, you're so—I forgot how big—" Her bottom lip quivered and her eyes locked on mine, tears racing down her temples toward her ears.

"Kels—baby, am I—am I hurting you?" I asked, already pulling back.

She shook her head and wrapped her legs tight around my back, heels digging into my ass to prevent my escape. Once she was satisfied I wasn't going anywhere, she brought her hand up to my cheek, her fingertips moving over an old scar beneath my left eye.

"There you are—" She paused, gulping back a broken sob before whispering, "I thought I'd lost you."

It was the same thing I'd said to her after the wreck, but instead of pain, there was wonder in her voice. Like she was seeing me for the first time. Not the physical me, but the version I'd spent the final years of our marriage pretending no longer existed—the man who'd loved her without reservation, without walls, without the burden of grief and guilt pressing down on my shoulders every waking moment. A man who made promises to her and kept them.

Something cracked wide open in my chest. A fissure that had been sealed shut for years, protecting the most vulnerable parts of me from the world. From her. But I didn't need it anymore. Not with Kelsey looking at me the way she did when we were kids.

"Right here, Kels," I agreed roughly, pressing my forehead to hers as I sank deeper. "Not going anywhere."

Her walls stretched around me, hot and slick and tight—so goddamn tight—I had to grit my teeth to keep it together. It was almost too much. Like, after years of wandering from place to place, I'd finally come home.

Kelsey slid her fingers down my jaw and neck, pressing them to the name scarred over my heart before exhaling another soft sob.

"I know, baby." I brushed the tears from the sides of her face with my thumbs, my hips beginning to move in slow, deliberate strokes. "I know."

My hair fell around us, creating a curtain that blocked out the rest of the world. Just Kelsey and me, the way it had always been—the way it was always supposed to be.

"Look at me," I ordered softly, and her eyes fluttered open, green and glassy and so fucking full of love it made my chest ache. "Stay with me, Kels. Right here."

She gave me a shaky nod and held on tight as I picked up the pace. The wet sound of our bodies meeting filled the room, mixing with her soft moans and my ragged breathing.

"Never letting you go again," I vowed, grabbing her hip and rocking deeper. "Never, you hear me?"

"I've always been yours… only yours." She groaned as I shifted angles, her walls beginning to contract around me. "Oh God, right there. Don't stop—"

"Not stopping," I promised, reaching between us to find her clit with my thumb. "Not until you come for me."

I shifted my weight, freeing one hand to slip between us. My thumb found her clit, already swollen and sensitive from before, and I circled it in time with my thrusts.

The reaction was instantaneous—a full-body shudder that rippled through her from head to toe. I clenched my jaw as her pussy gripped me like a goddamn vise, my pulse thundering in my ears.

I couldn't tear my gaze away from her face—the way her mouth fell open, eyes rolling back in her head, cheeks flushed pink with pleasure.

Christ, she was gorgeous when she came.

But I wasn't done with her yet.

Before she could come down, I pulled out and flipped her onto her stomach, hauling her hips up until she was on her knees. She made a surprised sound that turned into a guttural moan when I slammed back into her from behind.

Kelsey clawed wildly at the sheets, adding an extra eight or nine syllables to the word 'Yes' as she thrust her hips back to meet me.

"This what you need, baby?" I growled, roughly squeezing her ass cheeks before spreading them wide to savor the sight of my cock splitting her open.

"Yes, yes, yes," she chanted mindlessly, arching her back and forcing me even deeper.

"Wait, baby, baby—" I ground out, trying to hold her still—trying to stop the pressure rapidly building at the base of my spine.

But it was too late.

Kelsey tipped her head back, and the sounds she made—Christ, they were obscene.

My balls drew up tight, her raw, needy moans destroying what was left of my control. I emptied myself inside her with a roar, my hips jerking from the force of my release.

For a brief second, my entire body locked up, the world going white-hot behind my eyelids. I didn't care if my heart gave out from the strain—if this was how I died, so be it. There was no better way to go than while buried deep inside my Ol' Lady, her name tattooed across my chest and seared into every fucking strand of my DNA.

"Jesus Christ, Teddy," Kelsey collapsed onto her forearms with a shaky laugh. "Should have known better. You've never been able to last in this position."

I couldn't even argue. It was a known weakness of mine—had been since the first time she'd graced me with that particular view back when we were still finessing the logistics of what went where.

"And what the hell was that noise—" She gasped for air and tried to compose herself before doubling over again with a loud snort. "You sounded like… like an animal caught in a trap!"

"Shut up," I panted, nipping at her shoulder with a breathless chuckle. "Not my fault you've got an ass that won't quit."

She let out a sharp squeak before dissolving into another fit of giggles, and I couldn't help but grin despite the embarrassment heating my face.

This was us—the real us. Not the broken, grieving couple who'd forgotten how to touch each other. Not the strangers who'd signed divorce papers in some sterile office. Just Teddy and Kelsey, laughing in bed after mind-blowing sex.

Or, in my case, *because* of the mind-blowing sex.

"You're already regretting asking me to move in, aren't you?" she teased, still trying to catch her breath.

"Oh yeah, huge mistake," I deadpanned, rolling onto my side and pulling her back against my chest. "Clearly, I've lost my mind."

"Mm, probably," she purred, wiggling against my spent dick. "Good thing I like you crazy."

I hissed through my teeth at the contact, still incredibly sensitive. My whole body felt wrung out, muscles trembling from exertion and something deeper—relief, maybe. Or just the bone-deep satisfaction of finally, finally having her here where she belonged.

Before long, the old injury in my shoulder flared to life, forcing me to shift onto my back before tugging her close again. Kelsey came willingly, relaxing against me with a contented sigh.

For a long moment, we just lay there, her cheek pressed to my heart and fingers tracing lazy patterns through the hair below my navel.

"Hey, Teddy?"

"Hmm?" I asked, cracking an eyelid open.

"Think you dislocated my hip," she muttered with a wince. "Apparently, my joints don't appreciate being folded like a pretzel anymore."

I chuckled. "Welcome to sex in your fifties, baby. Try being on your knees on the hardwood floors. Pretty sure I left some cartilage in the kitchen yesterday."

"If we're being honest," she said, shifting against me with a small groan. "I think the sex injuries started in our thirties."

I pressed a kiss to the top of her head. "Might need to invest in some of those foam pads people use for gardening."

Kelsey's nose scrunched up. "Yeah, because nothing screams romance like orthopedic accessories."

"Hey, at our age, romance is finding someone willing to rub Icy Hot on your back after sex."

"Oh God," she gasped, burying her face in my chest with a snort. "Teddy, we're old. How did this happen?"

"Speak for yourself, baby. I'm in my prime."

She lifted her head, one eyebrow arched in challenge. "Your prime? That's a pretty bold statement for a man who came in under two minutes."

"Oof. That's a low blow, woman." I tried to look offended but couldn't quite manage it. Not when she was looking at me like that—soft and teasing and so goddamn beautiful it made my chest hurt.

"Just stating facts. Maybe we need to work on your stamina," she said, letting out a strangled yelp when I grabbed her around the waist and hauled her on top of me.

"You think you're real cute, don't you?" I asked, ignoring the protest from the muscles in my lower back.

She nodded solemnly, lips twitching wildly as she pressed a light kiss beneath my chin. "Mm hmm. Just one of the many reasons why you love me."

"That so?" I murmured, my hands sliding down to cup her ass. "And what are the other reasons?"

"Well..." She pretended to think about it, tapping her chin with one finger. "There's my sparkling personality, obviously."

"Obviously," I echoed dryly.

"Then there's my excellent taste in movies, my cooking skills, my ability to make the ugliest Christmas tree in the world look fabulous, and...oh! My amazing ass, of course."

I gave it a playful swat. "Should have put that at the top of the list, baby. I could recite sonnets about this ass."

"I think those are called dirty limericks—not sonnets—and please don't." Her expression softened, fading into something more vulnerable. "Promise me something?"

"Anything."

"Promise me we won't lose this again. The laughing. The fun. Even when it gets hard—because it will—promise we'll still find ways to be stupid together."

The admission hit me square in the chest. We had a track record of fucking things up when shit got heavy. Of retreating to our separate corners instead of fighting for each other.

"Hey." I cupped her face in my hands. "I promise to make embarrassing animal noises during sex for the rest of our lives if it makes you laugh like that."

She swatted my chest, but she was smiling—a real one that crinkled the corners of her eyes. The same one I'd been chasing for thirty-six years. "That's not what I—"

"Know exactly what you meant." I tucked her head under my chin, breathing in the scent of her hair. "But here's the thing—we're not the same people we were before. And this time, I promise you, no more running. No more hiding from each other and pretending we're fine when we're not. I'm all in, darlin'—"

"Even when you think I'm being ridiculous?" she whispered

I exhaled a soft laugh. "Especially then. Baby, I'd take your ridiculousness every day of the week over living without you again. Yeah, we're gonna fuck up and piss each other off. But I promise you, Kels—I promise I'll never stop trying. I'll fight for it. For you. For us. Fight every goddamn day if I have to. That's gotta count for something, right?"

Kelsey was quiet for a long moment, and I could practically hear her brain working, cataloging all the things that could go wrong.

I wanted to say something. Tell her how much I loved her, how there'd never been a single moment where I didn't want her. Not a damn one. Not even at the end, when we were sleeping in separate rooms and speaking to each other through our lawyers.

Instead, I waited, combing her hair with my fingers, content to hold her while she worked it out.

She pulled back, her gaze finding mine. Her cheeks were blotchy and her eyes still red from crying, but there was a peace in her expression I hadn't seen in years… or maybe ever. Her smile wobbled at the edges before she pressed her lips to mine—slow and sweet and tasting faintly of salt from her tears.

When she pulled back, she nodded to herself before whispering, "Okay. I'm all in."

19

kelsey

THE CERAMIC ANGEL had been crooked since 2019, when I'd launched her at Teddy's head during an argument about—honestly, I couldn't even remember what we'd been fighting about anymore.

Something that had felt earth-shattering at the time but was probably related to his spending either too much time at the club or the body shop he'd taken over after Phantom passed.

The angel had missed his skull by a solid three inches, thank God, and embedded itself in the drywall behind him with enough force to snap off her halo and crack her porcelain wings. Now she hung on the tree at a perpetual fifteen-degree angle, halo M.I.A., looking like she'd been hitting the communion wine a little too hard.

Like some kind of battle-scarred survivor of our marriage.

Which, I supposed, made two of us.

I reached out to straighten her, my fingers hovering over the gold-painted dress that had chipped away to reveal the white ceramic underneath. Then I pulled back. Let her stay crooked. She'd earned it.

Late afternoon sunlight streamed through the windows, turning the snow-covered landscape beyond into something that belonged on a postcard. The kind of light that made everything look softer and cozier.

If someone had told me I'd be standing in my ex-husband's living room, wearing nothing but thick wool socks and one of his old Silent Phoenix T-shirts while *White Christmas* played on the TV, I would have told them pigs had a better chance at flying.

But here I was, fiddling with a Christmas tree that was—according to Teddy—'Perfectly fine, Kels. Jesus Christ, stop fucking with it,' while Bing Crosby and Danny Kaye performed "Sisters" in drag on the screen behind me.

A year ago, I would have been horrified at the lack of proper Christmas attire. That Kelsey had a closet full of holiday sweaters and blouses for every day of December. She'd insisted on picture-perfect family photos where everyone smiled just right, even when Levi was having a bad day, and Teddy was exhausted from work, and the girls just wanted to be literally anywhere but home.

That Kelsey had performed Christmas like it was an Olympic sport, and she was going for gold.

This Kelsey hadn't worn real pants in three days and was seriously considering making it a New Year's resolution.

From the kitchen came the unmistakable sound of Teddy moving around—cupboard doors closing with unnecessary force, the coffee maker beeping, his low grunt when he bent to get something from a lower shelf.

Living with him had always been a little like cohabitating with a bear. Not in a dangerous way, but in the sense that he took up space unapologetically, moved through the world with a kind of lumbering confidence that occasionally resulted in knocked-over coffee mugs and cabinet doors left hanging open.

I'd spent years trying to domesticate that wildness, to smooth his rough edges into something that fit better with my vision of what our life should look like. Funny how it had never occurred to me that maybe I was the one who needed smoothing.

The kitchen went quiet for a beat, then Teddy emerged carrying a plate of gingerbread cookies in one hand and two mugs of coffee in the other. The jeans he'd thrown on when we finally emerged from the bedroom rode dangerously low on his hips, revealing a V of muscle that had no business existing on a fifty-three-year-old man. His hair was pulled back in a messy low knot, and he hadn't bothered with a shirt because why would he cover up all that.

If my ovaries hadn't been decommissioned, they absolutely would have given a standing ovation.

I'd spent two years at the gym trying to reclaim some version of my body that I'd lost to pregnancy and three decades of stress-eating and yo-yo dieting, and here he was looking like a Calvin Klein ad for the AARP crowd.

It felt like a tragedy that we'd spent the remainder of the morning and most of the afternoon sleeping like the dead and not having a sex marathon.

"You're staring," he said, a knowing grin spreading across his features as he set the coffee and cookies on the table beside the couch.

I planted a hand on my hip and scoffed, "You're half-naked in my living room, Theodore. Where else should I look?"

His tongue clicked against his teeth. "*Your* living room, huh? That was fast."

"You're the one who invited me to move in approximately—" I bit the inside of my cheek, squinting to read the clock on the oven. "—what, eight hours ago? I'm just practicing."

"Practice makes perfect, baby." He set the mugs on the coffee table and dropped onto the couch with an emphatic groan.

"Need your Life Alert, Grandpa?" I asked cheekily.

He shot me a look that could have melted steel. "Keep it up, Kels. See where that smart mouth gets you."

"Don't threaten me with a good time." I turned back to the tree, fighting the smile threatening to break free.

I felt lighter than I had in years. Like someone had taken the forty-pound weighted vest I'd been wearing since Levi died and finally let me shrug it off. My shoulders didn't ache. My jaw wasn't clenched. The constant background hum of anxiety that had been my companion for so long had quieted to something manageable.

"Careful with that one," Teddy rumbled as my fingers moved back to the angel. "Lost her halo and almost took my eye out last time you handled her. Starting to think maybe she's not as angelic as advertised."

When I glanced over my shoulder, he was watching me in the way only someone with three decades of context could—equal parts fondness and exasperation.

"Maybe she was just tired of being perfect," I'd said it jokingly, but the truth was, I was tired of being perfect. Exhausted by it, actually.

"Maybe she was," he agreed softly.

I ran my index finger over the crack in the wings, ostensibly to give the angel one final adjustment, but really because I needed a second to collect myself.

I'd spent most of my life scared of being anything less than perfect. Because perfect meant safe. Perfect meant no one could criticize or find me lacking.

A damaged ornament never would have made it onto old Kelsey's tree. I would have spent hours ensuring everything was perfect and matched that year's color theme.

The old me would have been up since dawn, meal-prepping something elaborate and Instagram-worthy. She would have been counting the carbs in those gingerbread cookies, calculating how many miles she'd need to run to burn them off. She would have been frantically checking in with the girls and mentally cataloging everything that still needed to be done before the holiday could be properly enjoyed.

Matching pajamas.

Raspberry-cream cheese Danishes made with crescent rolls and shaped into candy canes.

Christmas newsletters where I made our life sound like a Hallmark movie when the reality was anything but.

Perfect meant doing everything and still never feeling like it was enough.

The leather on the couch creaked as Teddy got up and crossed the living room. He came up behind me, banding both arms around my shoulders and pulling me back against his hard body.

"Know what I see when I look at that angel?" he asked, his voice low and rough.

"Evidence of my terrible aim?"

He huffed out a laugh. "See a woman who loved me enough to throw shit at my head when I was being an asshole. See someone who fought for us, even when fighting meant breaking things."

I craned my neck to find his hazel eyes. Warm and open and so full of love it took my breath away.

"You're being serious," I said, not quite a question.

Teddy pointed to a mercury glass ornament, our reflections staring back at us in the metallic, mirrored finish. "I see you, Kels—no makeup on, hair a mess, wearing my shirt—this is the girl I fell in love with. Not some perfect version you thought you needed to be. Just you."

He pressed a smacking kiss against my cheek and swatted my backside before returning to the couch. "Now, quit fucking with the goddamn tree and come eat your dinner."

A laugh bubbled up. "Gingerbread cookies and coffee constitute dinner now?"

"Hey, we're empty nesters living in sin. We can eat whatever the hell we want." With the plate balanced on his thigh, he picked up one of the cookies—one of the Christmas light ones that bore an unfortunate resemblance to a butt plug—and took a bite.

The lamp on the side table caught the silver threads running through his beard, turning them platinum in the golden light.

Teddy was beautiful. Devastating, really, in the way that dangerous things often were. All that barely contained power wrapped in tattooed muscle and the kind of confidence that came from knowing exactly who you were and refusing to apologize for it.

And he was mine. Again. Still. Always.

I padded over, hyperaware of how his gaze tracked the movement of my bare legs. A week ago, I would have been self-conscious about the way my thighs touched, about the cellulite and spider veins that had appeared after pregnancy, about all the ways my fifty-one-year-old body wasn't what it used to be.

Now, though? I felt like a model walking a runway with the way he was looking at me.

"Had to ice these damn things all by myself yesterday," he said, patting the empty space beside him on the couch. "Least you can do is enjoy 'em with me."

Heat crept up my throat as I recalled the reason he'd had to do it all by himself. How I'd ended up sprawled across his kitchen island, limbs still quaking and unable to move after my fourth or maybe fifth orgasm, while he whipped up the royal icing with a smug expression.

I stopped in front of the couch, and before he could say anything, I plucked the plate from his lap before sliding onto it myself.

One arm automatically went around my shoulders while the other went to my bare legs, fingers splaying wide across my skin. "What're you doing, baby?" he asked, his voice dropping an octave.

I selected a gingerbread cookie shaped like a candy cane and bit off the tip while keeping my expression perfectly innocent. "Eating dinner. Like you said."

"Uh-huh." His fingers pressed into the soft flesh of my inner thighs, not quite tickling but close enough to make me squirm. "And you had to sit on my lap to do that?"

"You know, it just doesn't feel like Christmas until I've sat on a bearded man's lap to tell him what I want." I licked a stray bit of icing from my thumb, watching his pupils dilate. "Isn't that the tradition?"

His grip tightened, pulling me closer until I could feel exactly how much he appreciated my choice of seating. "That so?"

"Mm hmm." I set the plate on the coffee table and turned to straddle him properly, my thighs bracketing his hips. "So, Santa... have I been a good girl this year?"

He raised an eyebrow, a slow grin spreading across his face—all teeth and trouble. The kind of smile that had gotten me into more compromising positions than I could count over the past three decades.

"That's a loaded question, baby." His hands spanned my waist before sliding down over the curve of my hips.

With deliberate slowness, I reached for the hem of my—his—T-shirt and lifted it just enough to reveal that I wasn't wearing anything underneath.

"What do you think, Santa?" I ground against him, feeling his erection strain against his jeans. The rough denim created the perfect amount of friction against my bare skin. "Is this nice... or naughty?" I asked, unable to quite suppress the small gasp that escaped.

His fingers dug into my hips hard enough to bruise, holding me still even as I tried to rock against him. "Jesus, Kels."

"That wasn't an answer." I traced the waistband of his jeans with one finger, popping the button free. "Come on, big guy. I need to know if I'm naughty or nice."

"Think we both know the answer to that," he forced out through clenched teeth. "But I'm real interested in hearing what's on your Christmas list... see if you can't change old Santa's mind."

I pulled the shirt over my head and tossed it aside, leaving me in nothing but the socks. The cool air hit my skin, pebbling my nipples, but Teddy's gaze was hot enough to keep me warm.

I felt powerful. Alive. Like I could do and say anything without fear of him judging or thinking less of me over it. This was what I'd needed—the freedom to be shameless. To want without apology.

"Well," I began, leaning in close enough that my breath ghosted across his lips. "First, I want you to come down my chimney."

He barked out a sharp, startled laugh before catching himself. "I see," he managed through twitching lips. "Go on."

"Then, I want you to stuff my stocking." I punctuated the words by grinding against his erection and licking a line up his throat to his beard. "Stuff it so full there's no room left for anything else. Until it's overflowing."

The growl that rumbled through his chest went straight between my legs. "Keep talking like that, and Santa's gonna give you everything on your list," he rasped, his hands already moving to cup my breasts. "Even if you have been on the naughty list since 1989."

I could hear Bing and the gang singing "Snow" as they took the train to Vermont. But I wasn't dreaming of snow. I was dreaming of Teddy—of his hands on my body, his mouth on my skin, his voice in my ear telling me all the filthy things he wanted to do to me.

"Fucking soaking my jeans," he murmured, showing me the dark patch I'd left. "Getting yourself all nice and wet for me."

I'd never had a problem in that area, although I'd expected it to go the other way during menopause. Given the hell my faulty reproductive organs had put me through for decades, I'd earned the reprieve.

"What else is on that list?" he prompted, rolling one nipple between his thumb and forefinger before brushing my hair back to take the other in his mouth.

Pleasure flooded my body, making my thoughts hazy and hard to grasp, but I fought through the fog to moan, "Want you to jingle my bells… all the way. Really make 'em ring."

"Christ, it just keeps getting worse," Teddy muttered with a low chuckle, sliding his fingers between my legs. "And no panties? Santa's gonna have to keep you on the naughty list for sure."

"Good." I gasped when his thumb found my clit, my forehead dropping to his shoulder. He worked me with steady, deliberate pressure, knowing exactly how to touch me—the speed, the angle. An art form he'd perfected over thirty years.

"That everything on your list?"

"No. Want you to—oh God—make it a not so silent night," I gasped out, my thighs starting to shake. "And hang your—your ornament on my—"

I couldn't finish. His fingers slipped inside me, one at first, then two, stretching me in a way that made my eyes roll back.

I was already close, embarrassingly so. But I didn't care. Didn't care that I was grinding against him like a teenager in heat, didn't care that I was spouting increasingly ridiculous Christmas euphemisms, didn't care about anything except the way his fingers felt as they worked me over.

"That's it, baby," he praised, his voice like gravel. "Look at you, riding my hand, begging for it. You gonna show Santa what a naughty girl you've been?"

I nodded frantically, beyond words now, just sensation and heat and the coiling pressure building low in my belly.

His free hand came up to cup the back of my neck, pulling me down for a kiss that was all tongue and teeth. "Let me hear you."

I bit my lip, trying to stay quiet because old habits died hard and some part of me still worried about being too loud, too needy, too much. But then his hand slid up to tangle in my hair, tugging gently until I met his eyes.

"Said, let me hear you, Kels," he repeated, his expression making it clear it wasn't a request.

"Yes," I whimpered, chanting and moaning the word on repeat.

"Then take it," he commanded, adding a third finger and curling them just right while his thumb maintained pressure on my clit.

My movements became erratic. "Teddy, I'm—oh fuck, I'm—"

"Yeah? You gonna come all over my hand like a good girl? Show me, baby."

That did it. I came with a breathless sob, my body clenching and pulsing around his fingers.

Teddy's mouth moved over my temple, my cheek, my jaw, drawing out the orgasm until I was shaking and oversensitive, and clinging to his shoulders to keep myself upright.

He withdrew his fingers slowly, bringing them to his mouth and sucking them clean. "There's one item off your list. What else you want, baby?"

I pulled back enough to meet his eyes—the man who'd been my husband, my ex-husband, and was now somehow both and neither, something new we were still figuring out—and felt something shift low in my belly.

A warmth that had nothing to do with the orgasm I'd just had, and everything to do with the way he was looking at me.

"You," I whispered shakily, reaching between us to free him from his jeans. "Just you."

His dick sprang free, thick and hard and already leaking at the tip. "You've got me, Kels."

I wrapped my hand around him, stroking once, twice. "Wanna take a ride on your Polar Express."

That startled another laugh out of him as well as a raised brow. "Polar Express? Really?"

"Would you prefer candy cane?" I rose up on my knees and positioned myself over him, teasing us both by dragging the head of his cock through my wetness. "Because that implies a curve that might be concerning. Might need to see a doct—"

"Just shut up and ride me," he growled.

20

kelsey

I EXHALED ROUGHLY AS he bucked his hips, pushing the blunt head of his dick past my entrance. Beads of sweat formed on his furrowed brow as he eased me down, inch by torturous inch.

Even after this morning, it took some effort to accommodate him. Some things never changed, no matter how many decades we'd been doing this.

His mouth fell open slightly, and a low groan escaped—the kind of sound that made me clench around him involuntarily.

Teddy leaned forward to suck a puckered nipple between his teeth, the sudden change in position forcing him even deeper.

I hissed out a curse when he bottomed out, clutching his head to my breast. For a long moment, neither of us moved while my body adjusted to the stretch.

"Wait, Kels," he groaned against my skin, the vein in his neck visibly pulsing. "Trying not to come."

I'd never been one for porn, but if I had, I doubted any video could compete with the sight of a man like Teddy fighting not to come undone beneath me.

There was something addicting about having that much control over a man so wild and famously ungovernable—something that made me want to push him to his breaking point. Just to see if I could.

I tightened around him again, enjoying the way his breath hitched, and his eyes rolled back in his skull.

"Fuck," he muttered, sinking his teeth into the sensitive flesh of my throat.

Goosebumps spread across my skin, and I braced my hands against his chest with a shiver before rocking against him. I fought a smile as the slow, sensual grind of my hips drew another sharp inhale from him.

"You good, baby?" I asked innocently, continuing to torment him. "Comfortable?"

"Could be on a bed of nails, and I doubt I'd notice. You feel so goddamn good," he growled, before tugging my mouth down to meet his in a rough kiss.

"Think we should probably avoid any more hard surfaces for the time being," I said, sucking in a ragged breath when his thumbs brushed over my nipples, making me arch into his touch. "My back is still achy from the kitchen island."

"But the look on your face when you came that first time—fuck, I'll be thinking about that for years."

"Mm… what else will you be thinking about?" I asked, lifting my hips until just the head of his cock remained inside before taking him deep again.

"This," he said, his eyes tracking the bounce of my breasts. "You taking what you want. Not holding back. Looking at me—just like that —like I'm yours."

"You are mine, Riggs," I said fiercely, surprising myself with the possessiveness in my voice.

He pushed up into me with a barely restrained growl. "What about you, Kels? What's going through that pretty head?"

"Mm, I'm trying to remember if there's still some of the potato casserole left in the fridge," I panted as we moved together in a rhythm that felt more like dancing than sex. "Or did we finish it all last night?"

Teddy's hips faltered, and he barked out an incredulous laugh. "Seriously? You're thinking about food right now?"

"What? I'm—" I trailed off when he hit a particularly good angle. "I'm hungry. A growing girl needs to eat."

"Growing girl?" he questioned through gritted teeth. "Baby, you're the same—fuck, do that again—the same height you were in high school."

"No, horizontally, I mean." I gestured to my hips and thighs, which had expanded over the years.

"Good. Gives me more to hold onto," Teddy grunted, giving both a rough squeeze before reaching forward to snag a gingerbread cookie from the plate on the coffee table. He broke a piece off and held it to my lips. "This oughta tide you over for a bit. Open."

I took a bite, chewing while watching me with an expression that suggested he couldn't quite believe this was his life now.

"Good?" he asked, pushing his index finger past my lips as he offered me another bite.

"So good," I said, swirling my tongue around the digit, tasting myself as much as the spices. "Can't believe we never brought food into the bedroom when we were married."

"This some long-unfulfilled fantasy for you, Kels—riding my dick while I feed you gingerbread?"

I chuckled. "Absolutely not. Old Kelsey would have had a coronary. Crumbs in the bed... cookies for dinner? The horror."

"Old Kelsey was wound tighter than an eight-day clock," Teddy dryly stated as he brushed crumbs off my lip.

"She was exhausting," I agreed. "And frankly, kind of a pain in the ass."

"Nah, you were doing your best."

"Was I though?" The question came out lighter than I intended. "Or was I just... performing? Like everything had to be Pinterest-perfect or the world would end?"

"You were trying to hold us together," he said quietly. "Only way you knew how."

"Fat lot of good it did," I mumbled around another mouthful of cookie.

"Might've taken the scenic route through Hell, baby, but we're still here," Teddy said, huffing out a strained breath when I reached back toward the coffee table.

"Scenic route's one way to put it," I deadpanned as I selected a handful of cookies, feeling him soften in me. Not all the way—just enough that I registered the loss of fullness.

It had been a frequent occurrence in the years before the divorce, when stress and grief and exhaustion had taken their toll on both of us. Before, it would have sent me spiraling into insecurity, wondering if I wasn't attractive enough, wasn't sexy enough, wasn't enough period.

Now I just engaged my inner muscles to hold him inside me before settling more comfortably in his lap.

"Think this is your handiwork," I said, holding up a gingerbread snowflake with a missing point before bringing it to his mouth.

The rigid expression on Teddy's face softened into something like gratitude or maybe even relief. Like he'd been bracing for me to pull away and make it A Thing.

"Those were all you, baby," Teddy drawled, taking a bite.

"Me?" I exclaimed, placing my hand against my chest in feigned horror. "I would never make such a mistake, Theodore."

"Oh, really?" His eyebrows raised mockingly as he took another bite of the cookie, crumbs tumbling down his bare chest. "Seem to recall someone saying she was too high-brow for anything but the snowflakes and trees."

I rolled my eyes, unable to suppress a grin. "Fine, maybe I delegated the more… phallic-shaped cookies to you initially. But need I remind you that you were responsible for more than a few of those little artistic creations while I—"

"Recovered from seven orgasms?" Teddy helpfully supplied, his eyes twinkling with mischief.

The playful back-and-forth was absurd and perfect and exactly what I hadn't known I needed—the easy intimacy, the comfort with our bodies and their limitations, the ability to be completely ourselves without pretense or performance.

We continued like that, between kisses and bites of gingerbread, until his cock slid free of my body.

Feeling the tension return to his muscles, I reached between us to take him in my hand. "Wanna know what I'm thinking about now?" I whispered, my lips brushing the shell of his ear.

A shudder rippled through his body. "What's that, baby?"

"I'm thinking about all those nights after the divorce when I couldn't sleep. When I'd lie in bed, hand between my legs, trying to get myself off."

His grip on my hips tightened, fingers digging into flesh hard enough to leave marks I'd admire later. "Yeah?"

"Mm hmm," I hummed, feeling him twitch against my palm. "Tried everything—bought toys, read books, bought sexy lingerie—but I couldn't do it. Nothing worked unless I pictured you."

"Kels—" His voice came out strangled as I stroked him from root to tip.

"Had this recurring fantasy. You'd show up at the house, coming through the door like you still owned the place. You'd find me spread out on the bed with my hand between my legs." I paused to adjust my grip, smearing the wetness over the head of his cock before continuing,

"Without a word, you'd drop into that old armchair in the corner before telling me exactly how you wanted me to touch myself." I pressed open-mouthed kisses along his jaw, down his throat.

"Would imagine your fingers digging into the arms of that chair while you told me slower... faster... deeper. Your voice getting rougher the closer I got."

"Fuck, Kels," he groaned, his head falling back against the couch.

I sucked hard on the spot where his neck met his shoulder, marking him the way I used to when we were teenagers. "Sometimes I imagined being with someone else, and you finding out. You'd get jealous. Show up and claim me, letting him see who I really belonged to, as you made me beg for it. Used to get myself off thinking about that one at least twice a week."

His dick pulsed in my hand, fully hard again. I traced the prominent vein running along his shaft with my thumb, watching the way his jaw clenched.

"Now I don't have to imagine anymore," I whispered as I lifted my hips and took him to the hilt with a groaned curse.

"Lean back," he ordered, voice suddenly rougher. "Hands behind you. Wanna see you."

I obeyed, planting my palms on his thighs and arching my back until he was hitting my G-spot with every roll of my hips.

The temperature in the room skyrocketed. What had started as playful, lazy lovemaking shifted into something else entirely. Something almost desperate.

"Fuck, that's pretty," Teddy growled, his eyes locked on where our bodies joined. "Look at you, Kels. Taking every inch of my dick like a good girl."

Heat crawled up my chest and neck. There it was. Not the praise, necessarily, but the rough edge creeping into his voice. Teddy had always enjoyed being in control when it came to sex, but his bossy side paired with his biker side did something shameful to me.

One hand slid up my ribcage before wrapping around my breast, squeezing while his other remained anchored on my hip, controlling my speed.

"You have any idea what these tits do to me?" He rolled my nipple between his thumb and index finger before dipping his head to drag his tongue over it.

"Didn't matter if I was at school, at the shop, in church, on a club run—didn't matter where I was, I was constantly thinking about these perfect tits. How they feel in my hands, in my mouth. How they bounce when you ride me like this." He sucked one nipple into his mouth, hard enough to make me cry out.

Teddy immediately pulled back, catching himself. "Shit, Kels. I'm sorry—"

"Don't." I caught his face between my palms, forcing him to look at me. "Don't apologize for that."

His brows pinched together, hazel eyes searching mine like he was trying to solve a puzzle. "But I—"

"I liked it," I whispered, feeling heat flood my cheeks at the admission. "The biker side—the dirty talk. I've always liked it."

Teddy went completely still beneath me, his expression shifting from apologetic to utterly dumbfounded. "You what?"

"I said I liked it," I repeated, more firmly this time. "When you get like that—all rough and filthy—it makes me feel..." I trailed off, searching for the right words. "I don't know—desired. Wanted. Like you can't help yourself."

"Kels, I've spent over thirty years trying not to talk to you like—" He stopped, jaw working. "Didn't want you to think I was disrespecting you. Treating you like some club whore instead of my wife."

"But I didn't feel disrespected," I argued, rocking against him to emphasize my point. "I felt powerful. Knowing I could make you lose control like that? That I was the reason you couldn't keep it together?" I bit my lip. "God, Teddy, that's incredibly hot."

"You're telling me you wanted me to talk dirty to you, but you never..." He trailed off, looking almost more confused than before. "You always seemed to pull away or go quiet on me—"

"Because I was embarrassed!" I swallowed past the sudden lump in my throat. "We had kids, Teddy. I was Perfect Kelsey, mother of three. Mothers aren't supposed to get wet when their husbands come home from a club run, all sweat and testosterone. Or want their husband to call them filthy names and manhandle them during sex. I thought there was something wrong with me, like it was wrong to want the things I did sexually."

I wanted to take it back as soon as I said it, to laugh the entire thing off as a joke, and retreat to safer ground. After years of feeling invisible, of moving through life like a ghost in my own story, being suddenly seen was like staring into the sun.

"There's nothing—no, eyes on me, baby—don't pull away." Teddy sat up straighter, one arm banding behind my back to keep me in place. "Not a goddamn thing wrong with you. You're allowed to want. You're allowed to be more than one thing at once. Jesus, I held back after Addie came along, thinking you wanted something else. Thinking you needed me to be someone I wasn't."

My tongue darted out to wet my lips. "I just—I just wanted you, Teddy", I whispered. "However you came."

We stared at each other, processing the weight of what we'd both just admitted. All those years of just existing in the same space and going through the motions, trying to be what we thought the other needed instead of just being ourselves.

Something snapped behind his eyes—some restraint he'd been holding onto for decades, finally giving way. He pistoned his hips up into me. Hard.

"So what you're saying," he rasped, catching my hair in his fist and tugging my head back until my throat was exposed to his teeth, "is that we wasted a lot of fucking time being polite to each other in bed."

"We've got time to make up for it now, figure out what we like." My breaths were coming in short gasps as I rode him faster, chasing the heat building in my lower belly. "All the things we were too scared or too tired or too stuck in our patterns to—oh God, right there. Don't stop—" I moaned, loud and shameless.

From somewhere outside came the low rumble of machinery—probably a snowplow clearing one of the access roads, finally—but I couldn't focus on it, couldn't concentrate on anything except Teddy's words and his hands and his mouth.

"That's it, baby. Ride it. Take what you need." His voice went gravelly. "You're so goddamn wet for me, Kels. Can you hear it?"

I dragged my fingernails down his thick thighs, babbling something that may or may not have been a response.

My glutes and thighs were burning from the exertion, muscles trembling with the effort of keeping pace, but I was too far gone to care.

"Teddy," I gasped, my movements becoming erratic as the pressure built. "I'm—I'm close—"

"Keep doing that, and I'm not gonna last."

"Don't you dare stop," I begged, one hand dropping between my legs while Teddy's hips snapped up to meet mine.

"I've got you. Take what you need." He brushed my hand aside to strum my clit with his thumb while pressing his fingers into my lower belly, right over his dick.

"Come on, baby," he gritted out, visibly hanging on by a thread. "Need you to get there. Come for me."

I frantically moved my hips forward, like I was scooting up to a table before coming apart. Black spots danced in front of my eyes, and

I was vaguely aware of Teddy's hips stuttering and me loudly sobbing his name as my body pulsed around him in waves.

Which is likely why neither of us noticed the rumbling outside growing louder until it was too late.

The front door burst open with a bang that would have sent us flying apart if we hadn't been so tangled together.

"Surprise! Guess who's—oh my Jesus!"

21

kelsey

FOR ONE HORRIFYING MOMENT, the world hung suspended. I sat frozen on Teddy's lap like some kind of pornographic statue, still feeling him twitching inside me.

And standing in the doorway—mere feet from us—their expressions morphing from excitement to identical masks of horror were our adult daughters.

"Oh God, oh God, oh God!" Addie's hands flew up to cover her face.

Sky made a sound like a wounded animal and spun toward the wall. "My eyes! My sweet, innocent eyes!"

The spell broke. I scrambled off Teddy's lap with all the grace of a baby giraffe learning to walk, nearly kneeing him in a very unfortunate location in the process. He caught me before I could face-plant, shielding me with his body while simultaneously trying to get his jeans up.

"What the hell are y'all doing here?" Teddy shouted, his face a shade of red I'd never seen before.

"Not looking!" Addie shrieked, already backing toward the door.

"We are absolutely not looking at whatever that was. We're leaving, we're so sorry—so, so sorry!"

"That's our dad and our mom!" Sky wailed, stumbling out after her sister. "Why are there no clothes? Where are everybody's clothes?"

The door slammed shut behind them hard enough to rattle the windows.

For approximately three seconds, the cabin was utterly silent except for our ragged breathing and the now almost cartoonish sounds of "White Christmas" still playing on the TV.

"Merry Christmas, girls," I muttered under my breath, scrambling to find the T-shirt I'd tossed off my body without a care in the world. Back when I was carefree, and my biggest concern was whether we ate all the casserole, not whether my children—who were supposed to be in Texas—would be popping in unexpectedly. "Maybe call ahead next time."

I turned back to find Teddy tugging his zipper up and trying very hard not to laugh.

"Don't even think about it," I warned, fighting the persistent tug at the corner of my lips.

"Right. Sorry. This is serious," he managed in a strained voice, the corners of his eyes crinkling.

"Theodore Riggs—"

He doubled over, his entire body convulsing with laughter so hard no sound came out at first. Just this silent, shaking thing that made him look like he was choking.

"Stop," I gasped, locating the T-shirt and tugging it over my head even as my own laughter bubbled up. "This isn't funny. Our daughters just—they saw—"

"Your face," he wheezed, tears streaming down his cheeks. "When the door opened—you looked like you'd been caught robbing a bank."

"I was naked!" I shrieked, smacking his arm. "On your lap! Mid-orgasm! What face was I supposed to make?"

That set him off again, and this time I couldn't help it—I dissolved into hysterical laughter right along with him.

"Sky called them her sweet, innocent eyes," I choked out between giggles. "Oh my God."

"Same girl who, at sixteen, thought we wouldn't find out she was watching Game of Thrones because she logged in through her laptop and not the TV. Ain't nothing innocent about that one."

We collapsed against each other, laughing so hard we could barely breathe. Every time we'd start to calm down, one of us would repeat something the girls had said, and we'd be off again.

Eventually, we managed to pull ourselves together enough to get fully dressed, my pants-free lifestyle ending almost as abruptly as it had begun.

Once we were both presentable—or as presentable as two people could be after being walked in on mid-orgasm by their adult children—we opened the front door to find our daughters huddled together like refugees in a war zone.

"It's safe," Teddy announced dryly. "We're decent."

"Are you sure?" Sky asked through her hands. "Do you have clothes on? All the clothes? Like, not just pants, but shirts, too? Because I just saw your—"

I cut her off. "Skylar Jade Riggs, do not finish that sentence and get in here before you both freeze. And next time, maybe knock first?"

"Next time, maybe lock the door," she retorted with a raised brow. "Or I dunno, keep your clothes on outside the bedroom?"

"Wasn't exactly expecting company," Teddy gritted out before raking a hand over his face.

Addie stomped the snow off her boots before brushing past us with a shudder. "There are some things a child should never have to witness, and her parents 'celebrating Christmas' is definitely one of them."

"Was actually more of a sitting on Santa's lap type thing," Teddy began before I elbowed him hard in the ribs.

"Not helping," I hissed, then turned to our daughters. "What are you two even doing here?"

"We were worried!" Sky burst out, still refusing to make direct eye contact, so it appeared she was yelling at the coffee table. "Mom, you sent that text—"

"What text?" Teddy asked, and my stomach dropped.

Addie pulled out her phone, scrolling before reading aloud:

"Ahem, 'Your dad's built a life here. He's the president of the Colorado chapter. We can't just pretend that doesn't change everything. We're not the same people anymore, and I'm just not sure there's room for—'"

She looked up. "And then nothing. You just stopped mid-sentence."

I watched as Teddy's expression went from amused to carefully neutral in the span of a heartbeat. The kind of neutral that meant he was working very hard to keep whatever he was feeling off his face.

"I was texting them back this morning, when you were on the phone with your mom," I explained with a wince. That half-formed text, sent in a moment of panic before I understood what the president patch really meant. Before Teddy had made it abundantly clear that nothing—not the club, not the distance, not our own spectacular capacity for self-destruction—mattered more than us.

"It wasn't—I didn't even mean to send it. I was spiraling, but we… we worked it out."

"Clearly," Sky said, gesturing vaguely at the couch with a traumatized expression, "Thoroughly. On the furniture. Where people sit."

"My couch. I can use it how I want," Teddy said, earning a disgusted groan from the girls.

"Gross, Dad," Addie muttered before narrowing her eyes at both of us. "Seriously, we tried calling and texting y'all like a hundred times, and when no one answered, we thought you two must have gotten into some massive fight."

"So naturally," Teddy said, crossing his arms, "you decided to drive five hundred miles from Lubbock. Makes sense."

"About that," she started, then stopped, clearly trying to figure out how to explain. She and Sky exchanged a look that put me on high alert immediately. I recognized that guilty expression—it was the same one they'd worn after spilling a bottle of red nail polish on the living room carpet.

Something wasn't adding up. I'd sent that text hours ago, right before Teddy distracted me with his declaration of love and invitation to move in. They would have had to have left Lubbock the second they received it.

"Wait. Did all the special orders get delivered?" I asked, my internal mom-manager mode kicking in despite everything.

"Kels, there are folks still stranded out at DIA," Teddy said, staring at me like that was supposed to mean something. "Even if the girls miraculously found a flight on Christmas Eve, I-70's shut down at the Eisenhower Tunnel."

I raised my shoulder in a half-shrug, trying and failing to make the connection in my sex-addled brain. "Not sure what the airport has to do with customers in Lubbock getting their orders."

"Because the girls weren't in Lubbock," he said gently, his eyes tracking between our daughters and me. "It's a nine-hour drive in good weather. 50, along with damn near everything else south of Summit County, is shut down; they'd have made it as far as Pueblo before having to turn around."

Sky suddenly became very interested in the tree, and Addie's face went through several expressions—panic, calculation, resignation—before she straightened her shoulders. "Okay, fine. We haven't been in Texas."

"No shit, Sherlock," Teddy replied dryly. "Care to tell us where you actually were?"

"We've been here," Addie admitted with a heavy sigh. "In Summit Ridge."

The words hung in the air for a moment while I tried to make sense of them. "You've been... what?"

"We got in the day before you did," Sky added, wincing. "We've been staying at the ski resort."

"The ski resort," I repeated slowly, feeling like I was still several steps behind in a conversation I should have been helping Teddy lead.

Addie nodded. "We just—we had this plan, and we thought if we could get you and Dad in the same place for a few days, you could reconnect. Really reconnect—"

"Mission fucking accomplished," Teddy muttered, sidestepping me before I could elbow him in the ribs again. "You commandeer a snowplow as part of your little con, too, Addie Grace?"

"No, a Sno-Cat!" Sky answered, her face lighting up with the glee of someone who—according to her—'had the tea.'

"You what?" I exclaimed, already mentally working out if Teddy's connections would be enough to keep our daughters out of jail for auto theft or whatever the hell a Sno-Cat would be classified as.

"Cal gave us a ride on his Sno-Cat," Sky said, then shot a pointed look at her sister. "From the resort. He was very concerned about Addie's safety."

Addie made a show of adjusting her glasses to hide the red creeping into her cheeks. "He was being polite. He works there; it's his job to—"

"Yeah, I didn't see him offering to let any other guests take a ride on his Sno-Cat." Sky waggled her eyebrows suggestively, just in case no one in the room understood the euphemism. "And on Christmas Eve afternoon, when I'm sure he had about a million other things to do."

"Shut up," Addie hissed. "He's just a stoner ski bum."

"A cute stoner ski bum, though," Sky continued, undeterred. "He's, like, this blond mountain god type with really good bone structure—like Chris Hemsworth playing Thor if he gave up Asgaard for snowboarding. And I think he's in love with our little Addie Waddie."

"He is absolutely not. I barely interacted with the guy."

"Barely interacted? Yesterday, you talked for three hours straight about books. He has opinions about Dostoevsky, Addison! Dostoevsky!"

"I will murder you in your sleep." My eldest daughter—always so composed, always so in control—was completely unraveling over a ski bum with opinions about Russian literature.

"Cal drove you," Teddy cut in. "As in, Callan Wright?"

"Well, most people call him Cali," Sky answered, oblivious to the dangerous edge in her father's voice.

"What? You know him?" Addie asked, suddenly looking nervous.

"Know him?" Teddy laughed, but it was apparent he wasn't particularly amused. "Kid owns half the resort. Also happens to be a member of my chapter."

Sky cackled. "Oh my God, you've been treating him like some burnout, and he's actually—"

"In the club," Addie finished, the color draining from her face. "He conveniently failed to mention that."

Teddy shrugged. "Probably didn't want to scare you off. He also runs the kids' programs on weekends and volunteers for ski patrol. But yeah, he's got money. Smart as hell, too. Engineering degree from Colorado School of Mines. Good guy, but he's a little too old for you."

I knew that tight smile all too well, and Cali—good guy or not—was in danger.

"He's like, what, mid-thirties?" Sky guessed. "Addie's twenty-five. It's not that big of a gap."

"Not dating him, not interested in dating him, so his age is irrelevant," Addie bit out, shooting her sister a look that could have curdled milk. "Can we please talk about literally anything else?"

Sky bobbed her head in agreement. "Yes. As much as I love watching Addie short-circuit, I need to know—" She pointed between Teddy and me. "Was that some weird, post-divorce booty call, slash, situationship—"

"For the love of God, don't say booty call or situationship when talking about our parents ever again, please," Addie pleaded softly, pressing her fingers to her eyelids beneath her glasses.

"I second that. Let's make a pact to never speak of what you saw," I suggested firmly. "Ever."

"So sorry to have offended everyone's virgin ears," Sky replied, looking anything but apologetic. "As I was saying, when we walked in on—"

"Skylar Jade," Teddy warned, raising his hand as if he were about to swat her, which would have been a more effective threat had he not been laughing as he said it.

"—the thing I've already forgotten," she finished smoothly, shielding herself behind Addie. "What even happened? I sure don't remember. Must've blocked it out. Anywho, are y'all back together or should we steal the keys to the Bronco and give you a little more time to think it over?"

Teddy and I exchanged a glance before he snaked an arm around my waist and pulled me snug against his side, briefly scrambling my brain again. Especially when I remembered where that hand had been less than an hour before.

Focus, Kelsey.

"Are we back together?" I repeated the question, pressing my tongue against the inside of my cheek when Teddy's fingers squeezed my hip in warning.

When I remained silent, he exhaled the long, drawn-out sigh of a man who just remembered how bratty his Ol' Lady could get. "Baby, you really gonna make me say it again?"

"Absolutely I am." I patted his chest with a solemn nod, enjoying the way his jaw ticked with barely restrained exasperation, knowing I'd pay for it later. "For the girls."

"Asked your mama to move in with me this morning," he said, his voice carrying the gruff edge that still did things to my insides even after thirty-plus years.

"And I said yes," I confirmed, arching up onto my toes to kiss his jaw. "We're getting back together."

The words felt surreal even as they left my mouth. Two weeks ago, I'd been standing in my empty Texas kitchen, stirring my coffee and wondering if the hollow existence I'd carved out was all I had left to look forward to.

Sky lurched forward with an ear-piercing shriek, wrapping her arms around both of us in a tackle-hug that nearly sent all three of us toppling over. "This is the best Christmas present ever!"

Addie was only marginally more composed, her eyes suspiciously bright as she joined the group hug. "I knew it would work," she said, her voice muffled against my shoulder.

"And we didn't even have to pretend to be each other and swap places—"

"Because we're not twins, Skylar."

"Y'all are so grounded for this," I informed them, but I was smiling, unable to help myself. "Like, forever."

"Nuh-uh," Sky replied cheerfully. "It's Christmas Eve. Nobody gets grounded on Christmas Eve. Besides, we were just responsible for getting you in the same room. It's not like we created back-to-back blizzards. That was just a lucky coincidence... or, I guess, unlucky, since you crashed the rental."

The light from the tree suddenly caught one of the ornaments just right, making it glint. My throat tightened when I saw it was one of Levi's snow globes. "Or maybe you two had a little help," I said, not bothering to hide the emotion in my voice. "Your brother always wanted to be a meteorologist."

Teddy followed my gaze to the tree before huffing out a soft laugh. "Wouldn't be a damn bit surprised if he pulled a few strings with the man upstairs, making sure we got the full parent trap experience."

"That totally sounds like something Levi would do," Addie said quietly, her voice thick.

Sky swiped at her eyes. "And you know he would have been so smug about it, too."

I laughed despite the tears threatening to spill. "He never could resist taking credit for a good scheme."

We were talking about him. Not tiptoeing around his memory or changing the subject when his name came up—just talking about our boy, making him a part of this moment.

Because he was.

The irony, of course, was that this had always been Levi's superpower—to make his presence known in every room, even after he was gone.

Because he had been so much more than the illness that took him from us. Levi loved conducting science experiments, from the glitter volcano he made in the bathroom sink to the elaborate Rube Goldberg machine he constructed on the staircase. It felt right that even now, he'd managed to orchestrate the most mortifying homecoming possible.

Sky nudged me with her hip. "I can't believe you're moving to Colorado. You are moving, right? This isn't like a retaliation prank, is it?" she asked, her eyes wide and earnest.

I looked at Teddy and caught the faintest twitch of nerves in his jaw. President of the club, leader of men, unbreakable force—and still so goddamn hungry for reassurance that I was staying.

"I am," I said, surprised by how easy it was. No jolt of anxiety. No second thoughts. Just a feeling of rightness in every fiber of my being.

I looked at my daughters—one wild and messy, the other wound tight as piano wire—and realized that, for the first time since Levi died, we were all right. Resilient, if not entirely functional. The world hadn't ended when our lives blew up; it just took a blizzard and some daughterly sabotage for us to discover that we could build something new from the shrapnel.

"I'm really glad you're happy," Addie said, coloring a little. "Y'all deserve it."

I thought of all the years I'd spent trying to be a perfect wife, mother, Christmas automaton. The years I'd spent thinking that happiness was something you finished earning, like a degree. The years after Levi, when it seemed impossible that any of us could ever be happy again, let alone together.

"Me too, kiddo," I whispered, blinking back sudden tears. "Me too."

epilogue
Christmas Morning

kelsey

THE KITCHEN CLOCK read 12:26 AM, officially making it Christmas morning, though it certainly didn't resemble any that I'd experienced most of my fifty-one years of life.

The counters were littered with dirty dinner dishes and a healthy dusting of cocoa powder and sugar. Before, I would have been elbow deep in suds or wiping down every sticky surface. I would have tuned out the conversations happening around me, occasionally asking someone to repeat a question when it was directed at me, but mostly stuck checking items off my mental to-do list.

Now, I sat with my feet tucked up under me, wearing one of Teddy's Metallica shirts from the nineties and a pair of his sweatpants I'd had to roll three times at the waist, feeling more content than I had in years.

No frantic last-minute wrapping

No matching Christmas pajamas.

No staging the living room for a Martha Stewart-worthy photoshoot as if a bunch of strangers on the internet really cared what my tree looked like.

Just three women gathered around a kitchen table, drinking spiked hot chocolate that Sky had topped with an ungodly amount of whipped cream and marshmallows.

"So then Cali asks Addie if she wants to see the sunrise from the summit," Sky said, pushing up the sleeves of an oversized bright orange hoodie with the phrase "*Send Noods*" above a cartoon cat eating a bowl of ramen that she'd paired with camo joggers. "And she's all, 'Oh, I don't do mornings.'"

"Um, because I don't?" Addie retorted, making a show of rubbing her nose with her middle finger. Unlike her sister, she'd chosen a thermal-pajama set in all black, her signature color.

"I'm just saying, if a hot mountain man with opinions about Russian literature wanted to show me a sunrise—"

"Please!" Addie interjected with a snort. "He's a trust fund kid who owns a ski resort and cosplays as a biker to seem edgy."

I wrapped both hands around my mug, letting the warmth seep into my palms while listening to the girls playfully bicker back and forth.

"He looked so disappointed, Mom," Sky added, pushing her lips out in an exaggerated pout. "Like a golden retriever who'd been told there would be no walkies."

"Well, other than when she was a newborn, your sister's never been much of a morning person. God help any man who gets in the way of her sleep."

Addie clinked her mug against mine in agreement. "Hear, hear."

"Speaking of newborns..." Sky tapped her phone screen before sighing. "Come on, baby Riggs. We'd like to go to sleep sometime tonight."

Dane had texted just after seven o'clock to let us know that Piper's water had broken in the middle of Christmas Eve dinner and that they were on their way to the hospital.

I scrolled through the updates, checking the timestamps to gauge her progress. "Let's see. She was dilated to a six a couple of hours ago, so it could be any time now. Second babies don't typically take as long as first ones."

"Or could be hours still," Addie said, ever the practical one.

"Poor Piper," Sky murmured, wincing. "I can't even imagine."

"It's totally worth it, though," I said automatically, before pausing to reconsider.

Because was it? The question felt blasphemous, the kind of thing Good Mothers weren't supposed to think, let alone say out loud.

The girls both looked at me, waiting for me to finish the thought.

"I mean, obviously it's worth it," I added. "But the process itself? Labor and delivery, and the complete destruction of your pelvic floor? That part's awful, and anyone who tells you otherwise is selling something."

"Yeah, no thanks. I like my coochie intact," Sky said with the kind of dramatic disdain only a twenty-two-year-old could muster.

"And that's why you've gotta avoid those golden retriever ski bum mountain gods," I deadpanned, causing her to spit out her hot chocolate in shock.

"Jesus, Mom! Warn a girl next time!"

Addie passed her a handful of napkins with a snort.

This was new territory for us—this easy banter, this comfort with saying things that weren't perfectly curated.

Before, I would have given them the sanitized version. Would have told them that every moment of pain had been transcendent, that I'd never felt more connected to the universe than when I was pushing a human being out of my body.

Which was utter bullshit.

I'd felt connected to an epidural and a very sincere desire never to do it again.

"How did Dad do when you were in labor?" Addie asked, genuine curiosity in her voice.

I laughed, remembering Teddy pacing the hospital room like a caged animal. "With your birth, he lost his shit when the anesthesiologist had trouble with the epidural and almost got himself thrown out for creatively describing exactly how he'd end him if he didn't get it on the second try. Your grandfather had to physically remove him from the room."

Sky snorted at the visual before squirting a mountain of whipped cream directly into her mouth.

"Took Poppy and three of the guys from the club to convince him that threatening medical staff wasn't gonna make the process go any faster." I smiled at the memory, remembering how mature we thought we were at twenty-six and twenty-eight and how completely unprepared we were for what parenthood would mean.

"But he came back, right?" Addie asked with a concerned expression.

A soft smile tugged at my lips. "Didn't leave my side after that. Held my hand and told me I was doing great, even when I was definitely not doing great."

We fell into comfortable silence, the only sounds the occasional notification from their phones and the steady thump of Teddy splitting logs out back for the fire.

Sky finished sending a text before leaning back in her chair. "So, what's the plan, Mom?"

I finished swallowing the boozy chocolate in my mouth before asking, "For what, Christmas Day?"

"No, with you moving in with Dad," Addie answered.

"Oh, I don't know," I said, shrugging as I licked a dollop of whipped cream off my lip. "Haven't gotten that far yet."

Both girls froze mid-sip, their eyes going comically wide over the rims of their mugs.

"You... don't have a plan?" Addie repeated slowly, like I'd just announced I was joining the circus.

"Nope." I popped the 'p' and took another drink, enjoying their shocked expressions more than I probably should have.

Sky made a surprised sound and set her mug down. "What do you mean? Shouldn't you have a timeline? Or at least decide whether you're going to list the house or try to rent it out?"

"Sure. Eventually."

Addie leaned forward, studying me like I was a particularly confusing passage in one of her textbooks. "Mom, this is, like, your literal job—helping people plan every detail of a major life change," she said, referring to my career as a senior transition specialist and estate organizer—a career I'd started twenty years ago after helping my parents downsize and relocate to Florida.

"*Home Again Transitions* handles everything so you can move forward with ease," Sky added on the off-chance I'd forgotten my own slogan. "You have systems and binders for this very thing…"

I grinned, reaching for another marshmallow from the bag on the table. "Mm hmm."

The silence that followed was profound. Both girls stared at me like I'd grown a second head.

"Are you feeling okay?" Sky leaned across the table to inspect the healing cut near my hairline. "It doesn't look infected. Do you know if you were concussed?"

I batted her hand away with a laugh. "I'm fine. Better than fine, actually."

"But you always have a plan," Addie insisted, her brow furrowed in genuine concern. "Like, always. Even Grandpa Jack likes to joke that you were born with a five-year plan in your hand."

She'd inherited that from me, though watching her now—hair twisted into a neat bun, matching pajamas somehow looking put-together despite the late hour—I wondered if maybe I'd passed on too much of my need for control.

The thought didn't sit well. I didn't want my daughters to spend their lives the way I had, white-knuckling their way through every moment, terrified of letting anything be less than perfect.

"Yeah, and look where it got me," I said, the words coming out gentler than they might have even a week ago. "I planned every detail of our lives to the nth degree for over thirty years. Scheduled family time, coordinated everyone's calendars, made sure every holiday was picture-perfect."

"Mom—" Sky started, but I shook my head.

"I'm not saying this to make you feel bad or to be dramatic," I said gently. "I'm just… I'm tired, girls. I'm tired of trying to control everything. I spent years thinking that if I could just control enough variables, keep all the plates spinning, nothing bad would happen."

My throat tightened slightly, but I pushed through. "But it did. Levi still died. Your dad and I still got divorced. All that planning, all that desperate need for control—it didn't prevent a single loss. It just left me feeling burned out and disconnected from what actually mattered."

I'd missed too many moments, worried about the next thing, more concerned with checking items off a list than with being present.

Addie's eyes were suspiciously bright. "So what are you going to do?"

"I'm gonna take it one day at a time," I said, and even as I said it, I felt something loosen in my chest. "I'll figure out the house when I need to figure out the house. I'll handle the logistics of the move when it's time. Right now, I'm just going to be here. With your dad. With you two. Actually enjoying Christmas instead of trying to manage it."

Sky's mouth opened and closed like a fish. "Who are you, and what have you done with our mother?" she demanded.

"She's right here," I said matter-of-factly. "Maybe just a slightly different version than the one you're used to. One who's learning that it's okay not to know what's coming next. It's okay not to have it all figured out."

Addie reached across the table and squeezed my hand. "But what about your business? Will you keep doing that here?"

"I don't know yet," I admitted. "Maybe. Maybe not. Maybe I'll do something completely different. Take up pottery. Learn to ski. Become one of those women who hikes mountains at sunrise with golden retriever mountain gods."

Sky giggled at the comment while Addie let her head fall back with a groan.

The back door opened with a gust of frigid air, and Teddy stomped in carrying an armload of firewood, his cheeks ruddy from the cold. He'd thrown on his jacket but hadn't bothered to zip it, and I could see his breath clouding in the cold air that followed him in.

"Cold enough to freeze the balls off a brass monkey," he announced, before disappearing into the living room. I heard the metallic clang of the fireplace screen being moved, then the solid thud of logs being added.

When he returned to the kitchen, he planted a kiss on the top of my head before snagging my mug and taking a long drink. "Better not be the good whiskey, Skylar Jade," he said, smacking his lips together as he placed it back on the table.

"No, sir. Even though the recipe called for Maker's Mark, I just used the cheap crap you keep on the bottom shelf."

"Sure went quiet in a hurry in here," Teddy observed as he pulled out the empty chair next to mine and sat down, immediately draping his arm across my shoulders. "Y'all talking about me again?"

Sky nodded emphatically. "Always. Actually, we just learned that Mom's considering taking up sunrise hiking with Cali, and I for one would love to know your thoughts on that."

Teddy's hand, which had been idly playing with the ends of my hair, went still. "That so?"

I kicked Sky under the table, earning a yelp, but the damage was already done. His fingers tightened on my shoulder—not painfully, but enough that I felt the possessive edge creeping in.

"She's joking," I said in my best warning tone—the one that used to make the kids straighten up immediately. "I was making a point about not having everything planned out."

"Mm," Teddy grunted, the muscle in his jaw flexing. "And this point required mentioning Wright specifically?"

"It was more about the concept of spontaneity," Addie offered diplomatically, though I could see her fighting a smile. "The sunrise was just an example."

"Right. An example." He took another deliberate sip of my hot chocolate, his eyes never leaving mine. "Baby, you wanna go watch a sunrise, I'll take you. Don't need some thirty-five-year-old pretty boy showing you around my mountain."

"Your mountain?" I repeated, arching an eyebrow.

"My mountain," he confirmed, utterly serious. "My woman. My sunrise."

Sky dissolved into giggles while Addie pressed her lips together, clearly trying not to laugh.

"Theodore, it was hypothetical—"

His arm slid from my shoulders to band around my waist, hauling me closer until I was practically in his lap. "You wanna see him hypothetically buried on the side of a mountain, Kels?"

I bit back a smile at his growly tone. "I thought you said he was a good guy."

Shannon Myers

"He is," he agreed. "Which is why it'd be a damn fucking shame to have to kill him."

I could have pointed out that he was being ridiculous. That I had zero interest in going anywhere with a man I didn't know, much less at sunrise. That his caveman routine was unnecessary and borderline absurd.

But the truth was, I kind of liked it. Liked being wanted this fiercely, this unapologetically. Liked that even the hypothetical idea of another man showing me a sunrise made him pull me closer.

"That's very sweet, but I'm not actually planning to—"

"Good," he interjected, the tension in his shoulders easing slightly, though the possessive gleam in his eyes remained. "Because I ain't big on sharing, especially when it comes to you, baby."

"Not exactly breaking news," I murmured before tipping my face up to kiss him. Right in front of our daughters, with my hands cupping his bearded jaw and my tongue sliding against his until he made that low, rumbling sound in his chest I'd loved hearing since we were teenagers.

Sky made a gagging sound. "And we're back to the gross couple stuff. You guys are at an eleven, and I'm gonna need you to dial it back to like a six. Think you can do that?"

"No," Teddy and I said at the same time.

"C'mon, keep it PG, you two," Addie chimed in. "There are children present."

"Children who orchestrated an elaborate con to get us back together," Teddy pointed out dryly. "Pretty sure you forfeited the right to pearl-clutch about our relationship, kiddo."

"There's a difference between wanting you back together and wanting front-row seats to—" Sky gestured vaguely at us. "—all of that."

Before I could formulate a smart-ass remark, our phones began buzzing in rapid succession, a cascade of notifications that could only mean one thing.

Sky lunged for hers first, nearly knocking over her mug in her excitement. "It's from Uncle Dane," she squealed. "He's here! We have a new cousin!"

I covered my mouth, my heart squeezing as I opened the attached photos. The baby was perfect, with a shock of dark hair and a scrunched-up little face. He had one tiny fist mashed against his cheek, lips pursed as if he wasn't thrilled he'd been evicted from his warm, cozy home.

Piper looked exhausted but somehow still radiant, and Dane—who took after his oldest brother in both build and appearance—had tears streaming down his face as he cradled them both.

Dane

Oliver Paul Riggs was born at 1:24 AM. 8 lbs. 10 oz, 21 inches. Piper made it through like a warrior goddess and is doing great. Meanwhile, I think I've cried more than Oliver in the past twenty minutes. Merry Christmas!

Oliver *Paul*, after the patriarch of the family, Paul "Wolverine" Riggs. A man who'd raised his four sons to be as tough as they were loyal, who'd taught them that family came first, always. Even when that family expanded to include an entire motorcycle club. The man who'd pulled Teddy off Dane in the funeral home parking lot at Levi's visitation, fighting to keep everybody together despite his own grief.

Sky let out a soft "aww" while Addie typed rapidly on her phone, probably already composing the perfect congratulatory message. "Poppy's going to cry. You know he will."

"Hundred percent," Sky agreed. "Remember when Levi was born, and he held him for the first time?"

I smiled at the memory of the gruff biker insisting on counting my son's toes to ensure he had all ten before discreetly wiping his eyes on the swaddling blanket.

Teddy zoomed in on the photo, studying his nephew with an expression that made my throat tighten. He'd worn the same look when each of our children was born—wonder and terror mixed with a love so fierce it could level mountains.

"He's perfect," I whispered, leaning into his warmth.

"Yeah," he said quietly, his thumb tracing over the screen. "He is."

The kitchen suddenly felt smaller, excitement dampening into something more complicated. His eyes seemed to stare straight through the screen into another delivery room, another December baby. He drummed his fingers restlessly against the table—index to pinky, repeatedly, a nervous tic I knew all too well.

Before I could probe further, he was already standing, his chair scraping against the floor.

"Gonna add another log to the fire," he announced, even though it was burning fine.

The girls felt the shift as much as I did, and Addie shot me a questioning look, eyebrows raised. *What's wrong with him?* she mouthed.

I shook my head slightly, watching Teddy's broad shoulders as he prodded at the embers, the flames casting flickering shadows across his furrowed brows. In another life, I would have stormed across the room, demanding he talk to me. I would have convinced myself I could fix the distant look in his eyes and instead made his withdrawal about me.

But if I'd learned anything over the past few days, it was that sometimes people needed space to feel whatever they were feeling. That love didn't mean trying to fix everything and everyone.

I rose from the table and padded over to where he crouched. My hand found the space between his shoulder blades, palm flat against the warm cotton of his shirt. I felt the tension coiled there, the tightness in muscles that should have been relaxed.

New life on Christmas morning. After everything we'd lost, everything we'd survived, it was proof that the world kept turning. That life continued. That families could heal.

But grief and joy were sometimes impossible to separate, each often making the other more intense. So while welcoming our new nephew to the world was a blessing, it was also a reminder of all the milestones we'd never get to experience, like watching our son graduate or become a meteorologist. We'd never get to see him get married or start a family. We'd never get to know how he would have turned out, what kind of man he would have become.

"Hey," I said softly, scrunching my nose to hold back the tears that wanted to fall.

Teddy glanced up at me, and for just a second, I saw something vulnerable flash across his face before he masked it. "Hey, yourself."

I carefully knelt beside him in front of the hearth, my knees crackling almost as loudly as the logs in the fireplace. My hand moved over his, lacing our fingers together before raising it to my mouth. I pressed a kiss to each scarred knuckle before loosening my grip in case he wanted to pull away.

He held on. Tight enough that my rings dug into my fingers, but I didn't complain.

"First time I held Levi," Teddy said suddenly, "he grabbed my finger. Just wrapped his whole fist around it and wouldn't let go. The nurse said it was just reflexes, but I thought…" He trailed off, staring into the fire in silence for several seconds. "Thought it meant something. Like he was telling me that he trusted me to keep him safe."

"And you did," I said simply. "Every day you could."

He jerked his chin in an abrupt nod before pressing his lips to my temple. "Thank you."

I leaned my head against his shoulder, breathing him in with a contented sigh. "I love you."

"Love you too, baby."

We stayed like that for a moment longer before Teddy cleared his throat and stood, pulling me up with him. When we turned back to the table, both girls were pretending to be engrossed in their phones, though Sky's eyes were suspiciously shiny.

"All right," he announced, his voice still rough but steadier. "It's after one. Y'all should get some sleep."

"But what about presents?" Sky protested, gesturing to the pile of wrapped packages under the tree. "We always open them first thing Christmas morning."

"First thing being a reasonable hour," I interjected. "Like nine or ten. Not the middle of the night."

Addie yawned, covering her mouth with her hand. "Actually, sleep sounds amazing right now. I think all the late-night plotting is catching up with me."

"Mm, that reminds me. You're both on kitchen duty tomorrow," I said as I gathered the empty mugs and carried them over to the sink.

"Working on Christmas?" Sky questioned with a theatrical gasp, as if it was the first she was hearing about it. "How very Ebenezer Scrooge of you."

"Look, while we appreciate the thought behind your little plan, it doesn't change the fact that you lied to us about where you were for days," I said, filling the sink with hot, soapy water before deciding the dishes could wait until morning. "Consider it your penance."

"Worth it," she declared with a smug smirk. "Seeing you two finally get your shit together was the best Christmas gift we could have asked for."

"Language," I said automatically before remembering I was talking to the child who'd been born without a filter.

Teddy snorted. "Baby, that ship sailed about twenty-one years ago when her first word was 'fuck' because someone couldn't watch her potty mouth around the baby."

"That was your fault!" I protested, smacking his arm. "You're the one who taught her that."

Addie stood, stretching with a groan that belonged on someone twice her age. "Okay, before this devolves into another round of 'who corrupted Skylar first,' I'm going to bed."

She paused at the foot of the stairs and primly adjusted her glasses, her mannerisms so like mine it was scary. "I just wanna say that I'm not sorry we meddled. You two were miserable apart and too damn stubborn to ever admit it."

"Great. Doesn't change the fact that you're still grounded," Teddy said, crossing his arms over his chest.

"Can't ground adults," Sky sing-songed as she headed for the stairs. "We have jobs and apartments and pay our own bills."

"Watch me, brat," he called after her, but she was already halfway up, Addie following close behind.

"Night, Mom! Night, Dad!" Addie said over her shoulder. "And remember, the living room couch is considered a public space and should remain family-friendly."

"Yeah, keep it in the bedroom, you two!" Sky added. "Some of us might need water in the middle of the night and would prefer not to be traumatized again!"

Their footsteps thundered up the stairs—how two relatively small women could sound like a herd of elephants was beyond me.

"Better hurry, or Santa won't come!" I called after them, unable to resist one last joke.

"Mom!" came the mortified chorus from upstairs, followed by Sky's muffled, "I'm sending you my therapy bill!"

I shook my head and moved through the kitchen, folding the dish towel over the oven handle and switching off the lights.

"Think Santa already came."

I turned at the sound of Teddy's low voice, ready with a quip about how that was a terrible line even for him. The words died in my throat.

He stood in the doorway between the kitchen and living room, backlit by the fireplace and twinkling tree lights. In his hand was a small velvet box, navy blue and battered at the corners, like it had been waiting a long time for this moment.

My hands came up over my mouth. "Teddy? What—"

He held up his free hand, a slight tremor in his fingers betraying his nerves. "Just... let me get this out before I lose my nerve."

Even in the dim light, I could see the nervous energy radiating off him—the way he shifted his weight from foot to foot, the tight set of his jaw.

"Bought this right after Irish offered me a spot here. Thought maybe..." He trailed off, dragging one hand through his hair. "Thought maybe if I showed you I was serious about starting over, about building something new here together, you'd give us another shot. Thought maybe if I could just get you away from there, we'd find our way back to each other."

I thought back to that horrible time period, remembering the way he'd come home talking about the mountains and the chapter and how much I'd resented him for running away when I'd needed him most.

He'd been trying to save us, to help us heal, and I'd handed him divorce papers.

"Had this whole plan to bring you here for our anniversary, show you the mountains and the life we could build, but it all went to shit before I could even bring it up." He swallowed, his nostrils flaring wide as he fought to hold back tears. "Thought about selling the ring or maybe chucking it into the Dillon Reservoir. But every time I took it out of the safe, I just… couldn't."

"Why?"

Teddy shrugged. "Guess some part of me never stopped hoping. Even when I was convinced we were over, even when I was drinking myself stupid and picking fights with anyone who looked at me wrong, some part of me knew. Knew that if you ever gave me another chance, if we ever found our way through all the shit and pain and mistakes, I wanted to have it."

The box opened with a soft squeak, revealing a ring that stole what little breath I had left. Not a diamond—he knew me better than that. The stone was a deep green; darker than the emerald I'd worn for three decades. It reminded me of a forest, with a vintage-gold setting—Art Deco, maybe—and tiny milgrain details.

"Tsavorite garnet," he explained, taking a step closer. "Jeweler suggested it, said they're formed under extreme heat and pressure that would destroy most things, but instead…" He lifted the ring from the box, twisting it to catch the tree lights. "Instead, it creates something that can last forever."

Teddy's eyes met mine again. "We've had more pain than any two people should have to carry. Lost more than…" His voice caught, and he had to stop, jaw flexing with emotion. "Lost our boy. Lost those babies that never got to be. Lost each other for a while there."

The other pregnancies. The ones we never talked about, that ended almost as soon as they began. Just one more thing we'd buried under silence and Perfect Kelsey's carefully maintained surface.

My throat felt tight, all the words I wanted to say stuck somewhere between my heart and my mouth.

"We did thirty years the hard way, baby," Teddy continued. "Fighting ourselves, fighting each other, fighting against what we both knew was true—that we're better together than apart. Like to try doing the next thirty different."

He reached for my hand, and at the last moment, I pulled back, unable to keep the smile from tugging at my lips even through tears. "Was there a question attached to that speech, Theodore?" I asked,

The side of his mouth tipped up. "Don't ask questions I already know the answer to," he said, gruff and certain. "You've been mine since I was seventeen, Kelsey Dawn. Ring's just making it official. Again."

"You're not getting down on one knee either?"

He stared at me for a long moment before shaking his head. "Baby, think we both know what would happen if I got on my knees right now," he said, his voice dropping low.

I playfully pushed against his chest, and he caught my hand, sliding the ring onto my finger before I could pull away. It fit perfectly, and I held my hand up, watching the way the stone caught the light, throwing tiny prisms across the walls.

He pulled me in for a kiss that started soft and turned heated within seconds, his hands tangling in my hair, mine grabbing at his shoulders. I could feel thirty-four years in that kiss—every first, every last, every moment we'd convinced ourselves was an ending when it turned out to be just another beginning.

We eventually migrated toward the fire, with Teddy making a quick detour to the liquor cabinet.

"Just one glass?" I asked when he returned with only one tumbler of whiskey.

"You plan on sitting across the room from me?"

"No," I admitted.

"Then we're sharing." He settled into the leather armchair near the fireplace before patting his thigh. "Come here."

I curled into his lap without hesitation, like I had a thousand times before the weight of the world convinced us we were too old for such things.

His arm came around me automatically, hand settling easily against my hip. The whiskey glass rested on the chair arm, within reach but forgotten for the moment.

My gaze drifted to the pile of presents beneath the tree. Wrapped in paper that hadn't come from the same roll. The ones I'd brought had elegant gold stripes. Others were wrapped in birthday paper and what appeared to be newspaper, decorated with a marker by someone—likely Teddy.

"I don't have anything for you," I said softly, guilt needling at me. "I didn't think about it. Didn't know any of this would happen."

Teddy's arm tightened around my waist, pulling me closer. "Baby, I got exactly what I wanted for Christmas."

"But—"

"Got my whole damn heart back," he continued, his voice a low growl against my shoulder. "Don't need anything else."

He paused, taking a sip of the whiskey before offering me the glass. I took it, letting the smoky caramel liquor warm me from the inside out while the man I'd loved since before I understood what love really meant watched me with a soft smile.

"Want you to understand something. I don't want you because we're trying to save something that's already broken. Don't want you because I feel obligated or because it's familiar or because we've got history," he said, his eyes holding mine.

"Want you the way I did when we were kids, Kels. Just because. Because you're the only woman I've ever wanted. The only one I'll ever want. And if that makes me sound like some obsessed teenager instead of a grown-ass man, then so be it."

We slipped into a comfortable silence, passing the glass back and forth. Sometimes he'd take a drink and kiss me immediately after. Once, I missed slightly, and a droplet clung to my bottom lip. He caught it with his thumb before bringing it to his mouth.

Outside, the world lay in frozen silence. Snow-covered pines climbing toward peaks I couldn't see in the darkness. A sky full of stars, more than I'd ever seen in Texas, scattered across the black like someone had spilled milky glitter.

I wasn't making mental to-do lists. Wasn't stressing about wrapping paper or the broken angel ornament or the disaster zone of a kitchen. Wasn't cataloging everything that needed to happen for the move, like finding a realtor, sorting through three decades of accumulated stuff, coordinating with the movers, finding a cardiologist, updating my address with approximately eight thousand different organizations and institutions.

For the first time in longer than I could remember, I was here.

Present in the moment, in this chair, with this man. Not five steps ahead or ten years in the past. Just here.

Someone once told me, in the fog of those first weeks after Levi died, that grief was just love with nowhere to go. At the time, I'd thought it was the most devastating thing I'd ever heard. All that love I had for my son, all those years of worry and hope and fear and joy—trapped inside me with no outlet, no destination, just endless circulation through a heart that didn't know how to let go.

I'd thought about it constantly after the divorce, wondering where I was supposed to store over three decades of love for a man who no longer shared my bed or my life. Where did love go when the person was still alive but no longer yours? Did it dissipate like smoke? Calcify into resentment? Transform into something else entirely?

It had taken me a long time, but I thought I finally understood what that well-meaning stranger had meant.

Grief was the price of love. It was the evidence that we once held something so profound and meaningful that it irrevocably changed our lives. You didn't get over it or move past or heal from it, not really.

It just changed shape. Found cracks to hide in, showing up where you least expected. Like finding one of Levi's socks under a couch cushion or seeing Skylar make the same face Teddy did when she was concentrating.

Just because it had nowhere to go didn't mean it disappeared.

Because that was the thing about love.

It waited. Patient and stubborn, it endured every winter, every sleepless night, every moment you thought would break you beyond repair. It showed you that you could hold both enormous joy and enormous loss in the same heart without one canceling out the other.

And sometimes, if you were impossibly lucky, all that love found its way home again.

"Merry Christmas, Kels," Teddy whispered, brushing a tear from my lashes.

"Merry Christmas, Teddy," I whispered before kissing the man who'd been my everything and my nothing and all the points between. Who'd given me three beautiful children and more pain than I'd thought survivable. Who'd loved me every way a person could—good and bad.

For the first time since losing Levi—maybe the first time ever—I let myself believe in a future again.

Not a perfect one. Not the carefully curated version I would have planned once upon a time, with contingency protocols and the desperate illusion of control that had destroyed us before. But a real one. Messy and uncertain and full of all the beautiful, terrible, ordinary moments that made up a life.

When Teddy's hand found mine in the darkness, squeezing gently, I squeezed back.

Merry Christmas to all, and to all a good life...
The End

Thank you for reading THE CHRISTMAS TRAP! I hope you loved Teddy and Kelsey's story.

Looking for more in the Silent Phoenix series? The ride begins with Grey & Celia's story in THE DESERTER, which is also where you'll be introduced to Riggs patriarch Wolverine and his Ol' Lady Lucy.

In the mood for a one-night stand, secret baby biker romance that can be read as a standalone? Check out Dane and Piper's story in THE KEEPER.

A one-night stand with a brooding biker turned my entire life upside down.

True to his name, Ghost disappeared without a trace.

Well, almost...

He left me with a permanent reminder of our night together...our daughter, Avery.

Almost two years later, our paths collide again at another book event, both of us still haunted by the tragic events that ripped us apart before. When he discovers he left behind more than regrets that night in the hotel, Ghost steps up, hellbent on reclaiming what's his.

But when the violence of his world bleeds over into mine, can I trust my biker to keep us safe?

Or will his darkness destroy everything I've fought to build?

Keep reading for an excerpt from The Keeper.

If you enjoyed this story, please consider leaving a review on Amazon. I appreciate your help in spreading the word, even if it's just telling a friend. Reviews help readers find new books to fall in love with.

Want to be the first to know when these stories are coming out? Sign up for my newsletter, join my Facebook group, and/or Follow me on BookBub!

the keeper

Piper

I WOVE through the vehicles parked in front of the valet and past a group of readers and authors getting their nicotine fix before the event. Their loud voices and boisterous laughter echoed off the walls of the hotel, assaulting my already frayed nerves.

It had been one year, nine months, and twenty-seven days since I'd woken up alone on a hotel room couch.

No note. No explanation. Nothing.

Since then, I'd often fantasized about what I would say to Dane if I ever saw him again. I envisioned boldly walking up to him and asking, *Why did you say you wanted to make it real and then leave without a word? Who the fuck does that?*

The daydreams varied, but most ended with me slapping the ever-loving shit out of him before waltzing off with my head held high, like a badass.

Now, faced with the reality of possibly seeing him again, my bravado crumbled. I couldn't do it. I wasn't ready to confront him over his actions if it meant seeing the rejection in his eyes when he learned the truth about our night together.

I'd spent most of the night and part of the morning with my head in the toilet, and exhaustion weighed on me like a lead blanket.

As I approached the entrance, I white-knuckled the strap of my purse, my palms growing clammy. The urge to flee back to my car and speed away from the entire asinine plan was overwhelming.

But my mama hadn't raised a coward.

An idiot, maybe. But not a coward.

So, with my heart pounding out a staccato rhythm, I took a deep breath and entered the lobby like a woman walking to her own execution, wincing when I caught sight of my haggard reflection in an ornate mirror.

Awesome. I looked as wrecked as I felt.

Dark smudges stained the pale skin beneath my green eyes, mocking my futile attempts to conceal them with makeup. The long, wispy bangs I spontaneously gave myself a few days ago looked less trendy and more like a cry for help.

Long months of worry and anxiety had taken a physical toll on me as much as an emotional one. Last night was just another in a long line of sleepless nights spent tossing in rumpled sheets and second-guessing my decision to come. The uncertainty was etched into the lines of my face and the hollows of my cheeks, and I couldn't even remember the last time I'd managed to get four hours of solid, uninterrupted sleep. And the long hours I'd been putting in at the bakery lately weren't doing me any favors either.

On cue, my phone vibrated, pulling me away from the mirror and the shell of a woman who was, as Garth would say, much too young to feel this damn old.

Thinking it might be my mother, I hurriedly snatched it out of my purse, only to see it was a text from my boss, Derek. My jaw tightened as I read his message, another thinly-veiled demand masquerading as a request.

Derek
Got a last-minute order, and Terri called in sick.
I need you to come in this afternoon. You know
how it is.

Frustration simmered beneath my skin, a slow burn that threatened to ignite into a full-blown inferno. I requested the day off six months in advance and had already put in nearly fifty hours this week.

My thumbs hovered over the screen, itching to unleash a scathing reply to tell Derek exactly where he could shove his last-minute summons. But I resisted, knowing it was a battle I couldn't win.

Not if I wanted to keep my job anyway. I desperately needed to keep my job.

With a growl, I dropped the phone back into my purse and smoothed a hand over my long-sleeved dress.

The entire hotel bustled with activity, the sounds of book carts being wheeled toward the ballrooms echoing off the marble floors.

I scanned the crowded lobby, searching for familiar faces while simultaneously hoping to avoid them. My pulse kicked up a notch at every glimpse of dark hair or broad shoulders, and I was convinced it was him.

"Piper!" Ivy's voice cut through the chaos, and I turned to see her waving frantically near the back of a growing line.

I forced my lips into what I hoped was a convincing smile and made my way to her, my pulse racing. Every step closer to the ballroom felt like it was bringing me closer to my doom.

What if Dane was already inside?

What if he saw me first?

Or worse, what if he didn't come at all?

As I approached, I noticed Ivy didn't look much better than I did. A slight tremor ran through her body, and her wide blue eyes seemed to dart nervously around the room.

"Hey," I said, feeling the tension in her shoulders as I pulled her into a quick hug. "Sorry, I'm late. Traffic was—"

"Don't apologize!" she interjected a little too loudly. "You're here now, and that's all that matters."

We pulled apart, and I peered into her overly bright eyes with a frown. "You okay?"

"Me? I'm fine!" She let out a startled shriek and spun around, startling the poor woman in line behind us.

"Sorry!" the woman exclaimed, jerking her hand back. "I was just trying to let you know the line was moving."

"Thank you," I told her. After inching forward to close the gap, I turned to Ivy with a raised brow. "Are you sure you're okay? You seem…on edge."

"Just excited and maybe a tad bit overcaffeinated," she insisted, squaring her shoulders with a brittle laugh. "This is fun. I can't remember the last time we had a weekend with just us."

Before I could press further, a familiar figure emerged from the ballroom, and my stomach dropped.

GQ moved with the casual grace of a man used to commanding the attention of women everywhere. But now, the sight of him sent a jolt of panic through my veins because where he was, Dane couldn't be far behind.

Panic clawed its way up my throat, bitter and sharp. Without thinking, I grabbed Ivy's hand and squeezed.

"Piper, what—"

"We have to go," I hissed, my voice trembling. "I can't—I can't do this. I can't be here."

She searched my face, her eyes softening with understanding. "Okay, sweetie. Why don't you wait for me by the entrance, and I'll be right there."

I nodded gratefully and made my way back through the crowded lobby, my heart pounding in my ears.

Once I reached the relative safety of the hotel entrance, I pulled out my phone with shaking hands. I needed a distraction, something to ground me before I completely lost it.

Me

Just checking in. How are y'all doing?

The reply came through almost immediately.

Mom

We're perfectly fine and having fun like you should be, missy.

I stared at the screen, the words blurring as tears pricked the corners of my eyes. If my mother knew why I was here, she would have told me not to come. She would have said it wasn't worth the risk, the pain.

But I had to know, didn't I?

I had to see Dane one last time, even if it shattered me.

Ivy's soothing voice broke through my spiraling thoughts. "Hey, I found a volunteer to hold our spot. Let's get you some air."

"You know I hate when you use your therapy voice," I grumbled, as she took my hand and led me outside.

"I have no idea what you're talking about."

The cool air was a welcome relief against my flushed skin. I took a deep breath, willing my racing heart to slow.

"I know it's hard being away from her and doing something for yourself," she said, breaking the silence. "Just know it's completely normal—"

"That's what you think this is—separation anxiety?" I huffed out an annoyed breath and shook my head. "I work all the damn time and only see her three, maybe four hours a day. Sorry, Doctor, but any separation anxiety I may have had is long gone."

"Is it something at work then?" she asked, her voice taking on a dangerous edge. "Or Derek? I swear to all that is good and holy, Piper. All I need is five minutes and a hammer, and that fucking creeper wouldn't bother you anymore."

I choked on a laugh and deadpanned, "A hammer? That's not very love and light of you. Have you asked yourself if this is coming from a place of healing?"

"Screw healing," she growled, balling her hand into a fist. "Sometimes, karma takes too long, and it's up to us to teach the dickheads of the world a lesson."

The reaction was overkill, even for someone as fiercely protective of her friends as she was. I studied her face, noting the tightness around her eyes and how her gaze continuously shifted from one end of the hotel to the other as if she were searching for an unseen threat.

"I'm good," I said, knowing better than to press her over it. Getting Ivy to open up was like trying to break into Fort Knox armed with nothing but a spork. "I think it was just all the people crowding around us—I felt like I couldn't breathe."

"Really?" she asked, her tone skeptical. "You sure it doesn't have something to do with running into Ghost again?"

The blood drained from my face. "Dane's—he's here? You're sure?"

She nodded, watching me with a penetrative gaze that always made me feel like she was peering straight into my soul. "Yeah, I saw him carrying boxes in with GQ and Duke before you got here."

My legs buckled, and I latched onto her to remain upright. My instincts screamed at me to run—from the hotel, from the memories, from him.

"The biker—he's the reason you're on the verge of a panic attack?" she questioned, pulling the corner of her lip between her teeth and studying me like I was a puzzle to be solved.

She knew me all too well—could sense the turmoil churning beneath the surface of my carefully crafted facade.

"What am I missing? You hung out at the pool, and then he walked you back to the room. End of story. Why would seeing him again upset you? It's not like he's the deadbeat who knocked you up—" She stopped abruptly, her face draining of color. "Dane is Avery's father?" she whispered, her voice barely audible.

I managed a small nod, confirming her worst suspicions.

"Jesus Christ," Ivy breathed, running a hand through her hair. "Why didn't you tell me?"

"Because saying it out loud made it real." Tears burned behind my eyes, threatening to spill over. I swallowed past the lump in my throat. "And I wasn't ready for it to be real."

"Does he know?"

I shook my head, shame and guilt twisting in my gut. "I tried to find him after I found out I was pregnant, but without a last name or phone number, it was virtually impossible. Short of dropping by every clubhouse in the state to see if they knew a Ghost or a Dane, I didn't know what else to do."

"You should have come to me with this. I would have helped you find him."

I shrugged, unable to meet her gaze. "At first, I was too scared to face the reality of the situation. Then, as time went on, it just got harder and harder to bring it up. I told myself it was better this way—that Avery and I were doing fine on our own."

"But you're not fine," she pointed out in a gentle tone. "You're exhausted, overworked, and falling apart at the thought of running into Dane. This isn't healthy, Piper."

"I know," I said, my voice cracking again. "But what am I supposed to do now? Walk up to him and say, 'Hey, remember that night we spent together? Surprise! You have a daughter!'"

Ivy placed her hands on my shoulders, forcing me to look at her. "Yeah, that's exactly what you're going to do. He deserves to know, and more importantly, Avery deserves to know her father."

The thought of confronting him, of seeing the shock and potential anger on his face, made me want to vomit all over again.

"You don't understand," I choked out, shaking my head frantically. "I can't just drop this bomb on him out of nowhere."

"Then when, Piper? When Avery's graduating from high school? When she's looking for someone to walk her down the aisle?" Ivy's voice softened. "There's never going to be a right time, but the longer you wait, the harder it's going to be."

The full weight of her words sank in. She was right, of course. But knowing what I had to do and doing it were two very different things.

"What if he wants nothing to do with us? Oh my god. What if he tries to take her away?"

"Breathe," Ivy commanded. "You're catastrophizing. You don't know how he'll react until you tell him."

I paced back and forth across a small section of pavement. "That's just it. I don't know *him*. Not really. We spent one night together, and then he vanished. For all I know, he could be married with three kids."

She latched onto my arm, halting my frantic movement. "Then you need to find out so you can stop torturing yourself with the what-ifs. You also need to consider the possibility that he might want to be involved. Are you prepared for that?"

Was I prepared for Dane to want to be a part of Avery's life? To potentially disrupt the careful balance I'd constructed over the past year?

"Piper?"

I froze, my heart pounding so violently I thought it might burst from my chest. Time slowed to a crawl as I turned around, coming face to face with the man who haunted almost all my dreams.

Dane stood less than six feet away, looking even more devastatingly handsome than the last time I saw him. His dark eyes roamed over me, and memories of that night flashed through my mind like an uninvited guest.

"I thought that was you inside," he said, his presence as palpable as ever. The kutte he wore molded to his muscular frame like a second skin, while the black T-shirt underneath strained against his biceps and broad shoulders.

Had he always been this muscular, or was it a recent development? I couldn't remember.

He took a step closer. "It's been a while."

A while.

As if the past year and nine months could be summed up so casually. As if he hadn't knocked me up and disappeared without a trace.

Not that either of us had known I would end up pregnant when he slipped out in the middle of the night, but still. *A while?* That was the best he could come up with?

A vein pulsed in my forehead. My emotions were rapidly cycling between anger, hurt, confusion, and rage.

Heavy on the rage.

An awkward silence stretched between us, thick with unspoken words and lingering questions. I could feel Ivy's eyes darting between us, practically vibrating with the need to intervene.

I opened my mouth, but the words wouldn't come out. This was it —the moment I'd both dreaded and longed for. And I was completely unprepared.

"You look…" He trailed off, his brow furrowing as he studied me more closely. "Are you all right?"

No, I wanted to scream. *I'm not all right. I haven't been all right since the night you left.*

My throat was bone dry as I replied, "I'm fine."

Dane's eyes narrowed, clearly not buying what I was trying to sell. He took another step closer, close enough now I could smell the faint scent of leather and something distinctly him. My traitorous body reacted instantly, a familiar warmth spreading through my veins.

His forehead creased with concern. "You don't look fine. What's wrong?"

A hysterical laugh bubbled up in my chest. What wasn't wrong? My entire world had been turned upside down the moment I saw those two pink lines on the pregnancy test. And now here he was, standing in front of me like no time had passed at all, asking what was wrong as if he had any right to know.

"Nothing's wrong," I lied again, my voice trembling. "I just... I wasn't expecting to see you here."

His jaw tightened, a flicker of hurt flashing across his face before he schooled his features into a neutral expression. "Yeah, I wasn't sure if I'd be able to make it this year, but GQ convinced me to come at the last minute. It's good to see you."

Good to see me?

"Well, we better go before we lose our place in line. Bye, Dane." I turned and walked back inside, focusing on the click of my heeled boots against the pavement—anything to keep from looking back.

My mind replayed our brief encounter on a loop. The concern in his eyes and the way his voice softened when he asked if I was all right was almost enough to make me believe he cared.

Almost.

Read THE KEEPER now!

playlist
(In chronological order)

"Christmas Time is Here" by Vince Guaraldi Trio
"Winter Song" by Sara Bareilles and Ingrid Michaelson
"Better Days" by Goo Goo Dolls
"Christmas (Baby Please Come Home)" by Darlene Love
"Far Behind" by Candlebox
"My December" by Linkin Park
"Run" by Snow Patrol
"You Found Me" by The Fray
"Merry Christmas Darling" by The Carpenters
"All I Want" by Kodaline
"River" by Joni Mitchell
"Winter" by Joshua Radin
"'tis the damn season" by Taylor Swift
"Linger" by the Cranberries
"Come Away With Me" by Norah Jones
"Photograph" by Ed Sheeran
"Northern Attitude" by Noah Kahan and Hozier
"Love Song" by The Cure
"Baby It's Cold Outside" by Zooey Deschanel & Leon Redbone
"Everlong" by Foo Fighters

"Hurt" by Johnny Cash
"One More Light" Linkin Park
"The Night We Met" by Lord Huron
"Fix You" by Coldplay
"Where Are You Christmas?" by Faith Hill
"Have Yourself a Merry Little Christmas" by Judy Garland
"Francesca" by Hozier
"Say You Won't Let Go" by James Arthur
"Santa Baby" by Eartha Kitt
"Sleigh Ride" by The Ronettes
"Turning Out" by AJR
"The Christmas Waltz" by She & Him
"What Are You Doing New Year's Eve" by Ella Fitzgerald
"Like Real People Do" by Hozier
"Silent Night" by Bing Crosby

also by shannon myers

From This Day Forward Duet

(David & Elizabeth's Story)

From This Day Forward

Forsaking All Others

Operation Duet

(Dakota & Zane's Story)

Operation Fit-ish

(Kate and Nate's Story)

Operation Annulment

Silent Phoenix MC Series

(Main Storyline)

The Deserter (Book One)

The Protector (Book Two)

The Renegade (Book Three)

The Traitor (Book Four)

The Savior (Book Five)

Standalones within the SPMC universe

The Keeper

The Christmas Trap

Fairest Series (Can be read as standalones)

(Charm & Neve's Story)

Through The Woods

(Killian and Ari's Story)

Wait For It

<u>Fictioned Series</u>

(Hayden & Jake's Story)

Protagonized

about the author

Shannon is a born and raised Texan. She grew up inventing clever stories, usually to get herself out of trouble. Her mother was not amused. In junior high, she began writing fractured fairy tales from the villain's point of view and that was the moment she knew that she was going to use her powers for evil instead of good.

After an unplanned surgery in 2014 and a long pity party, she decided to pen a novel about the worst thing that could happen to a person to cheer herself up. She's twisted like that. Thus, From This Day Forward was born and the rest, as they say, is history.

She resides in the Texas desert with a posse of men (nothing like she'd imagined in her fantasies) and a plethora of fur babies.

Find her online at: http://shannonshaemyers.com
Or in her fan group: https://www.facebook.com/groups/630229377127363/

facebook.com/shannonmyersauthor
x.com/shannonsmyers
instagram.com/shannonsmyers

www.ingramcontent.com/pod-product-compliance
Lightning Source LLC
Chambersburg PA
CBHW031940010726
47493CB00007B/2007